MW00877073

TRACING TIME

THE PAST OUTLINES A LEGACY

SHELLY SNOW PORDEA

Thank you for the love and support!
Love Shelly

AUTHOR ACADEMY elite

All of the characters, organizations and events in this novel are either products of the author's imagination or are used fictitiously. All rights reserved. No part of this may be reproduced, stored in a retrieval system or transmitted in any form or by any means without the written prior consent of the publisher. The only exception is in brief quotations in printed reviews.

Published by Author Academy Elite
P.O. Box 43, Powell, OH43035

www.AuthorAcademyElite.com

Cover design by Andrei Bat

Copyright Tracing Time © 2016 Shelly Snow Pordea
All rights reserved.

ISBN–13: 978-1943526529
ISBN–10: 1943526524

Library of Congress Control Number: 2016909740

DEDICATION

To my forever love.

CONTENTS

ACKNOWLEDGMENTS

To my husband and three amazing children
who each inspire me to tell stories.

To my incredible tribe of family and friends
who always believe in me, push me to dream, and
give me reason to believe that anything is possible.

To Denise Kruse, friend and editor.
Without your skills and talents, this is a work
that may have still lain in its infancy.

To those who supported this project throughout the
entire process, thank you. I could have never gone forward without your love, encouragement, and support.

To Kary Oberbrunner who led me to seek again,
to find my identity in something bigger than myself,
and to pursue this endeavor. I will be forever grateful.

CHAPTER ONE

All four walls were so dark and cold. The truth is, they were painted as stark white as an operating room, but I had hung the curtains in layers. Dark curtains. Any light that shone through would cast a shadowy purple across the barren canvas, and I could do nothing other than sink further into my covers and hope for silence. That's all I craved. No more noise, faces, requests, duties. None of it made sense anymore.

It had been six years. I was so far from home that I couldn't find my way back if I had wanted to. At least, that's how it felt. David had taken all it away, and I had let him. Stupid me. I felt stupid, deceived, and utterly hopeless. How foolish was I? I wished that I could go back in time!

Soon after we finished college, David and I married. We were so young, so hopeful, so full of adventure. And that's what we decided to do–be adventurous. His background in geology led him to study glaciers from Iceland to Mongolia. And here we were, six full years and nothing. Not for me, anyway. David was busy doing his studies, and though I had brought along my books, computers, and now even had two small children to look after, I was sinking into a desperate loneliness I had not known before. I had never been the type to get depressed; I had never even considered it. I'm a get-it-done kind of gal, and that feeling was foreign to me. Sadness so heavy, all I knew to do was try to sleep it off. It didn't work.

"Anna, please. Let me get you something–anything!"

"David, I don't know what's wrong. I'm so sorry, I just can't shake this. My head hurts...I don't..." my voice drifted off. I didn't know what to tell him. That I hated him for taking me there? I didn't. Honestly, I loved him more than ever–I just hated his stupid job. Was it my fault for ever agreeing to go with him–to do nothing but serve his needs? Raise his children? This love for him was now filled with resentment and confusion, yet; I saw it in his eyes. He loved me. How could I tell him that the one thing he loved more than anything was the one thing in the whole world I despised? I wanted him to choose me, not his job. *But would he? If I packed up and left, would he follow me, or would his precious glaciers win again?* We were caught in a no-win situation. And I said nothing. Again.

"I'm taking you to the doctor, Anna. I can't watch you wither away to nothing."

The health care I would receive was scary to me. I didn't know the language, and people would be poking and picking at me without being able to listen to what was really wrong, but I couldn't argue. I knew something was wrong. I knew I needed help.

I braced myself for the long train ride that we would have to the city from our little village, and hoped that the ride would prepare me for one of my worst fears–having to stay in the hospital overnight. I tried not to think about it. The kids were at home with the sweet girl who had been trying to teach me the Khalkha dialect, but after about two years, I think she had given up and just decided to perfect her English. She had been a lifesaver for me. David would be gone for days–sometimes weeks at a time–and Oyoon was the only other adult who spoke English in our entire village. She had a loving heart and a big smile. My kids were safe in her care. At least *that* was a comfort to me. The children would be fine even if I wasn't.

I was on my way to Ulaanbaatar with David. Maybe I'd open up and share my true feelings. We had hours to discuss, to reconnect, and to just *be* together.

I should take advantage of these hours.

I laid my head on his chest and listened to the beat of his heart. "Anna," I used to whisper and tell him that his heart beat to the sound of my name. He would smile and kiss me. As I listened to that beat–the sound of my nearly audible name–the jostling of the train lulled me into a fatigue that began to take my mind into a sleepy recollection of happier days.

"Business or pleasure?"

I had been scrolling through my phone, looking at all of the pictures that people were posting of the lovely autumn days we had been having. It was my favorite time of year and I had been enjoying every second of it. I adjusted my soft scarf.

"I love Chicago, don't you?" I sighed. "Especially this time of year! It's as if all of the sweet memories drift in on the Chicago River, and the bad memories seem to fly off on the brown leaves that tussle past tall buildings, knowing that their place isn't in the big city." I smiled, and tilted my phone toward the person who had just greeted me so he could see the lovely photo that had caught my eye. I hadn't even looked at him.

I turned my head and smiled. That's when I saw him— the most beautiful man I'd ever seen. His bright hazel eyes stared back at me as if I had confused him beyond measure. I think I had responded too hastily.

But what had I said?

I didn't even remember; I had just rambled off the thoughts that were going on in my head, knowing someone had taken a seat next to me, and even greeted me. *How was I to know that I should have kept my big mouth shut? What was this man thinking now? What had he even asked?*

I leaned forward in surprise and squared my shoulders to address him directly. "Um, what was the question?" I asked sheepishly.

"Business or pleasure?" He grinned.

"Oh, business I guess." And I left it at that.

He laughed. It was a short, melodic laugh that let me know he thought I was goofy, and I am sure I almost melted in my seat.

"So, you have been here before, have you?" he asked in a chipper tone. I had a feeling that he was teasing me already and it made me smile.

I couldn't believe he wasn't ignoring me. There were a hundred other seats in the terminal, and he could have taken one of those. But no, he sat next to me, talked to me, teased me, and I had no choice but to respond. I had rarely ever been so intimidated by a man's beauty—okay— never before. I am not the type to notice a guy's features

4

before I would engage in a conversation with him, so the whole situation was a new experience for me. My palms felt a little clammy. I rubbed them on my jeans, breathed in, and decided that I would just treat him normally. I tried to pull myself together and act like he didn't faze me one bit.

"Chicago? Um, yes, I've been here. I did my undergrad at the University of Chicago and I am going to California for research. My professor says it's the only way to get what I really need, so I'm headed to UCLA. Well, he did recommend Columbia too, but I've never been to California, and New York just doesn't sound as warm this time of year, you know?"

He sat there smiling. *I had done it again. Babbled along in my silly way. Ugh, when would I learn?*

"Perfect! Maybe I can show you around a bit. I work at UCLA myself," he sounded genuinely pleased. His eyes were piercingly bright, and his light brown hair was just long enough on top to notice that he had slight curls that would be clipped at every visit to the salon.

Oh dear, a California boy. No wonder he looked so delicious.

"Wow, my own tour guide, I'll have to take you up on that, you know!" I said trying not to sound awkward.

He tilted his head slightly and shifted in his seat to lean in closer "It wasn't a hollow offer," he said smiling.

I think I melted again. *That smile. This was not okay.* I kept telling myself to look away, but I couldn't. I was mesmerized. *He's like no one I've ever met. I could stay in this seat forever.*

"I think we're boarding," he said as he began to stand, interrupting my infatuated stare.

"Oh, okay," I said, trying to shake my nerves.

I didn't even know what I was doing. Was I staring at him for the past three minutes? *I have got to get myself together.*

We stood and got out our boarding passes.

"I guess I'll see you in California then," I said, trying to sound as nonchalant as possible.

"Oh, yes. Of course." He extended his hand and gave mine a quick shake. "My name is David Sturgeon, and I'm in the geology department. Please, look me up. Maybe when we land I can give you a number where you can reach me?" he said as he tugged at his computer bag.

"Okay." I smiled again, not sure how else to respond. *My name might have been nice.* I briskly walked forward trying not to show my nerves, as I handed the gate agent my boarding pass. I rolled my bag along with my right hand and clenched the pass with my left as I began to head down the walkway making my way into the aircraft.

10C. It wasn't too far back; I'd be able to easily exit and wait to find David once we landed. Maybe I'd start with my name. *Good plan.*

"10A? Is that this one here?" A voice asked behind me. It sounded like David, and I was hoping that it was him, but not brave enough to turn around to see if it was.

In the brief moment of excited anticipation, I felt a hand on my shoulder as I was lifting my bag into the overhead compartment. I'm surprised I didn't drop it. *No one would even believe me.*

"May I help you with that?" David asked as he stood behind me already, reaching for my carry-on.

I nervously grinned and turned around as he was lifting my bag and placing it in the compartment.

"I guess we'll see each other before California, won't we?" I said smiling and tried to play it cool. "I'm Anna Wright."

I did it! I finally smiled comfortably, without feeling like I should be doing or thinking something else. He scooted past me to the window seat as we both sat down, casting a glance to seat 10B, hoping no one would invade our little row. No one did.

The plane soon started to jiggle and pick up speed. Until then we'd said nothing more, just adjusted ourselves in the seats and cast an occasional awkward look toward each other and the empty seat between us. I was beginning to think he was a little nervous too.

Probably not.

"Can I tell you a secret?" I whispered.

"I didn't know we were at the secret-telling stage in our relationship already," he joked, and flashed his beautiful smile.

I felt a warm sensation rising in my chest as my face flushed completely. I grinned.

"I'm really afraid of heights, and this is only my second time flying. That's why I requested the aisle seat. I want to be as far from the window as possible." There might have been a little despair in my voice because David looked at me with such concern in his eyes that it made me feel pitiful.

He unbuckled his seatbelt and quickly slinked his way into the seat next to me. "You can hold my hand if you want to," he said softly.

I was tempted to, but I didn't. I pretended like I didn't see his open palm on his knee and I closed my eyes, waiting for the plane to ascend. It only lasted a minute or two—all that rattling—but it was definitely enough to shake me up. I finally opened my eyes and turned my head to the left. He was there, smiling.

"See? It's not so bad, right?" he said lightheartedly and he shrugged his shoulders as if to encourage me to loosen up a bit.

"If you say so," I sighed, a little embarrassed, and I felt my face go warm again.

"So, Miss Anna Wright, how long have you been at U of C?"

"I did my undergraduate studies there but went to Purdue to take my master's degree. I was in Chicago for almost four years, but moved back to southern Illinois about a year and a half ago."

"But you love it–this time of year especially," he winked at me. And I felt a flush of color rushing into my cheeks again.

"Yes." I let out a happy sigh. *I can be real with him.* After all, he was teasing me already. I liked that.

"And you, Mr. David Sturgeon?" I said in the same tone he had used to say my full name. "What brought you to Chicago from LA?"

"Glaciers."

I laughed out loud right there in my seat, but he didn't. *Oh, no. He's not joking.*

"No, really, I study geology and its geography. Not as in what's-the-capital-city-of-Uzbekistan type stuff, but as in changes in glaciers, bodies of water, and exploring natural resources. It's my passion in life."

"So you want to change the world?" I smiled, half-teasing him myself.

"Well, I want to see how this whole thing works, at least. Find new and improved ways of living here, conserve, develop, and just explore. My mom calls it 'tracing glaciers–as if scientists can trace the glacier's existence instead of the other way around,' as she would put it." He grinned, as if he was remembering his mom shaking her head in disapproval about his passion in life.

"And which glacier, may I ask, brought you here?" I asked, still teasing. "Because I've been through some frigid Chicago winters, trust me, but I've yet to see a glacier!"

"True enough," he said as he nodded toward me, and he smiled again. I almost wished that he would stop flashing his gorgeous teeth at me, but how could I go on living in the world knowing that his beautiful smile existed and not seek ways to be around him each time a moment of joy would bring a happy grin to his countenance?

I sighed, and felt my heart leap in my chest and my face tingle as it rushed with color once again.

"The U of C was doing a seminar on melting ice caps, and since I'm completing my doctoral thesis with Professor Trinkton at UCLA, he asked me to bring a short lecture on our findings in Iceland last summer," David continued.

"Oh, so you were a guest lecturer? Impressive." And impressed I was.

"It's not as glamorous as it sounds, but it's a good start to get funding for our next project," he paused. "Greenland." The hope in his voice was almost tangible. I was being swept away on a whirlwind of hopeful dreams about icecaps and glaciers—silly almost.

"I hear it's amazingly beautiful," he continued, "I can hardly wait to get started. Exploring mountains and vast caverns is like nothing else on earth. Have you ever been?"

"To a glacier?" I laughed. "No, I've never been to a regular mountain, much less an icy one; although I have been to a few caves and caverns—just the basic guided-tour kind."

"You've never been to a mountain?" he asked with a hint of surprise.

9

He couldn't believe it. The big, wide world was mine to explore and I had gone no further than a few states away. I wasn't about to tell him that I was actually just a poor farm girl on an academic scholarship who hadn't traveled by plane more than once in her life.

But wait, had I already said that? For some reason I kept opening my mouth. For a girl who rarely shared her personal life with anyone—much less a stranger—I was giving up a whole lot of information fast. I couldn't help myself. I felt safe with him.

"Really. I actually grew up in a small town in southern Illinois. Other than one plane ride to Canada for us to visit Niagara Falls, I haven't been further than a few states away from home. There's always just a whole lot to do around the farm, and when you're not working, the only thing you have the energy to do is read. Well, for me anyway. My brothers weren't as enthusiastic about it, and they found many leisure activities that did *not* involve reading," I smirked.

He didn't respond with anything but a laugh, and his captivating smile. His face was long and tan with a high forehead and distinct jaw line. When he smiled, his chin would lengthen and his cheeks would sit high, exposing one slight dimple on the left. I found myself staring.

I was perplexed. What power did he have over me that I just freely gave out this information? I hadn't made it a habit of telling people right away that I was simple farm girl. Not that I was ashamed—goodness knows I loved my parents more than anything in the world—but I had wanted to be a city girl since I could remember, and I tried hard to fit in from the moment I arrived. But he charmed me so fast that I spilled the beans and couldn't stop.

"Mom was a school teacher, so the amount of books we had in our home was innumerable. Dad would build shelves that lined our basement, and mom would fill them with books. Every couple of years, he'd find a new spot, build some more, and work on making sure the basement was waterproof. Eventually he remodeled the entire thing into a library that would make some small bookstore owners envious. It was my haven."

I paused, and bit my lower lip. *Was I boring him?* But David nodded, his beautiful hazel eyes beckoning me to continue.

I went on. "During the cold winters, we'd all come into the kitchen, and Mom would start preparing a big meal after a long day. She'd assign chores, and we'd all come together to cook, eat, laugh, and just enjoy each other. Dad would call us into the den after dinner, and he'd send someone to fetch a book–Shakespeare, Dickens, Keats, and Austen–the classics were treasured things in our home. My three brothers and I would gather around the fireplace, and Dad would read. I don't remember how young we were when this tradition started, but my earliest memories are of Dad sitting in his wooden rocking chair reading us stories. They carried me to places I'd visit again and again. I have long been in love with the written word."

"Wow, that's cool, I'm kind of jealous! That kind of quiet country life sounds so appealing. I grew up in LA–everything is always moving and changing–the times to sit and read a good book are few and far between. I think I'd have liked growing up with your quiet life."

Oh, LA, are you kidding me? And the country life is appealing? Maybe we wouldn't understand each other as much as I thought we would.

I just grinned.

"So, what research are you going to do at UCLA?" he asked.

"It's not as much research as it is taking advantage of other people's research, I guess. My major was in English and Latin, so my master's is in foreign language and teaching English as a second language. Syntax and linguistics, you know?"

"No. I know glaciers and geology," he laughed.

"Well, I'm meeting with a Professor Dubois about some studies and programs she has implemented in a few city schools in LA; I'll get to participate in a classroom setting for a few days, take notes, and hopefully get a real feel for an exhaustive thesis."

"Sounds interesting."

"But not as interesting as tracing glaciers, I guess." I smiled at him, more at ease with every passing second.

For the duration of the flight, we talked. We discussed everything. I discovered that he had one brother and two sisters–the perfect foursome. He grew up in a suburb of LA; his father was a real estate mogul, and his mother a massage therapist. His love for nature, science, and exploration came early on, and his parents and siblings always encouraged him to pursue his studies and academic goals, even though they were more non-traditional in their professions.

When he turned the tables and enquired about my life, he got an honest and elaborate answer for every question he asked. It was almost surreal. I would scold him occasionally for having some mysterious quality which made me open the floodgates of disclosure upon my otherwise protected secrets. And then he'd smile.

Sigh.

The time seemed to speed by so quickly that I'd have never known the long flight was almost over had we not been interrupted by the captain's landing announcement cackling over the loud speakers.

David snickered at me as I listened intently to landing and deplaning instructions.

"I can help you when we get off the plane if you want," he offered.

"Thanks, I might need it," I laughed.

The plane began to descend and we shuffled a bit in our seats in preparation for the landing. The shaking and force of deceleration didn't seem to be as difficult to bear as I sat next to David who slipped his hand into mine and whispered, "It gets easier the more you fly."

I gripped his hand tightly, closing my eyes until we had come to a complete stop.

"Now you can breathe!" David exclaimed as he quickly unbuckled his seatbelt and motioned for me to move into the aisle. I sat motionless for a moment then picked up my purse from under the seat in front of me, breathed a sigh of relief, and smiled at him.

David grabbed my carry-on along with his own, and we exited the plane together. He asked me if I had checked any luggage, offering to walk me toward baggage claim.

"I have a wise friend who's traveled enough to let me know a short trip like this needs nothing more than what I can put in my carry-on." I said.

"Wise friend, indeed," he responded kindly. "Well, I guess I'll be on my way. I have a driver who's probably waiting for me. Is there any way I can help–can I give you a lift?" he offered.

"Oh, thank you so much, but I'll be fine. I've made arrangements for everything. I appreciate it, though."

We had made our way out of the plane and to the terminal where the busy hallway was aflutter with other passengers hurrying to their destinations. I moved my bag out of the way and shifted to the left trying to glance around for an exit sign.

David began to extend his arm for a handshake, but quickly opened both of his palms upward in a shrug.

"Look at us being all formal," he said, and he did that almost musical laugh again. "I feel like I poured out my heart and soul to you and now...may I at least hug you goodbye?" he asked so tenderly that I felt my knees go weak.

"Yes," I couldn't get out more than a whisper.

I took one step and was scooped up into his arms. I squeezed him tightly and whispered "thank you" in his ear. As I started to pull back, I felt his arm firmly around my waist and I looked into his hazel eyes for only a moment—because the next thing I saw was his lips. I couldn't help myself. I leaned in and kissed him. It was a rapturous moment, and a horrific one at the same time. I suddenly realized what I had done.

"I'm so sorry!" again, only a whisper. "I've never done that before!"

"You've never kissed a man?" he teased.

"Um...not a man I don't even *know*!" I could barely breathe.

"But you know *me*," he said without releasing me from his embrace.

CHAPTER TWO

"You slept a little."

It was nice to wake up in David's arms once again. It had been a long time since I had simply rested in his embrace. It was funny to awake from a dream that was just a memory of how David and I met. It made me feel safe, hopeful.

"Chris and Rebecca are going to meet us at the station. Chris was able to secure an appointment with a neurologist for us." David spoke, breaking my reverie.

"A neurologist?" I could barely get out a whisper. *Where was that hope I felt?* I started to cry; I couldn't help myself. A neurologist meant problems. Real problems, and there was nothing else I could do but admit weakness. I had always thought myself strong. Maybe it was a façade. I fancied myself as a smart-girl-who-gets-it-all-done, but I hadn't felt like myself in so long that I couldn't figure out how to act. What I did know was that I could no longer live my life wishing the light away, and immersing myself into down covers. I needed help; for the first time in my adulthood I felt I couldn't manage my problems at all. I felt like a child again. I wanted to return to the dream. To go back in time.

David held me tightly and let me weep. Not a word escaped his lips—just soft kisses on my forehead.

"Can I ask you something?" I muttered pitifully.

"Anything," he whispered.

"If this is bad, I mean, *really* bad, please take our kids back to my parents', and if you need to finish your work, I understand, but don't be gone too long, okay?" I pictured four-year-old Maggie's soft auburn curls bouncing around her full face and James' nearly two-year-old chubby fingers that he was always using to explore anything within reach, and I felt tears push through my eyes, then roll down my cheeks.

"Shh…we'll talk about that later," David said, stroking my hair.

"No, David, I want to talk about it now," I said sitting upright to look him in the face. "What if something is seriously wrong and I don't make it? They are talking brain tumors and MRIs at this point! Please don't pretend this is not a possibility. I am so tired of pretending! What is even real anymore?"

I had done it. I had opened my mouth with the complaint I'd been stifling for so long. Pretending…

"I don't mean to pretend, Anna. I just…I can't…I can't fix this myself!"

A tear trickled down his cheek, and I nuzzled in closer, placing my head on his strong chest. I didn't remember the last time that I had seen him cry.

"I know. I don't want anything to happen to either one of us, but we can't act like it isn't possible." I said.

We sat in silent thought for a moment.

David stroked my hair as he asked for explanation, "What do you mean by pretending, exactly? Do you mean more than pretending that you feel well when you don't? What more are you struggling with, Anna? I feel like there are things you aren't telling me," he probed with serious concern.

"You know I'm not thinking clearly, David, but I do want to be honest. I have to. I can't let things fester like I have in the past, and I don't mean to hurt you; please believe that!"

"Hurt me? Anna what are you saying?" David's voice trembled.

I struggled to find the right words to say and the strength to lift my head to speak them. "I just feel like I have to put on a happy face to stay here one more day, David. To wake up each morning to the biting cold temperatures and know that there's no hope of going back to a normal life any time soon," I said trying to articulate the struggles that I had been wrestling with in my mind for years, circulating in repetitive rhythm, occupying every moment of thought.

My eyes welled with tears as I stammered through my complaints. "To know that my kids are so far from my family and friends—so far from normal life. What will we do when they are school-aged? There are so many things, David. I feel like I pretend to be happy just to keep a smile on for our kids, and it drains me more than I can explain," I cried, lifting my head and sitting straight against the back of the high train seat.

"Do you feel like you have to pretend to want to be with *me?*" he asked with a tinge of fear.

I had hurt him with my words. I had not meant to, but it was true. There were days that I had to pretend to want to be with him. But he didn't understand. It wasn't just about him. This was about *me!* Wasn't that okay?

"I'm trying, David! I have my own wishes and desires, goals for my life, for our kids. I don't want to accuse you of being selfish, but that's how it feels sometimes. I am sacrificing areas–years, even–and it seems like you don't even care." I complained.

"I do care. I care immensely, Anna. I just don't have a solution. You know we can't afford to send you back every time you get homesick, but this wasn't my decision alone, you know! You agreed to do this. You wanted to come. I have tried to offer you ways to reach out, to feel at home…"

"This will never be home," I interrupted. I could sense the bitterness in my voice; I wondered if he could.

"I didn't mean it like that. I know. I do understand. I want to go back to a normal life, as you call it, but I don't have the means to do so right now. I can't leave it all, Anna. All that we've worked for these six years. Are you asking me to forfeit all that work in order to go back home? Or worse, for me to send you and the kids away?"

And there we stayed. Silent. At a standstill. I knew that I was being selfish too, but neither one of us could remove ourselves and our own desires from the equation. *Is there a solution?* To be together meant some sacrifice. Would I just melt away into the recesses of my mind, secluding myself more and more from the world around me, because it was the only way I could make sense of things? My head hurt. The dark circles around my eyes were deeper than ever and the pounding was incessant. I needed a doctor soon. I couldn't lift my head up all the way, so I just slumped back down into David's lap.

"I love you, David," I whispered as I glanced up at his face that was staring off into the distance. That face. Oh, how I loved it so! I watched as a silent tear rolled down his cheek as if in slow motion. I wasn't used to seeing him get emotional. It hurt to keep my eyes open. I found refuge in my sleep once again.

"Anna, sweetie, we're here. Wake up." A gentle shaking of my wrist and a soft whisper awoke me. David helped me stand and we stood in an embrace.

"I love you, Anna. I love you," he whispered as he held me.

If there was one thing I was sure of in this world it was that David Sturgeon loved me, and I loved him. For now, that would have to be enough. I was convinced that our love could survive any circumstance. I stayed in his arms for a few more seconds, then leaned into his face and kissed him. "I know you love me, David. It's what keeps me breathing."

We met Chris and Rebecca as soon as we stepped off of the train. They were waiting on the platform ready to help with our bags. We had all met at UCLA while David was finishing his doctorate. We were quite the foursome, back in the day. Who would have thought that it was really only eight years ago?

"Oh, Anna!" Rebecca hugged me tightly. She pulled her face back to look at me with her icy blue eyes. She seemed to be pained by my appearance. I had gained some weight from being in bed most days, my head drooped in heaviness, and the color of my skin was pale. She put her arm around my shoulders, pulled me in closely and said, "You won't have to do anything, I promise. I've arranged everything. You can stay with us, I know it'll be tight, but we'll make it work," she explained. "And we have two doctors' appointments lined up, okay? We're sure to get answers here," she calmly reassured me.

"Rebecca," I laid my head on her shoulder as we walked. "I've missed you."

"Anna...I have so much to tell you. But let's get you better first, okay? I'm sure things will be fine."

She smiled at me like we were still two college girls. The truth is I think we both felt like we were. Being twenty-eight felt no different than being twenty, except it felt totally different. Funny how that can happen. It seemed a world away, yet barely yesterday. It was as if my life had become one big contradiction. I had gone to college just before I turned seventeen, finished by nineteen, and on to my master's before I turned twenty. Married by the time I was twenty-one, and now I spent my time wondering why I had been in such a rush.

Things started to blur as we piled into a small car with Rebecca up front while David and Chris crammed in the back seat with me. Chris spoke to David in a brotherly tone, occasionally casting a glance at me. We rode along the crowded streets of Ulaanbaatar as they discussed plans that I couldn't quite keep up with. Their words had begun to sound muffled and distant. My mind couldn't focus enough to decipher all that they were saying, and my thoughts drifted.

David and Christopher were fellow scientists. They had both been assigned to work in Mongolia, but David's study required regular visits and hands-on observation of glaciers while Chris stayed at the Mongolian university, MIU, in Ulaanbaatar only to join David on certain expeditions. When we had first moved, we had all been assigned to the university in Ulaanbaatar. Our happy foursome stuck together from the time we had met. People would comment about how we each possessed a quality the other did not, and were the perfect blend of friends. Rebecca was tall and thin with hair that was naturally white blonde, while I stood five inches shorter than she did with dark brown hair and an athletic build. David and Chris were similar in height, but opposite in build. David was tall and beefy, and Chris was lean and long.

We had started out on our assignments together, but things quickly changed. Within the first three years, I had given birth to two babies in Ulaanbataar and Rebecca was my saving grace through it all. But, four years after we arrived on foreign soil, David came home and told me that he'd be moving us to a village closer to his work. I had to leave my closest friendship behind. We set out on a journey more than twenty hours away with our newborn baby boy and two-year-old girl. They became my comfort and companions when David wasn't around. It was a happy life for a while—a busy life that a young mother must face, but loneliness finally set in. Rebecca had a baby of her own a year later, and for each of us, young motherhood became overwhelming while the distance of the desert land kept us apart.

As I sat reflecting on our history, I tried to relish the fact that we were together once again, but I couldn't seem to verbalize what I was thinking with clarity. Sweet sleep was sought again.

I awoke in a hospital room. I was told that I had blacked out and had been admitted right away. It was my biggest fear living abroad–a night in their hospitals. The dark concrete room was bleak and miserable. The pain and sorrow left in the space by the room's past occupants was nearly palpable. I pleaded with the staff to run the tests, and then allow me to stay with my friends, assuring them that my fainting spell was more due to fatigue than any true problem. They wouldn't hear of it. After a day or two of testing, my vital signs were clear, my first CAT scan came back clean, and the MRI showed no abnormalities. I was healthy enough for them to allow me to leave, and Chris took us to a private clinic where he had set up other appointments for me. It was such a relief to see a more modern facility; I wanted to feel hopeful again.

Day after day of testing wore me out both physically and mentally. Rebecca was a culinary genius preparing delicious meals and engaging in comforting conversation during the evenings, but my frustrations were mounting. We had been there for seven days, each one feeling longer than the last, and we still had no answers. At the end of the week, just getting to the table to share a meal was exhausting, and I was at the end of my rope.

"Nothing. That's all they ever say to me. Nothing's wrong. All tests came back as normal. Blood work, CAT scans, MRIs…this last lady did everything but tell me it was all in my head and that I might be crazy," I sighed hopelessly.

Am I crazy?

David held my hand while Chris and Rebecca sat silently.

"I didn't mean to ruin dinner, you guys. Sorry." I stood up from the dinner table and walked toward the couch as I began to get dizzy and stumble.

David had followed me, and grabbed my elbow before I could fall. "Anna, please, it's fine…I know you must be extremely frustrated. But this is real, you are not crazy, and we will get to the bottom of it. I'm making plans tomorrow to send you home to your mom."

Home to mommy. It sounded so cliché, but it was what I needed. I couldn't go on there with the doctors doing yet another random test, telling me that all I needed was a good cup of coffee in the morning, or insinuating that I was just begging for attention.

David had made arrangements within twenty-four hours. "I've booked a flight, Anna. I went ahead and made plans for you to come back after a month, but if you need longer, we'll deal with it then, okay? We can always change the return date."

"But the kids…" my voice had gotten weaker.

"They'll be fine. As soon as I drop you off at the airport, I'll head to our house and bring them back here to stay with Chris and Rebecca."

"I'm happy to do it, Anna. They'll be just fine," Rebecca said as she walked over and sat on the couch next to me. *Rebecca to the rescue again!* How could I ever express what she meant to me?

"Okay," I muttered. I pulled my long brown hair out of its disheveled ponytail and slumped back onto the sofa. It was where I had stayed most of the time, and the days that had passed felt like weeks.

Later that day, Chris burst into the house after work with such exuberance that it startled me. "You guys! Can we try something? I mean, it can't hurt, right?" I peered my head above the back of the couch slowly. "Oh, I'm sorry! I didn't mean to wake you, Anna, were you sleeping?" he said excitedly.

"It's all right, what's the news?" I said, scooting myself forward to sit upright.

"I was talking to a guy at the university today and telling him a bit about your condition. He said that we might have been going about it all wrong. He said that you need to see this lady he knows, and that she can sense what traditional doctors tend to miss with regular tests. You don't leave until Tuesday, Anna. So come with me Monday to this guy's therapist. It can't hurt, right?"

He sounded so enthusiastic and empathetic at the same time. I glanced at David with a shrug, "What do you think, honey?"

"What can it hurt, babe? You want to try?" David asked returning the same shrug I had given him.

"Why not? I have nothing to lose," I sighed.

The three of us looked at each other and smiled, as if we knew that we needed a positive response after the negativity we had been confronting. From then on, each one of us seemed to have a new hope. I got up that evening and ate dinner at the table again. It was nice to be with friends.

Early Monday morning we headed to an apartment complex with Christopher and his interpreter. It was a small, dark residence with a corner in the living room set aside for this tiny Mongolian lady to take her clients into a quiet place amidst the bustle of her busy day and three children. It didn't look miraculous.

She was sending two of her children off to school when we arrived, then secured the littlest one in her playtime activities, and closed the doors on either side of the small room that connected to both sides of the apartment. The unassuming little space didn't seem like much. Certainly not like anything I was accustomed to. I became nervous.

"Hello, child," she greeted me. Her melodic voice seemed to contrast her small frame, but was such a comforting sound that it calmed my nerves instantly.

The smell of sweet basil and lilies permeated the small room.

"You speak English?" I asked in surprise.

"Yes, dear, my name is Ami," she responded with barely a hint of an accent.

She didn't speak often; she simply motioned for me to sit next to her on the floor with my legs crossed and my hands on my knees as if in mediation. It looked silly, but I kept reminding myself that I had nothing to lose.

Her bony hand pushed gently down my spine, then up my neck, after which she instructed me to lie down, face up. She proceeded to pop my back and neck in ways that I cannot even describe. After she had rubbed my neck she pulled firmly upward.

I could feel blood rushing to my head and my temples pulsing so rapidly that I had to stop her, "I don't think I'm okay," I said. The pain in my head was so intense that I thought I would possibly die right there, and I began to cry.

"It's all right, dear. Let it out," she said as she held her cold fingers tightly on the nape of my neck, elevating my head slightly as it sat cradled in her hands. An intense peace rushed over me, and I realized that I would not die that day. I understood that there was a healing taking place that I couldn't explain.

We had found it. My miracle.

After we left that small apartment, we cancelled the airline tickets and I stayed in Ulaanbaatar for another three weeks to rest and recover. I missed my little Maggie and James more than I could bear. David had arranged for us to get a hotel room for those weeks, and brought the kids to stay with us. I went for six more treatments. It was as if I was a new person.

Every time I saw Ami, I regained strength and hope. Initially, her sessions were painful, but they became relaxing by the time I had gone through a few. I had begun to feel like my old vibrant, athletic self again, and it was almost hard to believe that I had been so ill just days before.

CHAPTER THREE

After we returned to our house, life seemed to be back to normal. Our home was almost ten miles outside of Khvod along a dirt road that was not easily traveled. We had settled there because it was nearer the mountains that David had been studying, but still more than a ten-hour journey from where the glacial area he was studying lay.

The city of Khovd was large enough to have decent shopping and offered us some diversion from the mundane when we would get restless. Maggie, James, Oyoon and I would bundle up and ride mules or bikes into town just for fun some days. I would strap my little James in a baby wrap on my chest, and Maggie would ride in a little seat that attached to my bike. James was a preemie, small for his age at nearly two years old, and would try to wriggle his way out of the wrap, but four-year-old Maggie would fearlessly peek through her helmet and warm scarf as her tight curls peered out of the cap encircling her round face, and happily giggle as we bounced along the bumpy roads to the city and back to the village. I had tried to find my place in our community of sixty or so, but never did quite feel like I could be at ease. Language was the biggest barrier. Oyoon had begun testing me on my Khalkha words, and even she mentioned a noticeable change in my health. I was feeling content, but could never escape the bitterness I had toward David's job.

He was planning a three-week journey into the Altai Mountains for measurements in glacial changes to report back about his research of climate change. By that time, I was handling the tasks of everyday life better. Weeks had passed, and I was thinking more rationally. I carried about my business ignoring the little voice in my head that said to panic. I didn't want to act crazy. I wanted peace, and I knew that I'd have to do my best to stay active if I started to become depressed, so I decided to put on a smile and move my way through anything. I couldn't help but ask myself if I could handle another of David's absences.

"I love you, David. Please be careful." I wanted to send him off with no tears and just hope that his research would be so thorough that we'd be able to go back to Illinois, and some sort of familiar normalcy would return to our little family. There was so much that I didn't understand about geology and his constant treks into the wilderness made it even more difficult for me to accept. I found it hard to support his dreams of changing the world by studying climate change when it only felt like we were wasting time. He would talk about global effects and changing atmospheres, send all sorts of papers and theories back to the States, yet we would still stay in Mongolia for mission after mission. It seemed never-ending. It was as if the weather, erosion, emissions, and all the other factors that he had told me about his studies would be an ever-changing thing, and that his work would never be done. I was feeling stuck, and I missed everyone–everything that I knew as normal. I wanted to put all of the hardships behind us and go home.

I looked into his hazel eyes again with such passion I could feel it in my toes. He put his arms around my waist and pulled me close.

"Anna, I promise you that if this expedition goes well, I'll do what I can to get reassigned. I don't ever want to disappoint you. You are worth more to me than anything in this world, please know that."

"David, I know your work is important to you, and I don't want to hold you back. I am going to be open and honest with you about how I'm doing, and we'll deal with things as they come, okay?" I said sincerely.

"Deal," he gave a little side grin as he winked at me and tightened his grip around my waist.

Oh, that smile! He kissed me with his soft lips and gently rubbed his stubbly cheek against mine. His eyes were closed as I peeked up at him, trying to soak in every line of his face. In that moment, I experienced the same joy that overcame me when he asked me to be his wife. I wanted to never let him go! But off he went to journey into the distant mountains, and there I stayed.

A rare, temperate day was reason enough to take Maggie and James out to play in a field near the house. Most of the quiet Mongolian days were beautifully sunny–but cold, windy, or both. We had rarely gotten more than a six-week bout of comfortable weather over the summer, and even then, there could be a twenty-or-thirty-degree difference of temperature within a given week. So when the temperature was high, and the wind speed low, we would spend as many waking hours outside as possible.

I tried to capture photos of my children in as many lovely growing-up moments as I could. I snapped picture after picture, checking the lighting and angles of each shot and smiling at every facial expression I could see on the little screen that illuminated on the back of my camera. Maggie's tight auburn curls made the loveliest photos, and James' little blond head and chubby dimpled cheeks complimented his sister's soft features. I knew I was biased, but I had always thought that God could have never given me better babies than the ones he had.

I sat down and leaned backwards on my forearms to enjoy the warmth of the sunshine on my face and the laughter of my children around me. My life was feeling full; there were only fading memories of the darkness I had felt just weeks before. I truly was myself again.

"One more word?" Oyoon giggled.

"Oh, I suppose. You would think that I was one to study math or something and not one to have a language major, the way I struggle with your language, Oyoon!"

"Mrs. Sturgeon, you do well," she said in her sweet voice.

"Will you never call me Anna?" I teased.

She smiled. I was her elder—only by a few years, but an employer as well, technically, so her culture wouldn't allow her the intimacy of being on a first-name basis with me. It was something that seemed so antiquated. I had read many a book about different cultures and formal etiquette growing up, but I didn't think that I would ever live in a time and place where it was common practice. I began to remind myself how lucky I was to have the experience of being there. My life was indeed good, and I felt blessed. I leaned back fully, laid my head on our picnic blanket, and took a deep breath.

Oyoon had not yet responded with anything other than a grin. I rolled over onto my stomach and placed my chin in my hands, kicking my feet up in the air and crossing them, one over the other. "Oh, it's all right, Oyoon. I like that you respect your traditions of propriety. Go ahead, give me another word," I said, smiling at her.

"Anna!" A shout came over the small hill in a panic. Oyoon and I were stunned, and the children ran toward the blanket we were sitting on. "ANNA! ANNA!"

I sprang to my feet and shouted back. "Over here! What is it?!" I felt my stomach fall, hardly able to get the words out. My heart was pounding, and I could feel my pulse in my temples as I started to approach the sounds of the cries.

The faint figure of a man came running closer toward us. "Chris, is that you?" I said, as the man calling my name approached. "Christopher, what is going on?"

I immediately felt my heart drop. I was confused at how he could be there. It was more than a twenty-hour drive from Ulaanbataar to the city nearest our village, so a visit was never spontaneous.

What in the world would he be doing here if nothing was wrong?

Christopher ran closer, bending over as he tried to catch his breath, placing the palms of his hands on his knees. His eyes were red and his brows furrowed in concern. He stood panting, saying nothing as I approached him.

31

"Please just tell me David is okay, please, Christopher," I begged.

He did not respond; his face was weary and swollen. "Anna," he whispered. He tried to catch his breath. "I had to be the one to come and tell you. I couldn't...I couldn't..."

He hung his head and sobbed.

I stood and watched him for a moment. The world around me started to feel like it was moving in slow motion.

What do I do first? The kids shouldn't be here if something is terribly wrong.

I asked Oyoon to take the children and head down the hill toward the house; everyone was confused and had begun to cry. There was a sadness in the air, and I felt like I should have been weeping along with them in the confusion, but I hadn't yet begun to cry. I couldn't process the events quickly enough to be anything but stunned in the moment.

Christopher had begun to breathe normally as he stood with shoulders faintly slumped and head bowed low.

I have to know.

"Christopher, please, just tell me," I whispered. He finally looked me in the eyes and said nothing. He didn't have to.

He's gone! My sweet David! He's gone!

I gasped for air.

We stood on the side of the hill crying into each other's shoulders for a while. The two of us stayed there long enough to gain the strength to stroll back to the house. Our steps were long and heavy. We were silent.

The cold dread of despair that I had felt before seemed as if it was rushing over me. Gloomy drapes and heavy covers began to call out to me, and I felt drawn to the dark cave of my depression as if it was beckoning me with a force that could not be overcome. I walked silently into the house, reached for the cold knob of the heavy wooden door, swung it open and returned to my bed. I crawled in, buried myself under the familiar comforter and wept. My salty tears began to saturate the fluffy pillows, and I tried to wipe them away with my hands. As I pulled the thick blanket up to my face grasping it tightly in my hands, I heard someone come into the room and sit down quietly in the chair beside the bed.

"Anna, I'm so sorry!" Christopher sounded pitiful. "Please let me explain. I couldn't have known that seeing you would make this all ten times harder...I didn't even have a chance to tell you...I had it all prepared...what I was going to say...I imagined what you would say too... what you would do...nothing could have prepared me for seeing you in such pain."

I peered at him over the top of my covers, clutching the end of them at my chin. "Is he dead?" I whispered. *Of course he's dead, but how could he be? I would have known something was wrong!*

"There was an accident, Anna. It wasn't supposed to be this way, he wasn't supposed to..."

Chris put his hand on mine and wept softly. I was almost numb in that moment. I wasn't crying anymore. I didn't care that he was. It was my hurt. My husband. I just lay under my covers and stared up at the ceiling.

"Just leave," I mumbled. "Tell Oyoon to stay the night and take care of the kids, and just leave me to sleep."

I could hear myself being inconsiderate and irrational, but it didn't stop me from saying every heartless word. Christopher silently stood and slowly walked to the door of the bedroom. I watched him shuffle his feet across the room, dragging them in weighty sorrow. He stopped to look back at me.

"We'll talk in the morning, Anna."

We didn't. I did not come out of my room for days.

Over the next couple weeks, I was flooded with paper-work. There was nothing left for me in Mongolia, and I had made peace with the fact that I had to leave the land I had desired to vacate for so long, even if it meant that I was somehow leaving the remains of my love behind. Responsibilities of things usually David took care of were imposed upon me, and Chris and Rebecca were by my side through it all. They were a godsend. Rebecca had taken Maggie and James to her home back in the city, and Chris and I returned to Khovd after David's memorial service at MIU in Ulaanbataar so that I could settle our debts with the landlord of our cottage and pack the things I wanted to take with me. I had stopped into some of the offices at the university to retrieve items that he had left with a few of the collaborating professors, and I had heard a familiar story each time. It seemed like everyone had rehearsed the same exact speech.

I walked around the house in a daze. My eyelids were heavy as I closed and opened them over and over trying to relive the memories we had shared behind those thick concrete walls. They were happy days mingled with the hardest trials I had ever faced.

Something isn't right. I know that Christopher is hiding some-thing…maybe just details about the accident that the university doesn't want to get sued for, but still. I need the truth. No actual body to be found, no other explanation, no recovered equipment, no colleague by David's side as usual? There are elements that don't add up. Do I dare speak up now?

"Christopher, what happened?" I finally gained the courage to ask as I walked down the narrow hallway that led to the main living space.

"I told you, Anna, he was up on the mountain researching..." he started to explain stoically.

"Stop. Just stop it, Christopher! You have told me that same memorized speech how many times now? He fell off the side of a mountain tracing the global effects of his stupid glaciers? That's what you're telling me? What *aren't* you telling me? That's all I want to know. After all we've been through, Chris, don't you owe me that?" My tone had started in anger and fell to despair.

With a love story like David's and mine, I was convinced that I'd have felt in my heart the exact moment he left the earth. When he took his last breath, I would have gasped for another one on his behalf. *I would have known.*

Christopher looked at me, stunned. I hadn't spoken much since the moment he came to give me the news. I had never before voiced my suspicion that there was something intentionally being hidden from me. I was a desperate woman in search of some closure–some meaning–just anything–standing in front of him pleading for help.

"Anna..." his voice was just a whisper. "I can't..."

"Can't what? Tell me the truth, Christopher?" I said in desperation, raising my voice slightly. "Whatever it is, I promise you is better than the nightmare of questions I am haunted with daily!"

He stood squarely before me in the entrance of the living room, nearly blocking me from the rest of the house. Perhaps he was trying to prevent me from drilling him with the questions I wanted to unload.

"Please, Anna, let's just gather your things and go. You'll be back in Illinois in a few days, and you'll be able to cope with the reality of what has happened then. Please?" he begged in a low voice, and continued into the room, nervously picking up a couple of items that were on a table.

I felt like he questioned when he answered me, as if he was entirely unsure of how successful he'd been at diverting my curiosity. *Is he probing me to ask another question? Should I insist one more time? Would he break some strange vow of silence and allow the dam of information to collapse into my hungry ears?* I took the bait, whether that's what it was or not.

I put my hand on his elbow, pulled his arm to turn toward me, and looked him in the eyes. He towered over me by at least eight inches and I stared up into his face as my pitiful voice quivered, "Christopher, if you look at me and promise that you're telling me the whole story, then I'll let it go."

He jerked his arm away from me, as he quickly walked over to the sofa to sit down. Looking down at his knees, he rubbed his hands back and forth on his legs as I followed him to the couch and sat down. One of the most reserved men I've ever known collapsed in shambles on my couch, and began to weep. I sat next to him and took his hand. I couldn't help but cry myself. An hour or two could have passed, or maybe it was just a few minutes, but he finally regained his composure and began to speak.

"David was my best friend, Anna. I loved him like a brother, and he loved no other girl but you. Ever. I couldn't believe he was finally serious about a girl until I saw the two of you together. I hope you know that. But there was something that he loved more, at least, that's how it seemed. He always loved his geological studies. He was married to his work long before he married you, but I guess I don't have to tell you that."

He didn't. A brief grin came across both of our faces in an attempt to share an ironic memory weaved between the heaviness of grief.

"Anna, do you believe in God?" Chris asked.

"Of course, I do, Chris. How could I have hope through this otherwise?" I shrugged my shoulders.

"David didn't. Not at first, but his belief became quite strong after about a year of study."

"Really? Glaciers? I wouldn't have guessed," I said, unconvinced.

"It was never about glaciers, Anna. Well, maybe it was at first. But it became about something much more. Glaciers were just a good cover for some of the remotest places on earth for the experimentation we'd do." Christopher breathed deeply.

I was confused. A little breathless.

"On what? *Humans?*" my weak voice trembled.

"Sort of. Not really." He hesitated as if he was trying to figure out how much to tell me. "Let me explain."

I began to get weak in the knees and shivered with the familiar chill that had constantly haunted me in the cold, dry house of that remote Mongolian village. I began to have trouble breathing, sitting with my body slumped, head in hands. *What is happening? I feel like answers that I may not be prepared to hear are coming.* I pulled the blanket from the back of the couch over onto my lap and covered my toes. Christopher moved from the couch to the coffee table and sat in front of me.

"When we were still at UCLA, just months before having met you, David and I began a secret study with Professor Trinkton–remember him?"

I nodded nervously. *This has been a secret the whole time? Was my entire life a lie?*

"Well, after a trip to Greenland for our initial project, Professor Trinkton shared a notebook full of theories and possible solutions with David and me," he paused in thought.

"Solutions to *what?*" I whispered suspiciously. I pulled my feet up onto the couch, hugging my knees into my chest.

"Possible solutions for…" he paused. "For time travel, Anna."

"What?" I looked up at him over my knees and said it again before he could respond. "Wait. What?"

"I know, Anna. It's unbelievable. At first, we thought Trinkton was kidding–or crazy. But he explained that the colleague, Professor Bennett, who had left him the notebook, had disappeared six years earlier without a trace. Professor Trinkton was certain that Bennett had succeeded. The more we looked into it, the more we agreed. We have the vessel he traveled in–or at least we did."

I laid my head back against the couch, half-hoping that I'd sink into it forever. *This can't be real. Why would he think that making up a stupid story would be funny?* I couldn't believe his ecological study was all a pretext to some absurd obsession with time travel. Christopher talked, but I didn't hear him for a while; it was all a blurred, muffled mess.

"…It was more than likely that we could retrieve them…" he continued.

"What?" I had to stop and make an effort to listen. I had asked for the truth, and needed to hear it–I was hearing it and yet, *was this the truth?* "Retrieve? Retrieve whom?"

"You stopped listening, didn't you?" Christopher said with a sigh.

"Sorry, I can't believe what you are saying, Chris. I can't even process what you are telling me," I said in disbelief. "You're claiming that this Professor Bennett left in a *time machine?*" I said the words as absurdly as they sounded.

Anna, I know this is hard for you to grasp, but yes. He had sketches of evidence...notes of his experience in Victorian England...calculations of how the theory of time travel is not only possible–it is doable. We began testing Professor Bennett's theories and experimenting with the vessel–a rocket, really."

"A *rocket?*" my disbelief was palpable.

"Yes. You see, in the research we've found, most people believed that a machine could take them through time, and though not all wrong, they were approaching it from a terrestrial point of view. We knew we had to get above it, if you will. Above time."

My mind was reeling. Everything I'd ever known was somehow in this one moment brought to question. *Was any of it real?*

"Chris, are you telling me that David died in some rocket trying to get above space and time?"

He was silent. His eyes shifted from the side-to-side and then at the floor. I could tell he was sifting through the details in his mind trying to decide what to say–or what not to.

"Christopher?" I said desperately, as tears began to well up in my eyes, and I dropped my feet to the floor, crossing my arms in front of me.

"We did it, Anna. There is a place–a place between what's here and what we think is where we can only assume God dwells–above space and time. It's like a cosmic loophole. What *we* measure as time is just this linear motion on a ring-shaped conveyer belt–all existing at once. Well, if you're above it, only when you're *in* it do you have to measure it as time itself, and you do not have the ability to access it all at once. All we had to do was figure out how to insert ourselves into a place along that vast conveyer belt." He spoke with excitement.

"I can't even take this in, Christopher. Are you telling me that David is dead, or that he's lost in a black hole that you think is the 'space between,' or what?"

"I don't know, Anna. I don't know."

His voice was hushed and slow. I could handle no more details, and Christopher knew it. I leaned forward to place my head in my hands again. I began to slightly rock back and forth, rubbing my eyebrows with my fingers. My head was suddenly throbbing.

"Let's get the things we came for, Anna," he said patting my knee as if to urge me to rise.

I stood silently and walked toward the bedrooms. I wandered aimlessly for a bit and just looked around the small house, suddenly perplexed about why I was there. The bleak walls appeared closer to each other than ever before, and my senses seemed to be fading.

A few minutes after I had started roaming the house, Oyoon came to help me with the items I wanted to take from the kids' room. Tears welled up in her eyes a bit as she held Maggie's stuffed monkey. I couldn't speak anymore. I patted her shoulder and smiled through my tears. I knew she loved us. Oyoon had been my salvation in a barren land, and I her real-life source of adventurous stories from a world she had never experienced outside the cold desert. We didn't have to speak to know that we would miss each other.

For the rest of the morning, the three of us packed in virtual silence. An occasional glance reassured each of us that we were all going to be okay. Christopher loaded the four suitcases and three boxes I had decided to take with me, and Oyoon had a few bags and boxes to take home with her. She hugged me as I walked out the door. I was so surprised at the uncharacteristic gesture that I think I startled her, but I returned her sweet embrace and thanked her for keeping me sane amongst the insanity. Her warmth was a memory I wanted to carry with me always. I packed so much less than what I left behind that day, but I was happy that I'd not have to return to those icy quarters ever again.

We decided to grab lunch in Khovd, and then we all set out on the road to Ulaanbataar. Chris and I agreed that we would take Oyoon with us, since driving for twenty hours or more on roads that were sparsely marked was something we didn't want to venture without a native. We piled into the car saying little, and tried to sleep between taking turns driving. The days had already started to become longer with sunrises before 6 a.m. and sunsets well after 8 p.m. I sat back and let the rhythm of the road lull me to sleep, but my thoughts were fighting my rest.

We were all leaving Mongolia. Chris was asked to report back to UCLA after being told there would be an investigation into David's accident. Rebecca was just excited to be able to return home. We decided to take the journey together to Chicago, and then they would take another leg to LA. Chris had asked me to promise not to divulge anything to Rebecca, so I didn't. It felt unfair. Wrong. *Is*

Christopher going to continue this insane study? Had he actually gone on a successful trip to the past, or future, or whatever it was? New questions began to haunt me.

I tried not to care. I was ready to see my parents and family for the first time in over two years. I determined that I'd leave it all behind and never look back. I had to. *I just had to.*

CHAPTER FOUR

"Penny for your thoughts?" Dad stepped onto the back of the large old porch of the farmhouse with a tray of ice-cold beverages.

The backyard view was a peaceful sea of tall cornstalks in the summer. It was one of my favorite places in the world. The brick farmhouse had stood for generations, and the white porch with its square pillars and blue-green roof complemented the landscape superbly. The porch wrapped around the entire house. We would paint the beams, railing and lattice with the same white paint every few years just to watch it chip off again with time. I used to hate that task. But these days, I wouldn't have minded spending my hours mindlessly stroking the wood with whitewash. I sat outside as often as I could, remembering the days of the menial tasks of painting the porch or barn, popping peas, watching grandma knit, and seeing dad wait outside after each date I'd ever had as if to let any suitors know that a kiss goodnight would have an audience. There I was, listening to the old classical piano records that my parents played throughout my childhood, the dramatic music swells filling the home and spilling out onto the porch outside. I was sitting on my grandmother's antique rocker that my mom had painted a deep green to contrast well with the red brick. I sat gazing off into the distance–again.

"Thanks, Dad," I said as I took the lemonade from his extended hand and began to sip it down.

"My favorite on a hot, summer day!" he said in his ever-so-chipper voice.

"Mine too, Dad…I…"

There were long pauses of silence during those days. Everyone gave me time. *Time.* There it was again. A measurement that kept me apart from my love, from his memory, or possibly from his actual being…or was I just going crazy? The fact that somewhere in time, my lovely David could be living, breathing, and loving without me was haunting my every thought.

"You, what, Anna?"

"Hmm?" I said as I continued to stare just past the kitchen window.

"You said 'I', and then you stopped," Dad replied.

More silence. Dad moved in closer to see my face and make sure I was listening. I could see his eyes. I realized that it had been a long time since I had looked a person in the eye when speaking with them. "What is it, Anna, why don't you just talk about it–about him? David wouldn't want you to be this way. So silent. So withdrawn. *Please.*"

To see my dad pleading with me on bended knee, my hand in his, brought tears to my eyes.

"Oh, I don't know, Dad. What can be said?" I spoke softly.

He reached to swipe a tear from my eye, kissed my hand, and stood. As he returned to his big, cushioned wicker chair, I heard him breathe a heavy sigh of grief.

"Your vocabulary may be feeble at a time like this, Anna, but it's not the eloquence with which you grieve that matters. It's the fact that you must grieve, and that you mustn't do it alone that matters."

"And silence isn't a part of that, Dad? Being lonely?"

"If it moves toward acceptance, then I guess it is. I'm not telling you how to grieve, sweetie. I'm not even telling you *to* grieve, because you can't get away from grieving him. I'm just telling you that you are here and David is gone, and I don't know that you have even accepted that. You are here in body…but you're a million miles away. Those two children need a mother. I don't care if you don't believe what everyone says about being young and able to find true love and happiness again. I'm just concerned that you seem like you are living your life as if David is somehow going to knock on the front door and come back."

The doorbell rang.

Dad and I looked at each other in surprise, taken aback by the timing, and we both chuckled. Levity at that moment was just what I needed to lift the burden of guilt, if only momentarily, from not sharing my heart's struggles with my dear old dad.

"Well, if that *is* him, I guess I'll get it," I smirked and gave a flippant shrug as if to try to mask the fact that I was secretly hoping it *was* David.

I walked around the corner of the old porch to the front part of the house. It was the UPS man.

"Hello," I smiled. I was a little embarrassed at the stupidity of my thoughts, as if the man could read them.

45

"Hello, ma'am! You'll have to sign for this," he said cheerfully.

My name was written on the box he held with a Californian return address. My heart dropped.

It must be from Christopher and Rebecca. They had returned to California where Christopher was reassigned to other tasks at the university while he began taking part in an investigation that the college was launching into David's death. He was not allowed to be onsite in Mongolia while the investigation was underway on MIU's part, but remained in constant contact with both universities as they recovered all the documents that he was required to submit. Rebecca had asked me three times to join them in California, but I couldn't bring myself to face her. I wasn't sure I believed the outrageous story her husband had told me, and I certainly didn't want to be involved in an investigation if I didn't have to.

I had, however, sent my kids to see their Californian grandparents. Maggie and James had been gone for two days visiting David's family in California. David's mom swept into town and suggested that it would be good for me to have a week off. She assured me that it would be best for me to join them in LA the following week. I knew she had been concerned, but being with my kids and watching others shouldering the majority of their care while I did nothing more than sulk, was somehow a bit easier than having them so far away from me. Regardless, alone is what I *said* that I wanted, and alone is what I got.

After signing for the package and watching the brown truck move down the long driveway and toward the barn, kicking up white dust from the dry gravel, I stood frozen at the screen door. A million thoughts raced through my head, and I nearly felt the room spinning. All I could think of were scenarios about what could be in the heavy parcel. It was a white box with a flip-top lid, the size and weight of a large textbook. *Maybe it's just one of his old books that he used when he taught. Surely if they found his body, Christopher would have had the decency to call, to come, something.*

Dad had made his way from the back of the house to the front of the porch. "Anna? What is it?" he asked with a hint of concern.

"Oh, it's just a package. I think Christopher has sent me something of David's from the university. They must have cleared out what little he had left in the offices there. Or something...I apparently didn't know much about his work at all."

"Well, who among us can tell you even the most basic facts about glaciers?" Dad said sarcastically.

"They're cold," I joked.

Rescued by a bit of humor once again. I couldn't let on that I knew there was a story far different from the one that David had led us to believe. Glaciers were the cover story because, really, who would ever question that?

"Well?"

"Well, what, Dad?"

"Aren't you going to open it?" he asked.

"Oh, of course I am. But, if you don't mind, Dad, I'd like to be alone when I do. Please understand..."

"Of course, Anna. You don't have to say another word, I completely understand." Dad kissed my forehead and headed out to the barn.

Mom and two of my brothers had gone to the marketplace where they were selling some of the fresh produce that we grew, so the house was empty. Dad left me to be alone as requested.

I ran my fingers across my name on the box and headed up the stairs to my childhood room. I thought that it was far too country-style as a kid–always desiring an escape to the big city, but I couldn't have enjoyed the rustic charm more as an adult. As I sat on the bed, I covered my bare feet with the old quilt my grandmother had made for my wedding. Each square represented a story that she had read to me as a child. The thick squares had embroidered scenes, patches of letters, or simple color patterns to remind me of the childhood tales we would immerse ourselves in again and again.

I shivered. I always got so cold when I was nervous about impending events. A vent of central air sat directly above my bed; the air conditioning was something I could barely tolerate after having lived years in the frigid Gobi Desert. Cold air was something I never handled with any grace, so why people wanted a frosty breeze blowing on them indoors was beyond me. But the old house would probably have been suffocating for others without the convenience of temperature control.

"Okay, I'm ready," I whispered to myself. I slowly pulled the tape back from the package and opened the lid, revealing a thick, leather-bound book with a closed flap that was secured with a brass lock. A card was tied around it with my name on the envelope.

It was in David's handwriting.

I felt numb. I held it in my quivering hands silently, trying to decide if I was ready to read it. I wondered if he had left me a note because he knew something would most likely go wrong. I was angry about so much. I oscillated between denial and anger constantly, and I was unsure of everything. I was grieving in a way that I didn't know how to handle. The arrogance of his assumption made me furious–that he would assume it was okay to risk his own life or disappearance just for research.

I slammed the lid, bending the cardboard and shoved the package under my bed. "I'm not ready to do this. Not now," I said aloud.

I started to go downstairs, but halfway down, something stopped me. *What if there are answers? What if Chris's story is really what happened and this package holds the key to finding David? How can I go on being angry when my one love may be…just very well might be…alive?*

I stood on the steps, gripping the top of the thick oak banister. Heading back up the stairs slowly, I forced myself to breathe normally.

"You can do this, Anna. Whatever it is, you can get through it and just move on." I had to audibly reassure myself that moving on was necessary, just like everyone was telling me. I had to get past it.

As I walked into the room, I retrieved the box from underneath the bed and opened the flip-top lid. *The envelope or the notebook first?* It was a beautifully antique book with worn edges and a brass clasp that I could tell had been locked somehow. I tried to open it, turning it every which way to see how it was sealed, but I couldn't quite figure out how it worked.

The card it is, I guess. Taking a deep breath, I opened the envelope. The card itself was from my collection of vintage stationery that David had bought me during our first anniversary trip to Paris. He had whisked me away on a whirlwind six-day trip that was one of the most romantic weeks I had ever spent with him. We walked the streets and shops every afternoon as we chose set after set of cards or writing paper that I loved.

I opened the card slowly. Red-hot tears immediately filled my eyes as I read "Dear Anna…" I clutched the note to my chest and wept a silent, deep cry. My chest heaved and my shoulders shook in guttural agony. I could not manage to let out a single sound. My voice was locked in heartbreak, and I felt as if I could cry no more tears.

Oh, how I had longed for the sound of his voice—for the simple calling of my name—"Dear Anna!" My dearest love had penned those words and I sat hopelessly in my old bedroom, hardly surviving without him. How full my life had been because of him, and how empty I felt when he was gone…I had to force myself to read the rest of the words through cloudy tears.

Dear Anna,

Please know that if you receive this note, I realize the need for an apology. I am so sorry that I have left your side. It was never my intention. I knew the dangers my work might lead me to, and still I chose to forge on. You mean everything in the world to me, and I will love you forever—time without end. My birth month, your favorite number, Maggie's birthday, the month James took his first steps, and our wedding day—each moments in time which will lead you to memories of me. Find me, Anna, always and forever in your heart, may you find me.

David

It seemed like a fairly normal note, yet I knew that it meant something—it was chock-full of strange clues. But what they meant, I wasn't sure. "Time without end."

Was he talking about what Christopher was telling me...the perplexing time loop theory that lies above space on a conveyer belt that Chris was trying to explain? Because David never spoke in code—he was always very literal, very matter-of-fact. And find me? Does he actually mean for me to go in search of him, or that I'd always find him in my heart? But those moments? The numbers have to mean something!

I took a long, deep breath.

The numbers. I took out a piece of paper and began to write them down. David's birth month—nine, my favorite number—eleven, Maggie's birthday—the sixth, the month James took his first steps and surprised us all—ten, our wedding day—the seventeenth.

I took the notebook and reexamined the brass lock mechanism. Leather encased the entire book with a stiff rim that I could feel underneath the surface. The skin flowed over to create a flap that covered more than half of the topside of the notebook, which had a connecting strap that locked into a small brass rectangular lock. A round cog protruded slightly out of the bottom. I turned it to the right and heard a click. I figured it worked much like a combination lock, so I started to turn—nine to the right, eleven to the left, six to the right, ten to the left, seventeen to the right.

Nothing.

The cog felt a little wobbly as it clicked along, so I thought that if I lifted it, like winding a watch, it would then turn properly. I lifted and turned. 1, 2, 3, 4, 5, 6, 7, 8, 9 clicks. Just then, a tiny brass rod popped out of the side of the small brass box. I turned it, but there were no clicks; it was basically just loose and pointy.

Eleven? What could eleven mean here? There's no room for eleven clicks on anything. One and one, maybe.

I pushed the rod to the left, and then down to where it was lying flat against the leather, almost disappearing into the lock again. The strap released from the locking mechanism, and I pulled the flap back to open the book, but only revealed the brass casing that made up the book's solid rim. The top piece of leather stayed secure with a quarter-sized brass closure, and I was still unable to get it open. I noticed a flat piece of metal on the rim of the book had popped out. I attempted to turn the brass, but it started to click upward as I tried to move it. Six clicks up.

Nothing popped out this time. The long rim sealed the space where you'd see protruding pages on most other notebooks, and there was no opening that I could find. I looked closely, but didn't see anything that would click or move the number of times I needed it to. I still had ten and seventeen left. What was I supposed to do with those numbers?

Maybe if I move the cog again.

My attempts were futile. The notebook was locked and its contents concealed. I didn't want to just give, but I became so frustrated that I began to feel tears well up in my eyes. I pulled the quilt up over my head and burrowed my head deeply into the covers on the bed to try to drift off. Sleep, my sweet escape.

CHAPTER FIVE

In my steam-filled bathroom after a long, hot shower, my coping mechanism of choice to thaw my bones in the coldest winters of Mongolia, I slowly ran my fingers across my belly. There I stood, in front of my mirror, gazing at a woman who had been changed forever. Not in a bad way–not really. But nagging insecurity can linger even in the best of us. And I was certainly not the nineteen-year-old my sweet David had fallen in love with. I turned to the side and stroked the faint stretch marks that I could hide under clothes, but could never erase. I sighed long and heavy.

The door opened abruptly, and I flung my bathrobe onto my shoulders.

"Whew! It's steamy in here!" David exclaimed as he hurriedly entered the bathroom.

"I guess the water was too hot again, sorry," I said as I quickly pulled my robe closed.

"I wasn't talking about the shower!" David said chuckling as he pulled me as close to him as he could.

I smirked. "Yeah, hot, sexy woman with stretch marks and extra baby fat right here in your steamy bathroom!" I rolled my eyes at him.

He took my face in his hands, as I looked into his gorgeous eyes. The eyes I had never escaped—not since the first time we met. I was lost in them, as always.

"Yes, hot, sexy woman in my bathroom! What is sexier than the woman who has borne my children? The marks leave behind reminders of the fruit of a love like ours." He pulled me closer. "What is more attractive to me than the breasts that give sustenance to our offspring? The womb that caressed our little miracles for nine months, the arms that carry the weight of nurturing our family, our home, our *lives*?" He turned me around to face the mirror once again. "Let me be your mirror, Anna. See yourself through the reflection of my eyes! See yourself the way I see you! Every curve of your body, every inch of your skin, every part of you—for me—will always be perfection."

My eyes welled up with tears. One gentle stroke of David's hand wiped them from my cheeks as he pulled me again toward his face and kissed me. My knees went weak every time.

"Wear the signs of our love on your body as a badge of remembrance that David Sturgeon loves you always and forever. Time without end," he gently whispered.

I woke up in a cold sweat. *Time without end. How could I have known? Had David been hinting to me all along that his research led him to this time-loop theory and I never picked up on*

the clues? That had not just been a dream. It was a recollection an actual event. *But had he said those exact words, or is the unlikely story of a plausible time travel theory simply haunting me?* I felt like I was beginning to live a nightmare–persistent reminders that the one man who saw even my flaws as endearing was now gone–or at least infinitely far out of my reach. My eyes were wet with tears, and my head was throbbing from the crying. I must have been weeping in my sleep. I glanced around the room in confusion. The sun had set and the soft glow of the porch lights peered through the thin curtains of the upstairs bedroom, allowing just enough light for me to remember where I was.

The notebook.

I frantically searched under the bed, feeling around for the box. I took a deep breath. It was still there. I stood and turned on the light, looking into the mirror. My eyes were swollen and my face red. *I could use the mirror of David's eyes about now.*

I glanced at the clock.

8:30? Impossible…

I slowly peered out of my bedroom door to hear the sound of laughter and music rising up the staircase from the living room below. As I crossed the hall to go to the bathroom, I realized that my brother Lyndon had come to Mom and Dad's for dinner. He was the youngest. He worked the fields with Dad most days and went to school at night. He was ten years my junior. Lyndon didn't go off in search of adventure like I did. He loved the simplicity of farm life, and was just plain constant. I loved that about him. My two younger brothers, Brian and Lyndon, stuck around our small farming community and had built a couple of houses on the outermost acreage of Dad's property. My older brother Jim had gone to school, gotten married, and moved to Colorado to be a business consultant for a large agriculture firm long before I had left home, and Brian, who was only two years younger than I, had gotten married during his senior year of college after an injury that put his major league dreams to rest. Agriculture became a learned affection for him, and he possessed a natural knack for it that he must have inherited from my dad. But Lyndon...it was in his bones. Earth, plants, naturally simplistic living—he desired nothing more than that, and would spend any chance he got in the big brick home of our youth.

Mom and Dad would play dinner music and set an atmosphere that would beckon anyone to stay for long hours of eating, talking, laughing, and playing; and Lyndon was simply soaking in another delightful evening at home. I didn't know why they hadn't called me down to join them for a meal, but it must have been because Mom saw that I had fallen asleep. I walked to the bathroom, quickly splashed some water on my face, trying to rinse away the misery my countenance was donning, and quietly headed downstairs.

Lyndon's face lit up when he saw me enter the kitchen. "Hey, Sis!" he said grabbing my arm.

He squeezed me in one of his suffocating bear hug grips as I tried to wriggle away in protest. "Lyndon, you will never grow up!" I laughed.

"Geez, I hope not!" he countered.

Mom and Dad gave us both a grin and started clearing off the table, not before offering me copious amounts of home-cooked food that I had to refuse because of my waning appetite.

Lyndon and I slipped out onto the porch while Mom and Dad continued their three-and-a-half-decade-strong evening ritual of conversation, singing, and dishwashing. We sat on a wooden bench-swing that my grandpa had made when my dad was a kid.

"So, are you going to tell me?"

"Tell you what, Lyn?" I truly didn't know what he was asking.

"Whatever it is that is eating you alive, Ann. Don't get me wrong. I know that it's David. We all know, and we all miss him. Seeing your love for each other wasn't like other people we know…"

I nodded upwards toward the kitchen window where we could see and hear Mom and Dad singing softly in harmony while they laughed and whispered as if they were teenagers. *Really?*

"Well, they don't count. They are of a different generation. Even for their own generation, they are the exception, those crazy kids!" he teased.

It's true. We kids took for granted that our parents loved each other deeply and allowed us to believe in true love when so many around us never had the privilege. It was embarrassing as a teenager, but as an adult, it was something we longed to be around—to remind us all that life is good, a gift, and can be full of love if you look for it. And if we needed real evidence, all we had to do was to go home.

Lyndon and I both smiled and watched Mom and Dad for a few silent seconds. They were an unvarying comfort. He finally looked at me and broke the silence.

"I mean it, Sis. I feel like it's not just that you are missing a piece of your heart. It's like you're not even here sometimes."

"No, Lyn, I know what you mean. It's true. I feel like I will be myself again soon. I just…need some answers." I muttered.

"Answers?" he looked at me in confusion. "What do you mean? The 'whys' that you may be looking for might not be able to be answered, you know? Don't extend your agony, Sis," he urged.

"Yeah, but it's more than that, Lyn. It's…just more," I said cryptically.

Lyndon leaned back on the porch swing and pushed with his feet as we continued to go back and forth. He started to dig deeper.

"Dad said you got a package today. He thought it was from the university. Those kinds of answers?" he asked with raised eyebrows. "Answers of how a man can fall off a glacier and be killed doing God-knows-what?"

"Yeah, those kinds," I could barely get the words out. "Can I tell you something?" *Should I tell him something?*

"Anything, Ann, you know that."

I decided to play it kind of safe. "I got something from the university, that's true. But it wasn't just some of David's stuff. It was a notebook with a combination lock of some sort. I don't know if it's wishful thinking or if it's actually got information that will help me, Lyn, but it's just starting to drive me crazy. I need answers, but it seems like they keep eluding me!" I crossed my arms and let out a sigh. Lyndon stopped the methodic sway of the swing by locking his knees.

"Well, I'm here whenever you need help, Sis. I don't know what kind of answers you could get from a notebook, but if I can help, let me know," he said putting his arm around my shoulder and giving me a quick tug.

I looked at him with a helpless stare.

"Can I see the notebook? Maybe I can help with that, at least," he shrugged.

"I…well, I don't know if I'm prepared to see what's in it, Lyn, or if I want to share what I find, but…" I looked at my little brother's round face and blue eyes, and I smiled. "I guess if anyone were to help me, you'd be the one I want," I said with a soft smile.

He looked at me and gave me another side-squeeze and smirked in a way that made my little brother so endearing. He had a bright smile and square teeth that would light up any space. His beard was kept to a short whisker in the winter, and a nearly unfamiliar clean-shaven man would reappear during the warm days of summer. I patted his arm lightly and consented to his offer of help.

We headed to the staircase as Mom and Dad continued their task of kitchen clean up, and I began to slow my pace. As we ascended step by step, my face began to feel flushed, and heat started to rise from my chest. I was sure that my little brother was going to think I was nutty if he found out what I was looking for, but I was convinced that I had to search for answers no matter what.

Before I opened the door to the bedroom, I looked back at him. "I don't know if I can do this, Lyn," I whispered.

"Sure you can, Sis. We'll face it together," he assured me as we pushed the door open. I turned the light on, pulled the box out from under the bed and handed the hefty book to him.

"Okay?" he said examining the leather book. "It's heavy," he observed then he tugged on the flap with no success. Then he pointed to the brass circle on the top. "So what's the deal here?"

"Well, I'm not sure how it works. I think the combination is 9, 11, 6, 10, 17…but I haven't gotten past the six," I admitted.

"What does this do here?" he asked as he fiddled with the rod on the side.

"Well, if I knew that, Lyn…" I laughed.

"Yeah, sorry. Hang on, how did it start out?" he asked. "Was it closed more than this when you got it?"

I hadn't even thought of that. I wriggled and turned the brass casing and lock until I finally had it back in its original position. We started over. Nine clicks of the cog. The rod was one up, one down, then the flat piece went six clicks upwards, and I was left where I had been with little room to go anywhere with the numbers ten and seventeen.

Lyndon ran his fingers across the margins of notebook and found that a small cog had barely protruded from underneath the rim of the brass on the edge of the book after that sixth click.

"Hey, here! This should click ten times!" he said with such excitement that I could almost feel my hope hanging on every click. He reached ten. The brass lock on the top snapped, and we opened the leather flap to reveal the thinnest screen I had ever seen, attached by a latch that held it fastened to the brass rim.

"Seventeen?" Lyn asked me in bewilderment.

I just sighed. "Yeah. Or maybe try one and seven, like with the one-one for eleven!"

"Okay, but one which way? I'm afraid to force the latch."

"Just try," I said. There was nothing more I could suggest.

He pushed the latch to the left, the right, up then down. Finally, when he pushed down on the latch, it clicked into the rim. When he tried to release it, and go somewhere else seven times, it didn't budge.

"Hold it down and slide it," I said.

He set it on the dresser and held it firmly down as we started to count the clicks aloud as the right side of the brass casing slid upward. One turned into two, then to five, seven, and the whole of the brass side began to slide off. Sixteen clicks later, it was removed completely. "Well, one click down and sixteen clicks up the sides, you'll need to remember that!" Lyn said.

We stood in silence for a few seconds.

"What is it, Anna?"

"I'm not sure," I said with a short laugh, because I was the last person in the world to recognize new gadgets and technology, and certainly less likely to know than he was.

I cautiously touched a button on the front screen and it began to glow.

"That is the weirdest iPad I've ever seen," Lyndon said, his eyes darting between the glowing leather-bound book and me.

We were both in awe of this seemingly old leather notebook being a casing for an electronic device, that I nearly missed the invitation to enter a password until it chimed at me. I quickly entered the numbers nine–eleven–six–ten–seventeen. A home screen, much like any device would have, appeared with rows and rows of what looked like files. The background of the screen was a scene of majestic stars and a constellation–Orion the Hunter–David's favorite. I ran my fingers across the screen.

"I don't know where to begin, Lyn," I sighed in confusion.

"Well, maybe start with this," he said, lifting up the screen to find the older part of the notebook. There was an edge of an old paper sticking up out of the right corner that I hadn't even noticed. Lyndon had removed the tablet fairly simply and beneath it was a whole tray that the rim had attached to that was full of old notes and diagrams. It held a scientific journal with sketches, written formulas, and drawings. I didn't recognize any of the writing, and was surprised that it would have been sent to me from David.

"I'm not sure how to make sense of any of this, Lyn. I guess you have to be a scientist to appreciate the treasures here. It's just full of David's years of study, I would imagine. But it doesn't look like his handwriting," I said. "He always used the tiniest letters when he'd scribble notes onto things."

"Well, it must be someone else's research notes, I suppose. Look at this!" he exclaimed.

I felt my heart drop. If Lyndon found out that David was possibly studying time travel, I could get Christopher's cover blown, and my little brother would just think we were all insane.

I took the paper from Lyndon's hand timidly.

"What do you think it is, Sis? Who is this professor Bennett? Geez, he seems rather meticulous," he said as he ran his fingers down the columns of information written on the coarse pages.

"He probably was. He worked in David's department before Professor Trinkton is all I know, and they shared some of their findings," I said, trying to avoid eye contact.

"About glaciers or space? Because this looks like rocket science, not glacier stuff!" Lyn said in confusion as he rifled through pages.

I shook my head, shrugging my shoulders, then looked more closely at the sketches he was holding. Formulas were scratched and scribbled all along the edges of the paper. I looked at him in bewilderment.

"Since when did you become a rocket scientist, Lyndon Wright?" I joked.

"Since when did David?" he asked with a smile. "What does all of this mean, I wonder," he said with the same curiosity that was pervading my every thought.

"I wish I knew, Lyn," I sighed.

"We'll figure it out, Sis, it's okay," he reassured softly, draping his arm around my shoulder. I slightly flinched and shrunk away from him at the word *we*.

"What is it, Anna?" he asked as he lowered his arm, taking a step back.

I impulsively began to stack the papers, scrambling to put them away as Lyndon looked on with wide eyes. Stuffing them back into the tray, I flipped the leather strap and closed the top, leaned my hands on the dresser to catch my breath, and turned to look at my baby brother's face.

"I'm sorry, Lyn. I don't know what I was thinking. I can't do this," I said abruptly.

"Anna, it's all right. I didn't mean to upset you. I want you to know that I'm here to help whenever you need it," he said with concern.

"I know," I took a long sigh, "and I need it." I could no longer handle the emotion. I turned back toward the dresser and began to sob. Lyndon warmly took my hand and led me to the bed to sit down. I cried long enough to have scared anyone away, but he stayed, periodically handing me a tissue.

"Anna, won't you please talk to me?" he pleaded.

"Lyndon, I promised," I spoke through my tears, as I would occasionally catch a breath and sniffle into a tissue. I promised that I wouldn't tell!" I cried.

"Tell what, Anna? Is it really that serious?" He paused. "Illegal?" his eyes widened.

"I don't know," I muttered.

"Won't you please let me help?" he said, sounding desperate.

I took the notebook in my hands and reopened it. I began to spill the beans. Every last bit. I told Lyndon the entire story as he sat on the desk chair to the side of the bed, soaking in each word.

"So, this holds the answer?" He plucked the heavy notebook from my hands and put it on his lap.

"I guess," I shrugged in uncertainly. "I mean, if we can figure out what any of it means."

"Well, let's get started!" he said with enthusiasm.

I was stunned. It was not the reaction that I expected from a rational human being.

"Lyn! This is crazy! I mean...isn't this crazy? You aren't going to tell mom and dad to commit me to an asylum or something?"

"An *asylum?*" he said in a teasing voice. "Sis, who even uses that word anymore? And no. I'm going to help my big sister find answers to a pretty captivating mystery! Yes, that's kind of crazy. But I need a bit of mystery in my little hum-drum life!" he playfully exclaimed.

Over the next couple of evenings, Lyndon came over to help me sift through all of the information in the book. We set up an area to lay out our findings in the back of the big barn, where Dad had set up a space for a small office that held a workshop with all of his power tools. We began to separate the papers into sections: past, present, and future, ironically enough. We had found a tiny USB cable and power cord in a small pocket on the flap of the notebook, and were able to keep the tablet charged as we printed out some of the files which seemed to correlate to earlier findings. Dad had a busy season in the fields, so his inside workroom remained undisturbed for us to spread out the data.

The *past* section held conjecture and formulaic methods of previous time travel attempts along with theories written by Professor Bennett who had supposedly disappeared. *Present* held all the information that David and Professor Trinkton had gathered from what we could tell. *Future* held all the speculation each man had concluded about the future, many years beyond the two thousands. Charts and formulas were scribbled in various places across the pages with theories of reentry, calculations for what we assumed were rocket ship functions, and dates that indicated time travel far beyond the present day.

The lights in the old barn cast a yellow hue over the entire space as we worked late into the evening. There were reoccurring names listed at the corners of each page with data below that made little sense. "What should I do about these names, Anna?" Lyndon asked.

"I guess we should just make a running list of them and how many times they appear. It's so odd," I said, wondering what more names would have to do with anything, but since we were trying to be thorough, I decided that another list couldn't hurt.

"Yeah…so weird…I'll read them off to you, and you take notes, okay? Do you want the dates along with them? They seem to be reoccurring too."

"Sure." I typed as Lyndon dictated a list of about sixty names. The dates showed a pattern. Each time a name appeared, a date within a span of one single decade occurred.

"These are by decades, Lyn! Do you think that there are sixty different people within each decade who tried and succeeded at this time travel stuff, and this is the log of their travels?" I asked in bewilderment.

"Ann, I don't know what to think, to be honest. Anything I thought I knew is certainly coming into question now!" He leaned back on the large wooden desk chair that Dad kept in his workshop, crossed his arms, and exhaled deeply.

I sighed. I knew the feeling.

"Whatever it is, Anna, you have the information in front of you to ask Christopher for some real answers. If David is dead and he can assure you of that, then you will have the closure you need to move on."

"And if he can't?" I muttered, nearly breathless at the thought.

Lyndon stood, giving me a hug as I joined him, and handed me the stack of papers that we had printed, complied, and combed through for hours.

"Then you'll have to insist on answers about this information," he said tapping on the stack of papers he had put in my hands.

I knew he was right. I had too much knowledge on the subject to be ignored, and I wanted the truth. We began to clear out our workspace and pack things up as neatly as possible. The heavy leather notebook had given birth to so much information. We had gone through nearly everything—even many of the hand-sketched papers had been scanned and entered into the tablet for safekeeping. We had kept the originals as safe as possible, and printed as many as we could place into categories. *Lyndon's done everything that he can to help. Christopher will have no choice but to give me real answers. We've put too much of the puzzle together for him to not explain things.*

We gathered all the original papers and placed them with the tablet back into their rightful home in the beautiful leather-bound notebook and brass casing. Lyndon placed it atop a spiral-bound printout book of all of our findings.

"Well, you should go and pack your bags, Anna. And you make sure you give those two precious babies big hugs and kisses from Uncle Lyn-lyn!" he smiled.

My children. I had been so consumed with my own grief and finding answers, that I had barely even thought of them over the last few days. *What could this mean for them?* Panic threatened to set in, but I tried to keep it together.

"Yeah, I miss them so much!" I said with a heavy sigh. We started the quick walk back to the house.

"Me too!" he said. "What time do you have to leave here?" he asked.

"I'm taking a four o'clock flight from O'Hare to LA," I said looking at my watch and realizing that we had worked the entire night through. "I didn't even notice the sun coming up, Lyn."

He placed his arm around my shoulders as we walked, and smiled. "I guess that only gives you a couple hours to get your things together and head off to the airport." He kept his grip around my arm and whispered in my ear, "Be safe, will ya, Sis?"

I could hear deep concern hang on his voice. I knew this journey could hold dangers I had never imagined. So did he.

"I'll do my best," I replied tearfully.

Mom and Dad were already up and about getting ready for an early start to another summer day. I greeted both of them with a good morning peck on the cheek, and declined to sit with them for breakfast so I could start packing. Mom soon joined me in the bedroom.

"Emotional goodbye with Lyndon earlier, wasn't it?" she asked.

"Yeah, Mom, everything's emotional these days, I guess," I said shrugging my shoulders.

"Mm-hmm. It sure is, sweetie," she said quietly nodding her head. Mom didn't pry or push her way into anyone's business, but you could always tell if she had an insightful word of wisdom lingering beneath her soft-spoken surface.

"I love you, Mom. I do. No matter what happens," I put my arms around her and hung on tightly.

"Anna, you're going to California for a few weeks. I know it's going to be hard, but it's going to be all right!" she assured me with a smile. "We are here for you."

My mom. Always the optimist. I was thinking that I wanted to go and find my husband in a rocket ship in some kind of space journey to a black hole, and my mom was thinking of the meal she'd cook for my sweet kids and me when we arrived back from LA, deeply concerned that my grief was too heavy to carry alone, and silently hoping that this trip would give me closure. I took a breath, and smiled lovingly toward her.

"You're right. I'll see you when I get back, Mom," I said with a bit of confidence. "Are you sure you don't want to ride with Dad and me to the airport?"

"Oh, you know me, I don't like that long drive or those goodbyes at the airport. We'll have our time to say 'see you later' right here in the comfort of our own home!" she said lightheartedly and picked up a cardigan off of the chair. "Take this, that AC is a killer in airports."

"Thanks, Mom," I said as I took it from her hand and draped it over my purse.

We went down the stairs and out to the old white porch. I hugged my mom once more and met my dad at the car for him to take me to the airport. The long ride was strangely comforting as I watched the colors of the summer sun upon the horizon casting hues over each story and piece of advice my dad would give as he filled the time with his beautiful words. The rays of lasting sun would compliment each moment as if they were coloring his very conversation in beautiful illustration. I tried to soak in every word.

"You all right, kiddo?"

"Yes, Daddy, just enjoying listening to you talk. I am truly blessed," I said as I turned my head to see him.

My dad chuckled softly, and then went straight to solemn.

"The loss of David has changed us all, Anna. But making us all more appreciative of what we have is such a wonderful thing. I do pray that you get comfort and peace about your lot in life while you're in California that you couldn't get from what we offer you here at home, sweetie. We never could keep you tied down to the simple farm life, could we?" he smiled and chuckled again.

"And strangely, Dad, it's the one place I ache for each time I've been away too long," I grinned.

"Ah, that's not strange, that's just the phenomenon we call 'home,' my dear. And we truly are blessed to have it."

The five-hour drive to the airport went all too quickly for once. As we arrived at the terminal, I decided that I would keep a levelheaded approach to my finding answers. I would spend at least a few days with my children, drinking in every second of time I would have with them. Then I would explain to David's parents that I had business to wrap up at the university where I would approach Christopher. I was determined to put the whole thing to rest. There was a heavy load of information in my suitcase–information that at least three educated men had devoted their lives to. If their theory was possible, then maybe I wasn't losing my mind. If it was a waste of time, then I had lost my David for nothing, and it might just be easier to be angry about everything than to go on wondering.

This is how I will cope. It's how I will move past this and become the old Anna that everyone wants to see again. I'll demand answers.

"Be safe, Pumpkin. Call me when you land," Dad said as he grabbed my bag from the trunk, then hugging me.

"Dad, it'll be kind of late for you–I'll call you in the morning."

"You call me when you land; I'll sleep better having heard from you," he insisted.

"Okay, Daddy. I love you!"

My dad rarely gushed with loving proclamations, but this time he kissed my cheek, held me tight and said, "I love you, dear, come back safe."

Strangely, I couldn't promise him that. I couldn't assume that things would go as planned. I just smiled, kissed his cheek, rolled my bag behind me, walked toward the entrance, and began my journey.

CHAPTER SIX

"Anna! What are you doing here?" Chris answered the door and quickly slipped out into the long hallway of the university office space.

I placed my hand on the door, expecting him to invite me in. "Christopher, I had to come," I said, almost as if I was begging.

"I told you not to, Anna, please. You're making this more difficult than it has to be! I sent you the last of David's things here," he sternly whispered, keeping his hand tightly on the doorknob so I couldn't intrude, but I held my hand firmly on the door, pushing back. "I have already told you what I know over the phone," he said. "And it really is all I can do, Anna. I have to worry about the investigation now. It's not good for you to be here." Christopher held on firmly, trying to keep me from forcing the door open.

"Chris, what am I supposed to...?" I began to plead with him for some kind of help.

"Who is that?" I heard a voice asking from inside Christopher's office. Reaching a new level of frustration, I pushed the door open with my body to see who Chris had been hiding me from, attempting to nonchalantly introduce myself.

"Hi, my name is Anna Sturgeon, a friend of Christopher's," I said with as much ease as I could muster, extending my hand.

"Why, Christopher, you never told me David had such a lovely wife!" The man smiled. He knew exactly who I was. "I'm Professor Trinkton," he continued, firmly shaking my hand.

I took a slight step back, but the professor didn't release his grip. I was in shock; for some reason I thought he had died. I had assumed that he had taught Chris and David about impossible theories and then left them to continue a work that he had left behind. But there he stood–the man whose work I had been rummaging through for the past few days, and the person whom I blamed for the disappearance of my husband. I could feel rage rising up from my core. My face felt warm and my hands were sweaty. I held the briefcase in my hand as it suddenly became heavier at the thought of what I had come to show Christopher. I glanced his way. He shrugged his shoulders, giving me a wide-eyed look, shaking his head as if motioning that he had tried to tell me. I stumbled over my words.

"I...I've heard so much about you, Professor. I'm glad to finally meet you." Professor Trinkton was just what a professor should be. Grey-headed and handsome, wearing wiry glasses. His stature was tall, lean and perfectly intimidating. He wore an impeccable suit and a starched white shirt with an unbuttoned collar and shiny cuff links that protruded slightly out of the long sleeves of his jacket.

"And I, you, my dear," he kissed my hand, drawing it slowly to his lips and gently releasing it again. I shuddered and quickly drew my hand back to my side.

"Come, now, Mrs. Anna Sturgeon, let's have a chat. May I offer you a beverage?" The professor cordially made his way to a small coffee and drink bar set up on the left wall of the office.

I stood silently for a few seconds and then realized that the two men were looking at me, waiting for an answer.

"Oh, forgive me, I'll take a coffee if you have enough."

"Perfect! That's what I was preparing when you came in. Now let's all sit down and have a chat, shall we?" the professor asked as he tilted his head to one side, grinned, and squinted his eyes through his round glasses. He went to the counter to pour the coffee as he motioned for us to take a seat.

I watched as he made his way around the office as if it was his own before Christopher ever occupied it. The professor was the type of man that I would notice on the street and call David's attention to, as I'd whisper in his ear that I loved distinguished-looking, grey-headed men. I would tell David that I planned to be in love with him as much when he was older as I was when we were in our youth, as long as he aged well, of course. Then we'd laugh, and he would kiss my forehead.

"I'll love you forever, Anna," would always be his reply.

I felt a soft smile curl on my face at the memory of David, and my love for him eased the moment. I took a long breath as I sat down.

Christopher began, "Anna, I don't know why you came today, but since you did, maybe it will make things easier on the professor and me."

"Of course! While I am here, it is important that I speak with Mrs. Sturgeon, Christopher," the professor said cheerfully. "Who knows when my next visit will be? We should have spoken of this sooner!" The professor playfully scolded Christopher as he finished up the coffee and walked toward us carrying a tray of drinks.

"Oh! You don't live here in LA? That explains why I thought…" I realized that I was about to say that in my mind he was dead, so I let my thought trail off. I rubbed my clammy palms on my lap and took a breath.

"You presumed me to be dead, did you?" the professor teased.

"Well, yes, I thought so," I said shyly. "I thought you were one of the men who left behind studies for David and Christopher to carry on."

"As a matter of fact, I have. But my work is not yet done," he explained. "Cream and sugar, dear?"

"Just cream, please," I replied as the professor came and placed the tray on a square bistro table that was near the coffee bar where we had sat down.

The room fell strangely silent. I didn't know if I should break the ice and just open my heavy briefcase, or if there was something they'd tell me without my asking for it. I instantly became nervous, started fidgeting, and concluded that I had made a colossal mistake. *Why was it that I came here again?*

"Well, obviously I've disturbed you both," I said feeling more and more uncomfortable. "I…I guess we can talk later, Christopher. Maybe I'm fooling myself with thinking that this will all make sense to me anyway," I said as I grabbed for the briefcase that rested at my feet. I felt defeated. I wondered what I thought I would be accomplishing by coming to the university. *Maybe it's time for me to put this behind me and go to my sweet children.* I stood swiftly and awkwardly began to walk toward the door.

"Anna, wait," the professor admonished. "You will need to prepare yourself. You *can* find answers. But do you *want* them?" he asked.

"Professor, I don't mean to be rude, but I don't know you, and I don't trust you enough to tell you what I think I do or do not need to know. I just thought…Well, I thought all the studies and expeditions were a sham to convince my husband to believe in the nonsense that got him killed. Or lost. Or whatever this is, Professor," I paused and shook my head. "What *is* this? Do you intend to give me answers? Real answers?" I pleaded with him as he left the table where we had been sitting, and approached me.

He held my elbow, leading me to a couch by the bookshelf that lined the right side of the room. I felt the same cold chill run down my spine that I had felt when he kissed my hand. I was positive he couldn't be trusted.

Surely this was a mistake.

"Anna, what's in the briefcase?" Christopher asked.

I had almost forgotten that it was in my hand. I was clenching it tightly in a protective manner. I drew it close to my chest and hugged it. Sitting on the couch, I glanced up at them both shyly.

"Just some things I've been piecing together from the package you sent me, Chris. I came to show you evidence of what I think that I have found. And I guess I came to accuse you a bit. But I don't know if I even feel like slinging accusations now. I just want answers, guys," I said, not letting go of the treasure of information I cradled.

"Then answers you shall receive, Anna." The professor's voice was calm and reassuring, but I remained skeptical. I sat unmoved for a moment, looking at the two men—hoping that they could not see on my face what turmoil was happening in my soul. I didn't respond. They waited for a few moments as we all sat in silence.

"Well, then, I'll begin, I suppose," the professor said leaning back, and removing the thin glasses from his eyes and lifting them to his lips. "Anna, I believe I must properly introduce myself–I am Professor William Trinkton, successful time traveler."

What he said next was a mixture of muffled static and words I couldn't piece together. It felt very much like I was in a trance. Blurs of sounds and wave-like images ran through my head to cloud what he was saying, and I sat motionless, trying to feel the tips of my fingers as I stared at the grey bag on my lap. I lifted my head to see Christopher leaning in close to my face.

"Anna? Are you?"

"I'm sorry, am I?" I asked in confusion. "Am I what, Christopher?"

They both had a look of pity on their faces, as if they sympathized with my reaction.

"So, at what point did you stop listening?" the professor laughed.

"Um, when you said *successful time traveler*," I said, shaking my head. "Yeah, you lost me," I admitted.

The professor chuckled a bit, but still continued as if he understood my dilemma. "I am from the future, Anna."

"*What?*" I whispered incredulously. *The future?* I felt myself reeling. I needed a moment. I motioned with my hand for him to stop talking, and placed the grey briefcase on the floor next to the couch. I inhaled deeply. "Are you being serious?"

I sat looking at the two men, waiting for one of them to tell me that this was some ludicrous joke, or a cover-up for how David died so that the university wouldn't get sued.

"Completely serious, my dear." The pity in Professor Trinkton's voice was almost palpable. He must have done this before–been the one to reveal time travel secrets to a listening ear–or perhaps he was just patronizing me. I couldn't quite make up my mind about him.

"So how many people have you told about your successful time travel, Professor?" I had a sarcastic tone to my question, and I didn't care. I squinted my eyes, trying to subtly scan the professor for some kind of super-advanced gadgetry or high-tech beams that might give him away as a futuristic being, but he looked uninterestingly normal.

"Anna, I know this is hard to believe. I have traveled in time from the future three times, and there are very few people who know this information. I believe that you are trustworthy–someone who must know the facts at this point. You need answers, and I can give them," he said.

I leaned back on the couch and crossed my arms in disbelief.

"Okay, what year did you come from?" I asked, not really giving him time to respond. "How long do you stay in our time? And what in the world do you travel in?" Joke or no joke, I did want his answers.

The professor gestured toward the back of the office. "Anna, take your briefcase and come with me. I have something to show you, and you've obviously come prepared. You can do this."

Do what?!

I didn't know how else to respond, so I grabbed the bag and stood with him. Christopher, who had remained silent to allow the professor to take over the conversation, walked to the back of the room and pushed a button on the back wall near the coffee pot. A piece of the wall inconspicuously slid behind the second half of it, and an elevator door appeared. I stood bewildered and motionless until Christopher had to take my hand and lead me into the elevator.

The three of us stood silently as the door closed, and we slowly descended. From what I could tell, the office shouldn't have been more than couple stories above ground, since I had only walked up a small flight of stairs to get to there, but the descent seemed to be lengthy. We hadn't spoken. I wasn't sure if they weren't saying anything because they didn't know what to say, or if it was because they knew it would be best if I were left to simply take in my surroundings.

As we exited the elevator, we entered an enormously circular space, housing a balcony that jutted out over a sunken area that went at least another forty feet or more below us that held an oval-shaped spacecraft. The circular room was lined with digital screens, knobs, buttons, and transparent furniture. I stood motionless for a moment, trying to gather my thoughts.

"What is this?" I finally whispered moving slowly along the oval walkway, down a step to the slightly sunken control area, peering over the three-foot glass balcony wall, gazing at the spacecraft below. The craft sat in a large metal cradle that looked as if it was the beginning of a roller coaster track that would propel the vessel down a tunnel that sat to its left.

"Anna, would you like to show me the information you brought with you? I would love to know where to start, what you already know, and how to proceed." Professor Trinkton asked.

Does the world deserve to know that these things exist? That someone from the future visits us? How can I not be upset? Or am I just intrigued? And that would make me as insane as the men I am with. Wouldn't it?

"How to proceed, Professor?" I wasn't only confused at that point, but nearly frightened and eager to return above ground. I was ready to accuse. "You want to keep me quiet so that your little secret is safe?" I was nearly angry at that point.

"Are you telling me that UCLA knows about this, funds the operation, and the information I have is part of a legitimate time travel study?" I had been leaning over the glass staring at the stunning technology that surrounded me. "This is for *real*?" I asked, turning to look at the professor, and leaning myself up against the glass.

Christopher had been so uncharacteristically quiet for the most part that I had almost forgotten he was there. "Yes, Anna, this is for real," he said, "but it's not so much the secret we're concerned with keeping. Please don't be angry. We do understand why David left you clues, and we understand why you are here. We want to help you, we really do. Please let us."

"*Help?!* Christopher, you want to help me? When I begged you for answers and you eluded them until I thought I would go crazy, *that* was a big help! You give me vague explanations, tell me not to come here, and now you are *helping* me?" I was angry by then.

"Anna, please," Christopher said softly.

I could no longer take the emotions I was feeling. I put my face in my hands and began to cry. "I'm sorry. I don't mean to bite your head off, Chris," I said tearfully. "You really aren't just trying to manipulate me into believing a weird story and shut me up for good so you can continue this farce?" *Please tell me that I am not going completely mad.*

Professor Trinkton put his stiff, long fingers on my shoulder. "Anna, my dear, please understand something. UCLA does, in fact, know about our involvement. It is considered a secret, but it's not one that's hard to keep safe. Consider the facts, Anna." The professor spoke dryly. "Many have caused one scene or another about time travel, and they were very quickly written off. This workroom can easily be explained as a laboratory for scientific space study. The university will not look suspicious," he said confidently.

I began to feel myself calm down. Sometimes letting my tears wash away my emotions was my only release, and it definitely started to work. Christopher brought me to a chair that was placed at a long, rounded clear table that lined one section of the circular workspace.

"Let's begin, shall we?" the professor said with a smile.

I gave him a look of compliance, shrugged my shoulders and said, "We might as well."

The professor looked pleased. He tapped the long table and an integrated electronic device came to life as it lit up the table, the walls, and large screens that encased the walls. I had seen transparent screens before, but not of that magnitude, not in real life. It was as if the entire room was aglow with a strange blue shade and a million different twinkle lights. I began to focus on the images. There were photographs from what seemed like every era you could imagine. Lists of data, codes, and maps that depicted what I assumed were entry points from different time travelers.

"Let's see what you brought, dear."

Professor Trinkton reached for the bag, but I abruptly stopped him.

"I'll get it. I can explain as I take things out." I was still protective of the things David had left me.

I set the papers in folders that Lyn and I had created–organized by decade; by past, present, and future; and by professor–but when I took out the beautiful leather-bound book, I clutched it closely to my heart.

"David left me this. I guess you sent it, Christopher, but it's full of the information I printed out, and a simple 'I'm sorry' note." I slipped the heavy notebook back into my bag as I said it because somehow it was the one thing I couldn't relinquish. It was the last thing David's hands must have touched with intention of having it reach me after his departure; it was mine to guard forever.

We began to go through all of the papers. I had so many questions. *What is the circular spacecraft? Did David use something similar? Did they know where in time David was? Do they know if he survived? How did Professor Trinkton successfully go in and out of time periods? Where in time did he come from?*

But those questions would have to wait.

I combed through the vast amounts of information, explaining my conjectures, and, when they would ask, giving them numbers from the combination clue David left.

"I think it was just a combination to unlock the book," I explained, but that didn't stop them from using the numbers again and again as we rummaged through the mountain of information.

It took hours. At least, it felt like it did. I started asking the questions I had been pondering, and had so many more to add along the way. As we sifted through data, I asked more questions, but got very few responses from the two men who were too preoccupied with the information before them to stop and answer every little inquiry that

I had. They simply kept scouring the pages and pages of numbers, notes, and diagrams, typing information into the keyboard illuminated on both ends of the long table. They would repeat the sequence of numerals as they worked. "So…it's more than that?" I asked. "I mean, the numbers–the combination lock. Is it a code to where he is?" I asked, as I walked over to the corner where Christopher was studying the large screen in front of him.

"Anna, let's sit down. It's about time we explain a few things to you." I trusted Christopher, but I was scared. *Sit down? Is this where they break the news to me that I must now leave, David is dead, and thanks for cooperating and sharing the evidence?*

I reluctantly took a seat next to the long table as the professor rolled his chair over toward the two of us. "You'll have to be trained," Christopher said looking at me intensely.

"*Trained?* What are you talking about, Chris?" I had a feeling that I would not like what was coming.

"Anna," he sighed deeply, "just listen. We'll tell you everything–well, as much as we can–tonight, and you can make an informed decision within the next forty-eight hours. But if we want to find David, you'll have to be trained. There are rules. There are methods and there are real chances of fatality. But now that we know what you have, what you know, and how you have deciphered this information, we are sure that you can do this."

"*Do?* Do what, Christopher?"

"Find him yourself."

I felt the room spin.

"*Find him? Find David?*" I could only manage a whisper.

Christopher entered a command on the table, and as if a vending machine was connected, a small window on the wall opened and a bottle of sparkling water and a pack of pretzels appeared. He handed me the cold bottle and small bag, "Eat," he insisted.

"How can *I* help you find him?" I asked, confused at how I could possibly be qualified to go on the venture rather than one of them.

The professor grinned, pulling his chair closer to mine. "Anna, why don't we chat over a nice meal, hmm?" he said coyly.

I nodded in consent. It had been a long day, and I figured that having food could never hurt.

With a few swipes and taps of the professor's fingers along the wide table, dinner was ordered. Within ten minutes, we had our cuisine delivered in three parts through the same window that I had gotten the pretzels and mineral water from. The hot food was set on separate trays as if it had come directly from the university dining hall, but the food itself looked and smelled like a delicious home-cooked dinner. They invited me to dig in. I couldn't stomach more than my pretzels and lime-flavored soda water. I was ready for them to talk, and for me to sit and listen.

"Anna, I'll start by filling in some of the gaps about me, all right?" the professor began. "I have successfully traveled through time—the latest being when I traveled back to 1942. It was our first trial. There was barely enough technology to support my return, and though I met a few glitches along the way, I succeeded. I returned unscathed to my own time. I know that others have been successful as well, but I have not yet had a chance to meet them. I have only found their studies. You see, it's difficult to pinpoint a time traveler because you can't always enter the time period you intend to, and, well, it's the return that is the tricky part. If the fuels and methods do not exist in the time era in which you find yourself, the return flight proves to be much more difficult," he explained. "Also, there are certain rules. Because of the Guardians, I cannot tell you what year I was born, nor can I develop for you tactics and advances in technology–it's safer this way to remain inconspicuous–you must learn and develop ways yourself, and it makes returning back to where you began very tricky."

"What are you saying? Did David go into the past and just get lost there?"

"Anna, this is where you have to be trained. Educated, I guess. About the rules, the process and the explanation of things. You have heard of UFOs I'm sure." Christopher chimed in.

"UFOs?" *This is ridiculous.*

"Yes, the UFO sightings. It's us, Anna. Time travelers," the professor confirmed.

"So there are no such things as…aliens?" I asked with an incredulous tone. Our conversation was sounding extremely absurd to me, but something about it beckoned me to believe it may very well be true.

"Well, I have not been to another universe, Anna," the professor said. "I travel this one. What I am saying, though, is that our vessels travel through space and time and are sometimes noticed. Occasionally they are called UFOs, but they do in fact exist, and there are some who know exactly what they are."

He paused to study my face. I was soaking in each word. "There are dimensions that lie between where we are and what exists before us, and what will exist after us. I know you've done your homework, so I don't mean to condescend, but allow me to explain," the professor continued.

"Please do." I was no longer tempted to mistrust.

"There are what we know as 'black holes' in our universe. If you traveled outer space, you wouldn't live long enough to cross it, so there's no way we travel far enough to get 'above time,' as we say. But the holes in space that we have found are literally portals. Portals above time which can travel in a linear motion as each era exists simultaneously. And there are Guardians, Anna. The list of names you found and so astutely categorized into decades, I might add, are names of the Guardians of the Decades," he explained as he pushed his chair back from the long table, stood, and began tidying up the dinner mess. "There is a realm which interacts with ours, whether we choose to believe it or not. I don't know what your belief system is, but one journey through time opens your eyes to things you have only wondered about–or perhaps hoped for."

"But how…what about David?" It was fascinating to hear all the explanations and theories, but my one true desire was always only to find him. *My David.*

"There's a way for you to find him, Anna," the professor said.

"Me?" I sat back in my seat, assuming him to be joking. "You want me to drive a spacecraft through time portals?" I asked, chuckling in disbelief.

"Yes, of course," the professor said flatly.

"Why *me?* You said that you have done this three times!" It didn't make sense.

"It *must* be you, Anna. We will put too many people and events in danger if one of us attempts this. But no one will suspect you. There isn't evidence of anything more than a normal life that you have lived in this one single time period. I have told you that there are Guardians. We must protect…" his voice trembled and his brow furrowed in concern. "No, Anna, you are our best bet," the professor said decisively.

"But what *happened?*" I asked breathlessly.

Christopher began to explain, "David was sent on a mission. We have a colleague who worked with us back in grad school. I think you might have met her. Laura Francis?"

I nodded. We had met just once. She was tall, curvy, blonde, and intimidating. I remembered her vividly, because when I met her, I wondered what in the world David ever saw in me. "Yes, I do remember her, but she left LA for some remote study in the Amazon, I thought."

"That is the story, yes," Christopher nodded, "we believe she successfully made it through time, Anna. However, when she was supposed to return, she did not come, and David felt guilty. As if it was his own error that made the travel go awry. She was set to arrive in Mongolia—and that's one of the reasons we were there. It's why you moved to the remotest place in the mountain village—so Laura could have an undetected reentry."

Christopher paused and looked toward Professor Trinkton with a sigh. "When she didn't arrive...David just couldn't handle the feelings of guilt...he offered to go on the mission himself to get her back."

Christopher was becoming emotional, and I had felt a few slow tears drip down my own hardened face.

I stood and grabbed my bag. "I can't do any more of this—not tonight. I need to think. Please just take me back upstairs, Chris," I begged. My head was pounding and my heart was so heavy at the thought that David knowingly risked his life for this mission. I wanted to leave before it became impossible for me to suppress the dam of tears threatening to burst.

"Anna, wait," Chris stood and headed toward the elevator door to stop me.

"Christopher, no! He…he…he chose this over me?" It was too late. I could feel the tears streaming down my face. "*Her* over me? I am completely lost without him here! And for what? So that he could save your precious legacy of time travel study? Or what? Save a woman that took her own risks of being harmed or killed by her profession? How is that okay?" I said through the hot tears that streamed down my face. "I don't know what you expect from me, but I can't make any decisions now, nor can I handle any further information. Please. Just take me back. I'll call you tomorrow. I promise."

CHAPTER SEVEN

"Mommy!" Little Maggie greeted me at the door of my in-laws' spacious home. I scooped her up into my arms, held her tightly, and walked in. David's father greeted me warmly as he kissed my cheek.

"Hi, Pops," I smiled and leaned into his big hug. His shoulders were muscular and broad, and he was taller than me by a foot, it seemed. He was the sweetest guy; it was no wonder he raised my lovely David. Everyone who knew him called him Pops, and the name fit him well. He was always smiling, joking, laughing, and encouraging anyone who crossed his path. His nicknames were endless, and it seemed that he never met a stranger. I often wished I were more like him.

"Did you take care of everything at the university, sweetie?" he asked tenderly.

"Not exactly. I might have to return tomorrow. I think I'll need you to watch the kids again," I replied with a shrug.

"Okay, whatever you need, honey. We've got no better job in the world than grandparenting these days!" he said cheerfully.

James and Maggie ran toward me as I entered the kitchen, showering me with kisses. Their sweet voices made my defeated mood disappear, and I listened to James as he tried to mimic the sounds and words of his big sister. They begged me to let them stay up as my mother-in-law, Cheri, started to prepare us a smoothie to enjoy on the back porch.

The vast stone terrace wrapped around the rear of the entire house, with tall windows and doors leading to it from each room along the perimeter. The pool sparkled in the moonlight and the glow from the low lights surrounding us made the evening enchanting. I had almost forgotten what dreamy Californian evenings felt like.

"It's kind of late to have the kids up, Anna, won't you let me put them in bed?" my mother-in-law asked.

"No, Cheri, I'll do it. They can fall asleep here on the chaise watching the stars with me. Let me just enjoy them for a while tonight. I've seen so little of them lately!" I said, as I hoisted them up onto the long chair, giggling and kissing them playfully.

It was past nine o'clock, and little James with his soft curls and blonde hair, nuzzled into my chest and fell asleep within seconds, it seemed. He was turning two in a week, and his little round face had brought so much joy to my saddest days. Maggie was the boisterous one with her auburn hair, golden eyes, and tight curls. She looked so much like her dad that I could stare at her for hours.

Cheri handed me my smoothie before joining Pops on the sofa, as my kids and I sat on the large chaise next to the wall separating the veranda and the pool area, whispering about our day. Maggie, with a slight lisp and endearing toddler voice, told me all about her fun time with Pops and Mimi, how they played in the pool, took a walk to the park, and now insisted that she wasn't even tired.

Pops and Cheri snuggled on the outdoor sofa next to the long chaise the kids and I were sharing, and we enjoyed star-gazing for a few minutes until the best of the long day got to Maggie as well, and we sat in the quiet of the evening.

"Anna, did you know David was in danger?" Cheri broke the silence in a whisper. She must have been aching to ask me for weeks.

"No, Cheri, not really. I mean, I guess deep down there was always a nagging feeling that climbing and measuring all those high mountains and ice caps was, in fact, a dangerous job," I said, attempting to keep my emotion at bay. My voice trembled slightly. "But...no. I never imagined I'd lose him...that *we'd* lose him," I corrected myself with a sigh. The soft tears of agony spilled down my cheeks, realizing that I was forced to continue David's lie. My heart was heavy.

It was difficult for me to imagine what Cheri must have been feeling after having lost a son, so I tried to be sensitive to that. The loss of David was not mine alone. I had a two-and a four-year-old; I couldn't imagine having lived a life of watching them become adults and then losing them in a fatal accident. The thought was nearly unbearable.

Grieving was hard on us all. And there I was, entertaining the thought of leaving my suffering family and needy young children to go on an inconceivable expedition to find my possibly dead husband, and in the process probably get killed myself. *What was I thinking?* Reality and fiction seemed to blur.

Pops and Cheri lay silently on the sofa, not responding to my answer. Their silence was occasionally broken by sniffles and whispers and I decided to give them the privacy they needed.

"I'll put the kids in bed. Thanks for the smoothie, it really hit the spot, Cheri." I said gratefully.

"I'll come with you; you can't carry them both," said Pops, getting ready to stand and help.

"No, Pops, I'll take James first and come back for Maggie. It's all right. Just stay here and soak in the evening. I'm okay." I stood and kissed them both on the cheeks and thanked them again for all they did to help the kids and me.

I carried James, then Maggie to the bedroom next to mine. Pops and Cheri had fixed up two of the rooms in the house for any of their children to visit with their young families. There was a kids' room lined with bookshelves, toy cubbies, two small beds, a crib, and an adjacent bedroom with an en suite for the adults. I stood quietly watching the children sleep for a few extra moments, stroking their hair, and softly kissing foreheads a little longer that evening. I wanted to scoop them up and protect them from any heartache that the world could throw at them. I wanted to promise them that Daddy would someday return. But I couldn't.

I quietly returned to my room. It was a large, inviting suite, and I enjoyed the privacy. The fluffy covers beckoned me as usual, but that night I couldn't sleep. I couldn't even cry. I could barely settle myself to be still enough to rest. My thoughts kept me pacing. *What was David thinking going off into space on a mission to save some girl? This is absurd. I'm just stunned. I need to go back to the university to meet with Christopher and the professor. I won't rest until I hear every option, every explanation. I need to force myself to be unmoved by my emotions and just hear them out. I'm tortur-ing myself otherwise, and I can't live that way.* It was around three o'clock in the morning before I finally nodded off in exhaustion, but I was up again by six.

Cheri was in the kitchen, brewing coffee and prepar-ing her routine breakfast of oats, fruit, and nuts. She wore a long silk housecoat and braided hemp flip-flops. Even in her most casual style, she was an impressive woman, con-fidently donning her silvery white shoulder-length hair, which never seemed to be out of place. She smiled, "Good morning, dear. Can I pour you a cup of coffee?" she asked.

"Sure, thanks, Cheri," I softly said with a thankful smile.

"Pops said that you have more work at the univer-sity. Is there anything we can help with?" she asked. "Did David have items from his office that we need to remove or anything?"

"I don't think so, Cheri. It's more about paperwork and official stuff, really. Most of his personal belongings were removed when we left for Mongolia," I said. I knew that she was not only grieving his loss, but also lament-ing the years that she had missed while we were away. There was a lingering sadness and blame that I felt from her. Not that she tried to project that. But something had come between us since David had disappeared. She wanted him back. She wanted time back. And so did I.

"I can make you an egg or something," she lifted her eyebrows and nodded toward me with a smile.

"It's okay, Cheri. I'd like to get an early start. Can I take that coffee to go?" I wasn't sure if staying and savor-ing a cup of coffee would help mend the hurts between us, or if leaving her to be free from my presence was a better choice. But I was emotionally unprepared to devote energy to the former, so I chose to leave.

I still got to the office by quarter to seven. I was surprised to see the door open.

"Christopher?" I said cautiously, peering into the room to see who was there.

"Hey, Anna. Couldn't sleep?" he asked.

"No. You?" I asked, happy to see that the professor wasn't yet there.

"Not much," he said shaking his head. We sat quietly as Chris shared his hot coffee, sipping and pondering the events of the past twenty-four hours.

"Christopher, how do you explain this to Rebecca? She must know something is up," I asked, knowing that it was a secret that affected so many people.

"Yes, she does," he admitted. "I just told her that you're in town and there's so much of David's stuff to go through that it's making me uneasy. She wants to see you, you know."

"I miss her too," I said, hanging my head. I had been avoiding her; I knew I had. *How could I see one of my dearest friends in the world and not tell her the truth? Could I let her know that her husband is in danger of being sucked into space and time if he continues on like the others before him had? It sounds so stupid—so unbelievable. I can't face her.*

Christopher broke the awkward silence and stood to refill his coffee. "The professor should be here soon, Anna. He wanted to get an early start," he smiled through a short pause and nodded toward me, "he said you'd come back."

I rolled my eyes at him then gave a conceding grin, shrugging my shoulders.

Before the professor arrived, Chris began to explain how his and David's studies morphed from geology and ecology to where we were.

"The path wasn't that long, Anna," he said. The evidence we found intrigued us, and we were hooked within weeks. We only wanted answers. I never thought it would lead us here."

I felt Christopher's excitement and his regret all at once, and it made me understand my own emotions a little better as I listened to him speak. The professor soon arrived and led us to the elevator, which took us back down to the workroom.

"Just tell me what I need to know," I said as we arrived at the control center of the immense room. I was calmer, more calculated, and determined at that point. "Let's get things done."

The professor had not only a look of satisfaction on his face, but he appeared to be slightly excited, which, for the distinguished professor, was enough to make me smile. I grabbed a notebook and pen from my purse, and looked up at him.

"Well...okay, then. Let's do it," Christopher said.

"The first thing I need to do is tell you about how you travel. Your training will include a series of physical aptitude tests as well as timed exercise performance trials. Space travel will require physical stamina, but the combination of the time travel along with it will tax your mind and body as well. And, Anna, you have to be prepared for the Guardians. They protect their time, and the people within it.

"As long as you can go through unnoticed, there should be no problem, but they are there for a reason. When the craft arrives at the black hole, it is instantaneously transported to a band of light where one can literally *see* time. You will be wearing the equipment we give you, of course, but in that space, you can only survive twenty seconds. It is critical that you do exactly what we tell you to survive."

I had to interject. "So, if that's the case, what makes you think David survived?"

"There are codes. Numbers left behind to let us know that a time traveler is alive. That's how we knew Laura was still out there, and how we know David is. Kind of."

"Kind of? Chris, what do you mean 'kind of'?"

"With David, it seems that his codes are intertwined within Laura's and that's why we had to double-check. The numbers he left you with were not only the combination to unlock that notebook, but the numbers to plug into certain formulas for his location of entry, and a few other things. However, the calculations are not exactly turning out the way we expected. Our initial guess is he might have gotten Laura, and then tried to re-enter, but got either separated or propelled into time and inserted into the past more than two hundred years off target."

"Off target from today's date? You mean, he's somewhere in the 1800s? And how would you know that, or do you just assume?"

The Professor put his hand on my shoulder and sighed. It didn't make me shiver that time. I understood then that he was a kind man, but still so much of a mystery to me.

Christopher explained, "We assume some things, Anna, but others we know. There are subtle indications that we can leave in another time period without being noticed, if you know what to look for, that is. Laura had left such indicators, and we know that she was out there. We were shooting for 1977. That was one year before the traces of Laura had stopped. David felt that he had to be the one to help get her back.

"He and I sent Laura off ourselves, Anna, and we believe that David forgot to enter a calculation that may or may not have contributed to her failure to return. He was crushed. As you were in Mongolia, I received almost daily emails about how he was struggling so much there, how he wanted to go on a quick excursion to recover Laura, and then move back to the States. He was extremely concerned about the welfare of your family, Anna.

"But then…after he had left on the mission, not only had Laura's clues stopped in 1978, David's codes appeared in the 1850s. We assume that he retrieved her, but that they must be trapped in the nineteenth century because of some wrong computations."

"Codes on what? How do you get word from the 1800s that David might be there?" I asked.

"There are records of birth, marriages, baptisms, political propaganda, laws–many historical documents that we must comb through, but the codes are covertly left for us to track. David was trained well in the art of time travel coding," explained the professor. He paced back and forth, wringing his hands from time to time, taking long pauses. I just sat and listened. I could not fully absorb all the information as quickly as they were teaching me, so I began to scribble notes here and there.

"Something is just askew at this point, Anna. David is going off the book a bit, I think. There's a protocol to follow if you get lost in time. There are ways to leave the code without suspicion, because it can be dangerous to be in the time period you weren't destined to be in." He began to explain more about the Guardians' role, and how I would encounter many during the space portion of my travels. "You can be easily detected if you aren't trained properly, and the Guardians of the Decades, well…that's their job.

Each one is assigned to guard ten years, they are…angels, if you want to call them that. They have the possibility to appear as humans, but in space, you will see them for what they are. Very human-like, but with an ability to pass through space or time without equipment. You will be overwhelmed at the sights, Anna. Whether spirits float in and out of every decade on a whim and pass from heaven to earth, I am not sure, but one thing I do know is that you will see a multitude of 'people' up there. That is why you can enter and not be noticed right away."

I shifted in my seat and began chewing on the pen I had been writing notes with.

"But you said I can only survive there for twenty seconds," I said in confusion.

"Yes, you will have to count precisely in your mind, as no one measures time up there, but it takes them only about twenty seconds to notice a difference in their state. Since there's a perpetual state of motion, you can enter with ease, but they will quickly notice a foreigner, no matter how chaotic it looks to *you*."

I put my hand on my forehead and rested my elbow on the plastic furniture as I scribbled furiously in my notebook, trying to hide my bewilderment.

"Tell me again. Let me write some more of this down. Step by step. What do I need to know?"

"Okay. Christopher, you go ahead and take the space travel instruction," the professor motioned for Christopher to take over as he pushed his chair away from the table.

Christopher had pushed his rolling chair up against the rounded glass balcony wall as we were talking but as he began to explain, he walked to where I was sitting and began to tap and swipe at the table again, making different images of equipment appear in holographic form. They lit up the entire space. He moved around effortlessly, scrolling and swooping the figures with his fingers as if operating a control center from a sci-fi movie.

"This is the suit you will be wearing," he said, pointing at the holographic image that began to fill the circular area of the control room. "You will have to wear this hood and mask, as it will keep you alive for those critical twenty seconds. While you are in the craft, an extra helmet like this one will be worn." Illuminated outlines of each piece of space apparel floated in front of me as he explained.

"The controls will be automatic, so you won't have to know all the formulas for entry and reentry—we do that before you leave. But what you do have to remember is how to exit and enter the craft. This is of utmost importance, Anna. You must follow the procedure strictly."

I watched as the figure of the panel inside of the spacecraft began to rise from the table. No codes other than the numbers I had been given by David were necessary, but the wearing of the helmet and suit seemed to be of top priority. I continued to scribble instructions and sketch the images of the equipment as quickly as I could.

"We will set everything up. You won't have to worry about getting into space. That—if you can believe it—is the easy part. The pod travels a hundred times faster than any spacecraft NASA has ever put in space. You will experience some nausea, but the cabin has been updated and tweaked so much that the level of discomfort is minimal, and you won't feel the speed.

"Once you are inside, you will not be able to see much. Come take a look at the pod you'll be taking—this one right here," he said as we stood and walked a few

steps to the balcony to look down at the space pod, cradled in its metal frame.

Chris pointed to the top of the round craft. "You see
the extremely small windows? Now, that's your only point
of orientation, but it won't matter because it will be only for
the first twenty-four hours that you'll be able to see anything
anyway. After that, it will be completely black. Your gears will
illuminate some, but for another fifty hours or so, you will be
in darkness. You will have to be trained to handle that, Anna.
It can be mind-numbing. At hour eighty, or thereabouts, you
will see a stream of light. This is essential," he said walking
back toward the holograms and pointing out further instruction. "You will remove the helmet, and remain only in your
hood and under mask. You must look as inconspicuous as
possible. If they know you can't breathe up there, well, you'll
be immediately seized," Chris explained.

"Seized?! By what? The space police?" It made me
laugh out loud, but I was the only one laughing. "You're
not joking? Guys, c'mon…"

The professor shook his head. "No. No jokes. The
Guardians of the Decades will seize you. Two things
could happen: You could cease to exist, meaning you will
end your earthly journey, or you will be escorted back to a
day in your life before any knowledge of space travel was
known to you," he said as he stood gazing at the images
Chris had been displaying. "You may remain with some
subconscious memories of what may have happened from
the point of your knowledge of time travel to the point
you were captured. Most people do remain with some
memories. Nightmares, mostly. The Guardians are powerful," the professor explained pensively.

"And they are there to keep me from going into the
time period I wasn't intended to be in?" I fearfully asked,

raising my eyebrows, and taking a seat again at the long table.

"Yes," the professor said solemnly, "I speak from experience, Anna."

My eyes widened and I began to have a feeling of terror. I was unsure if I wanted to vomit or cry. I knew that I should have been scared about the mere thought of time travel, space travel, and all of the ridiculous things they had been saying from the beginning, but there was something cold and sinister in the professor's tone. It sent shivers down my spine as he explained.

"When I was in my late thirties, I started to have excruciating nightmares about getting sucked into an endless darkness, captured by aliens, and tortured. I began to have migraines that the doctors couldn't medicate, and our medicine is very, shall I say…capable. I began to look for clues as to why I was experiencing the repetitive haunting dreams and found a hypnotist who recorded my sessions." The professor paused, taking a seat on one of the hard plastic desk chairs along the sides of the circular room. "As I viewed the footage from one particular session, I began to remember that I was working on time travel study during that season of my professional life. The Guardians had captured me and returned me to a time in my life that I can't even pinpoint. But I remembered when the nightmares started, so I decided to locate a former colleague and he confirmed everything." The professor paused and sighed. "We started over, Anna. The second time my colleague and I were successful, but mostly because we were better trained."

I breathed deeply. "If you're trying to convince me that this is a good choice for me, then you are not doing a good job of it, Professor," I replied softly, shaking my head.

"That is not my intention, Anna. You will have to make this decision on your own, knowing that there are risks," he replied in somber tone.

Would the biggest risk of my life be dying and leaving my children completely orphaned, or being captured and having to relive the agony of losing my husband and facing the nightmares alone? What kind of mother could I be to my children either way? And what kind of mother am I being now? The inner conflict felt too heavy to bear.

"Then you'd better keep teaching me what this entails, guys. If I'm going to make a decision, I want to know all the factors," I said determinedly.

Christopher's mouth curled at one side and he nodded his head. He was clearly happy to hear that I wasn't backing out–at least not yet. I knew he wanted me to be the one to get David back, but it seemed like he wasn't considering all that this meant outside of science. The position I was putting James and Maggie in, not to mention my family and David's…but, personal factors were secondary to science for them, and I knew it.

"So where did I leave off?" The hologram of my sleek space suit lingered in the air and Christopher began further instruction.

"Ah, yes. This is what you will be wearing as you exit. This hood and mask are the most important things to secure, Anna." He pointed to a place on the adjacent wall that outlined the inner workings of the spacecraft.

"As you encounter the band of light, you will remove your helmet, secure your hood and mask, and then approach the exit, located here," he pointed to each part of the hologram as he explained. "Your mask will adjust to keep you from being blinded from the massive band of light. From the time it appears to the time you exit the pod, it will become increasingly bright and hot. Your suit will protect you, so do try not to let it scare you. Try to keep your focus. Okay?"

I nodded. I was attempting to study every bit of what he was pointing out.

"You will be in the band of light for ten to twelve seconds, if my calculations are correct."

"*If*? What do you mean, '*if*'?" my concern was heavy.

"We haven't quite figured out how to measure years, Anna. The Guardians mark decades, so that's our best guess of where you can be dropped off. I say ten to eight seconds to assure that you land somewhere in the right decade—the one David should have arrived in."

"The right *decade*? So I could arrive nine years before he did, and have to wait? Or worse, arrive after him, and he's somehow figured out how to get back, and isn't even there anymore?"

"That's always a risk."

I was stunned.

"But it's not the greatest risk."

"It's not?" I scoffed. "Me, the non-scientist stuck in an age that I don't know how to get out of alone? And for nothing since I didn't even find the one thing I came after? Then why bother? What's a greater risk than that?"

"That you won't be able to return, Anna. Ever," Chris said bluntly.

I sat motionless for a moment with my head in my hands. "How am I supposed to have a chance of survival if I exit the space pod, anyway, Christopher?" I worriedly asked, not lifting my gaze from my lap. "Getting stuck in the 1800s forever seems less bleak, to be honest."

"Okay, fair enough. But let's say that you do get out, survive the Guardians, even find David," his voice trailed off. "You...you may be forced to stay."

"Stay? Stay in the nineteenth century?" Then what's the point?"

"Anna, that's not the goal, of course. We want to help you have a successful mission and return safely, but you said that you wanted to know all of the factors," Chris explained. "You simply could get stuck there, just as David has."

"So what makes you think that I can get him out if he couldn't do it?" I asked.

"We believe that he's run out of fuel. Out of his suit's electrical charge, at least," the professor chimed in. We can send you with suits to get both David and Laura the equipment they need to return to the spacecraft and come home," the professor's voice was calm and hopeful.

"So how's your British accent?" Christopher asked.

"Wait, Christopher, let's not get ahead of ourselves," the professor interjected.

"British? What do you *mean*...I'll be arriving in *England?*" I sat, wide-eyed, pulling my legs up onto the chair to sit crisscross. "This just keeps getting crazier, you guys," I said.

"Most likely, yes. It will be somewhere in England. Again, we're getting ahead of ourselves. Get back to the procedures, Christopher," the professor instructed.

"Yes, I'm sorry. Okay, so...Anna," Chris continued, pointing to the section of the space pod that had a small door with a long, vertical control pad to its right. "As you approach the exit, open the hatch, and push the button–this

green one here–and tumble out. Literally roll, just like a sum-
mersault, okay? Then, count to ten, push the button on your
suit right above the left ribcage, and extend your arms, just
like you're a superhero. You should probably keep your eyes
closed so you can concentrate on counting. The sights, as the
professor mentioned, may tend to distract you completely.
Or blind you for a period of time.

"At that point, you should be home free, no pun
intended," he laughed a short, nerdy scientist chuckle
that I somehow found endearing. "Your suit, after a few
moments of free-falling, will release a parachute, and you
will eventually land. Probably somewhere north of London–or maybe west, depending on the wind. They didn't
record precise measurements of wind speed from the
records of the mid to late 1800s that we've found. So,
weather will play a bit of an unpredictable variable."

They spoke so matter-of-factly that I was often flab-
bergasted at their dryness. *As if this is a trip to London for
leisure!*

"So, assuming I land, and I actually do find myself in
England, I have to pretend I'm *from* there, not to be suspected?" I asked, supposing that had been why Christopher
broke the news to me about England by asking if I could
speak with an accent.

"In a way. But not necessarily," the professor took
the teaching baton at that point. "You must remember that we measure time our way, but it's not like things
started at year one. Our calculations could land you in
the 1840s or the early 1850s where people didn't travel
extremely often between continents. Do you know any of
your personal family history?"

"Actually, I do. Will it mean I have to change my
name and make up some story?"

"Well, that depends, tell me about your family's arrival in America."

"Okay, I know that my great-grandfather on my mom's side, however many greats back, came over on the *Mayflower*, and my great-grandmother came over three years later on the ship *Anne*. Then there was just a hodge-podge of marriages after that, but mostly Native American Indian, British, and some German. But does any of that really matter?" I asked, not seeing how the connection could help that much.

"Yes, actually, that's perfect. Your maiden name Wright will easily give you footing in England, and immediate social acceptance. You will be able to use some of your ancestry to connect your story," said the professor. "Your family ancestors will not have been in Europe for over two hundred years by the time you arrive, and that will be the perfect answer to why you have so little knowledge of the ways and customs of Old England, and why your accent may be off...though we know little of how and when the British accent turned American over the years, I highly doubt it would be as predominant as you speak with today."

"So brush up on my British lingo and accent, huh? I don't know how good at it I'll be at that!" I laughed.

"It doesn't matter immensely, you have come from America to find family members who remained after the initial departure in the 1620s. You're an educated, accomplished woman studying her lineage. Maybe you are a supporter of mother England. Whatever you want to say, own it well, and stick to your story. You should keep your name, Anna Wright, and even use some of your ancestors' names to confirm your story, if you know them." The professor leaned back in the rigid plastic chair and crossed one arm over his midsection, resting his other elbow on it, lifting his hand to his chin. "The British are fastidious about keeping baptismal records and such, so you should have no problem corroborating your family history if suspicion arises. Look more into that, and brush up on your knowledge of names, dates, and relational details. Ah, this is perfect," he said, well-pleased with the convenience my lineage offered their story.

The professor stood, clasped his hands in delight, and began pacing again. I sat wide-eyed, writing down more details, and trying to recall the names of the relatives I knew about, making notes to remind myself to look up more people that might help me explain my unexpected arrival.

"But, wait a second," I paused and looked up from my notes. "I mean, great that I have a story, but if I'm down on the ground—and I exit the pod to freefall—that means, I don't take the craft with me. I can't ever get back anyway! Where does it go?"

"The pod remains, Anna. It goes virtually unnoticed, sort of like a piece of space debris. Whatever is in that band of light is an incredible power source. Everything within the pod is fueled electrically from that source, and the power of the light can refuel the pod for up to a year in just a few minutes," the professor explained returning to his seat at the table.

"We will program the pod to descend to an altitude of one hundred feet for four-point-three seconds at an exact interval every two days," Christopher interrupted. "It will come in a flash, and then leave almost as quickly."

The professor continued, "You *must* be there to reenter. Now, because there are slight discrepancies, we will give you four different locations, not far from each other—within fifty miles—but you have to remember that people did not easily travel in those days, and fifty miles could be quite the trek. But it if you miss one chance to board the craft, you go on to the next location, and keep going to different spots, or choose just one and go multiple times at two day intervals if you wish. We can send the pod back up to be re-fueled every two hundred days or so, and that means that it will make a virtually undetectable descent every two days within the four locations we've chosen, without having to travel all the way back very often. We won't have to program it to hover too far above the earth because at that point in history, air travel was not a factor. That, of course, makes re-fueling virtually unnecessary," he paused. "Unless you take longer than two hundred days initially."

"Well, then, that's good! There's no problem getting back to the pod; we just have to worry about finding them, and getting them to it, right?" I said.

Of course it wasn't that simple.

"Yes, that would take away a complication of epic proportions if you could find them right away. Get to the pod with David and Laura, and reenter. That is the goal, after all."

"*But…?*" I asked. I just knew there had to be a "but" attached to it.

The professor gave me a little smirk and sighed. "*But…*the suit has to be charged too, Anna. It will be charged only for the seconds you remain in that band, no fewer than ten seconds, no more than twenty." He rolled his chair closer to me and glanced over the notes I'd been writing. "Which, don't get me wrong, will be enough to power your flight down, release of the parachute, and even your reentry. Since the space craft appears for only four-point-three seconds, your suit is what will guarantee your safe entry." The professor stood and walked back to the illuminated image of the suit floating in the room. "If you see on the left rib cage, there's another button on the suit. This is what you will push as soon as you see the pod.

"Lie flat on the ground and wait until you see the craft, but push the button immediately. It will open a hatch of the spacecraft and literally transport you up from the ground to the pod in one second flat. And don't worry about pushing the button if you think you see it, just make sure it's activated, and if you were mistaken, deactivate it again. This is just to ensure that we keep as much stored energy as possible for your transportation back," he explained, standing next to the holographic suit.

I pulled one knee up onto the chair and close into my chest as I shifted in my seat, resting my chin on top of my knee.

"Then there are the suits for David and Laura," Christopher said plainly as he joined the professor on the opposite side of the glowing hologram. "Their suits will be charged before you leave, and they'll retain a little more power than yours since they won't use the energy yours will for the landing. We decided to store them on your back thighs," Christopher said as he pointed out an area on the thigh that looked like it had a built-in pocket for stuffing fake muscles, like on a superhero costume. "The suit must stay streamlined and you cannot carry much. So they will be in these small pouches here."

The professor removed a little vacuum-sealed packet from a solid white acrylic drawer that sat to the side of the table along the edge of an adjacent workspace. He stepped toward me and handed me the package. "The two suits for them will be sealed, and can be activated and expand once removed, okay? Never activate all three without intended reentry, Anna. The quickest way for a Guardian to measure foreign activity is from energy emissions from the Earth. They seem to monitor these things closely. You must either all three be together, or have abandoned the search, and attempt a solo return," the professor said solemnly.

It all sounded amazing, exciting, and ridiculously scary at that point. I was fascinated. "Okay," I sighed. "Maybe I can do this," I said nearly smiling with enthusiasm. "We'll practice, and you can train me; I'm a fast learner. I'll get it. I'll go in and get David and Laura, then we'll be back. Where is our point of reentry? Won't we be conspicuous in London?"

"Anna, don't get ahead of yourself. If your suit isn't powered up while you are on the ground, you can't get into the pod. You unfortunately don't have hundreds of days to do this—you have four. The suit will most likely not have enough power after that time, at least not enough to get you airborne. Unless you can come up with a plan to get harnessed electricity into that suit quickly, you have four days for this mission."

I didn't quite understand. "You just told me you could refuel every two hundred days...and now you're saying I have *four?*" I dropped both of my feet to the ground and stood to approach the holographic suit. "With all this technology, there is no way to power up the suit? C'mon, seriously?" I asked, pointing at the suit's capabilities they had just shown me. I turned my incredulous glance from the professor. "Christopher?"

"Seriously," he replied flatly. *Of course they were saving the bad news for last, and starting with the whole two-hundred-day story. Great.*

"Is there a way to have them solar-powered?" I asked. "I mean, the sun shone back then just as it does today, and we know how to harness that. It's practically the simplest technology, right?"

"No, it's not that simple, Anna." I could tell that Christopher was trying to explain in layman's terms, but simple science was what I knew.

Sun. Solar power. Problem solved. Right? Wrong, apparently.

"The amount of time it would take for the sun to power up the suit the way that the band of light can is about eighteen years," he explained. "We have been harnessing wind, water, and solar energy for decades exclusively for our own travels, Anna. It's just that we aren't *sure* the suit has more than four days of storage before it powers down. We are playing it on the safe side when we say that. We can speculate that there might be six to eight days of power, but we *know* there will be four."

"Based on previous experience, I suppose," I sighed, returning to my seat as the professor and Christopher walked to theirs.

"Yes," answered the professor.

Four days? How would that be possible? The two men spent more time that day teaching me, training me, and telling me how great of a shot they thought that I had at completing the mission; but what I remembered was *four days*. Just four. *Then what?* The hope I once felt was quickly turning into despair and I could feel the old clutches of debilitating depression call out to me. All I could think was that David had surely abandoned hope if all he had was four days. If it took eighteen years to power up the suit, he'd physically be forty-eight by the time the power was stored, and how could that have seemed doable? I was beginning to believe that maybe it was all hopeless.

I left later that day after trying to soak in what seemed like pointless information since the task that had begun to excite me became overwhelmingly daunting. I needed to head home. To spend some time with my loving family. To kiss my sweet babies. To make some decisions.

"Anna? May I come in?"

"Yes, Dad, you don't have to whisper. I'm up."

Dad entered my old room carrying a breakfast tray, and set it on the bed over my legs.

"Mom made her famous biscuits and gravy. I made the pancakes, though," he said with a smirk. "You *know* mine are the best!"

I smiled. "Of course they are." It was true. Something about the fluffy pancakes Dad made were always just so good that Mom had handed him the reins on that task long ago.

Dad bent over the bed and kissed my forehead. "Eat up. We have a busy day ahead of us! You have to be at the airport by noon!"

"The airport?"

"Yeah, Chris called yesterday and asked if I could drive you instead of having to hire a car to take you all the way there from here. Did you forget what day today is, sweetie?"

Forget? No. I was lying in bed contemplating the insane notion of a risky time travel mission. Of course I hadn't forgotten today's date! I just hadn't agreed to it. And I guess that wasn't a concern to Christopher and the Professor. They had obviously arranged my travel plans.

111

"Anna?" he paused, and his tone changed a bit. "Are you all right? You've only been home three days and you've barely said a word. I thought the trip to California would be good for you, but…"

"Oh, dad I'm okay. I asked Christopher to help me take care of the plans for me to finalize all of David's things out there; I just didn't expect it to be this soon. And it's all so real now. So very real."

"Yes, it is indeed. Whatever I can do to help…" his soft voice trailed off with a sigh.

"Thanks, Dad. I know." I knew he was concerned.

"Of course, I get the deplorable job of playing with my grandchildren and sending my sons off to work the fields without me," he laughed.

I smiled up at him. "Thank you, Dad. For everything. I think I'll talk to the Sturgeons and have you all come out to California for a while, okay? I have quite a few things to take care of out there with all of David's research and programs, so I might not be back right away. It would be nice if you could come and stay for a couple of weeks. The boys can handle the farm. Just put Lyn in charge. We all know he's the reliable one."

He grinned a grin of delight and sheer love. "That's true! We'll do whatever you'd like, honey. You know I'm just here to help!" I knew nothing gave him more pleasure than seeing Maggie and James romp and play. I could leave on the mission knowing that they were loved like I was my entire life. And that made things slightly easier.

Dad left the room, while I finished my breakfast and looked around the space crowded with neatly stacked boxes, reminding me of the life I had lived and the life I was possibly leaving behind. I knew I had to finish packing what I could, so I rummaged through the bits and pieces of things I was contemplating taking with me. I came across a picture of the time I had gone with David up the mountain on one of his studies. It was a cold, clear day. There was a burst of sunlight in the sky, and David and I sat high upon a cliff looking out into the mountainous distance. It had been one of my favorite pictures of the two of us, but somehow looking at it in that moment made me think not of the memory of when the photo was taken, but of a different moment in that exact space. Before I left Mongolia, I had run up to the cliffs where David was supposed to have been at the time of his disappearance. There, I had sat alone. Wondering. Searching. That photo now represented a place of loneliness to me, and I tried to convince myself that I was doing the right thing.

I knew David needed me. I placed the photo in the back pocket of my jeans, and headed downstairs.

Mom was in the kitchen cleaning up dishes and wiping down the countertops. Dad had replaced the old laminate counters with sleek quartz the summer before, and added the small island bar that mom had always wanted. She constantly wiped them to keep them shiny. She loved that kitchen. Some of my happiest memories were there, standing right next to her, learning how to cook everything from boiled eggs to fancy desserts. My heart ached, knowing I'd be leaving the very place I had so much longed for. I stood and cast my gaze around each inch of the room, trying to enjoy every moment I was blessed to be there.

"Good morning, dear," Mom greeted me sweetly as always.

"Good morning, Mom," I said, kissing her cheek. "Thanks for the breakfast, it was very thoughtful."

"You've been so tired and I just thought it'd be a nice treat," she said.

"It was," I grinned and put my head on her shoulder.

"What is it, Anna?"

"Oh, nothing, Ma. I just love you. I'm glad I was able to come home for a few days."

"Me too." She smiled a loving grin that warmed my heart like no other could. I was safe. It almost made it worse. Harder, at least. I was leaving my safe place. The place I had yearned for so much when I was away. I wanted to rest in its sweet comfort. Instead, I was plucked from its arms again by circumstance–yet by choice. I was making a conscious decision, and I had to live with that. I had hopes of going on a grand quest and returning unscathed with my husband, who had disappeared into oblivion. It was certainly too bizarre of a notion to share with my mom. So I said nothing but my goodbyes.

The kids had not yet awoken. They took after their father and would sleep long past seven o'clock each morning. It was a topic I didn't discuss with my friends, since most mommies were sleep-deprived half of the time, and I almost felt guilty for having little ones who enjoyed sleeping ten hours a night. But that morning, I was saddened by their habit. I peeked into the small bedroom they shared, kissing each resting cheek without waking them. I wasn't sure if it would've been harder to hear them beg me not to leave, or to sneak out in the early hours of the morning without hearing the sound of their toddler voices once more. Hot, silent tears trickled down my cheeks as I made my way to my dad's car.

The drive to the airport seemed longer than usual. Like I was going toward impending doom. I must have fallen asleep the moment I found my seat on the plane, because I only remember staring out the window watching the airport workers signal to each other back and forth a few times. I laid my head back, surrendering to fatigue and the sinking feeling that I may have made the most colossal mistake of my life.

CHAPTER EIGHT

"The training will be rigorous, Anna." The professor smiled, stood, and reached out across the broad desk in the university office and shook my hand, as if to seal the deal.

"I understand, Professor." I stood and returned the handshake.

"Okay, then. We will begin, but I need to make sure you are ready for this commitment. I don't wish to put you through the horrors of all of this again. So, let's get going."

The professor stepped out from behind the desk and began walking toward the large window near the wall by the hidden elevator.

"Again?" I said in almost a whisper. Something about what he said made no sense to me, yet I felt it had heavy significance. He tried to ignore me, or pretend that he hadn't heard me, and went chattering on with what the exercises would entail. I glanced around the office space and sat back down in the chair behind the large work desk.

"The physical fitness aspect is paramount to success," the professor continued. "You will have a personal trainer here daily. I think it's important to begin your morning routine with her. She's fantastic. But we're looking for more than resistance training here. You must be able to withstand some elements as well endure the physical stress that will come upon you.

"After that…"

I interrupted him, looking up from my blank stare. I hadn't really been paying attention to what he was saying. I had just been processing the encounter. "You said '*again*'…what did you mean by that?"

"Anna, I just meant that you have been through so much already, and…" he approached me taking a seat at the couch that sat between the desk and the opposite side of the room lined with bookcases.

"No. No, you didn't. Did you? Professor, have I tried this already and been captured by the Guardians?" I asked as I stepped closer to join him on the sofa. "That darkness. Those headaches. The strange woman in Mongolia who made it all go away? They sent me back to the time before I lost David and made me suffer this all over again? Didn't they, Professor?"

I was close to tears. So perplexed by the logistics of the possibility that I just might have already been in a place between time and space and failed to complete my mission, that I could hardly get out audible sentences.

"I think so. Yes, Anna," he admitted, bowing his head with a sigh.

"You *think?*" I stammered, gasping for air.

So much about what we were doing was simple conjecture that I became weary of it all. I slumped back in the seat.

"I'm about to give up, Professor. What else don't I know? Who was that Mongolian woman who helped put me out of my misery? Why would the Guardians prevent me from stopping David on that last mission if I had a second chance? Are they that cruel?" I choked out the questions one after the other. I began crying too hard to say anything else. The professor took my hand and knelt next to me.

"There's a lot about this that we don't know. Things that are hidden—or sometimes *taken* from us. Your memories about some of these happenings were erased. Ours were not. Christopher and I have not been affected like you have and…well, your arrival the first time to set out on the mission was faster than your second. And that's how we knew. You were back within three days of our sending you off to go and find David, and you knew nothing of our initial conversations. So, we had to assume that you had been captured and returned somewhere in time."

"You *knew*? Why didn't you say?" I whimpered.

"It would have just made it harder, Anna. We didn't say anything because we weren't planning on having you go through this again. Maybe you shouldn't. When you arrived this time, Christopher and I were thinking that perhaps we should leave well enough alone. Let you live your life with your children. Find love again. Chances are, David will have to do the same."

It was like a dagger to my heart. Thinking that David could be settling in, somewhere in the 1800s, destined to be married off to some English girl. Or worse, found on a street as a nobody, having to scrape and beg to survive. Or maybe he never even survived.

"David's circumstance could be as grim as a Dickens novel, or as frivolous as an Austen socialite tale. You said so yourself. That's what you told me, isn't it, Professor? That's what he could be in? Didn't you say that?" I begged for answers through each sob.

He bowed his head and sighed. "Yes."

"I have to know, Professor. I have to know where he is and what has become of him. I'll do it. I'll do it all again, if I have to. But if they send me back...back to that dark place, where I was before...at least I'll be with him for a little while. And maybe he'll listen to me and not go this time. Right?" I rubbed my swelling eyes, desperately pleading for answers.

"Perhaps," the professor whispered. "Perhaps."

The next few weeks were grueling. The professor, Chris, and I would meet in the mornings at the university office, then head down to *The Cave*, as I began to call it. An entire team was assigned to what they referred to as the underground space program, and the only discussions about time travel were when the three of us were alone. I had to undergo a slew of physical tests. The most nauseating part about it was the amount of blood they drew to run what I was told were necessary tests. My diet was strictly monitored. Everything I was allowed to eat was organic. I couldn't have anything with hormones or chemicals used after 1850. The detoxification was astonishing. I felt sick for the first two weeks, but after I got accustomed to the extremely low sugar and limited protein regimen, it became easier, and I began to feel better than ever.

No unnatural hair dyes were allowed. I had to go and have a hairdresser try to match my highlights back to the closest she could get to my natural light brown color. No one ever really knew what color to call it–sandy blonde, light brown, kind of generic and dull. But it was mine, and I had to own it. My nails were cleaned and buffed. I got used to leaving them bare, and studied how to pin my own hair and braid it up in a way that would at least resemble the "olden days," as I would refer to them. The professor would roll his eyes and shake his head with an exasperated grin.

My phone was taken away. No games, no texts, no calls. Not during the training hours, at least. I was allowed to use the phone for twenty minutes each afternoon to return any calls I had received and to get updates from Mom and Dad. But after the first week, they took me up on the idea to come out to LA to stay with David's parents so I could see them each night. Every morning, I'd dress in a fitted workout shirt and leggings, and another long day of training would begin.

"What's your skill set? Your talents?" Christopher asked after a morning weigh-in. We had been training for three weeks, and the focus began to include social aptitude as well as physical fitness.

He attached a couple of wires to my chest for the monitor and I began to walk on the high-tech treadmill. I knew the routine already, but it still amazed me to see the figure of my entire body emerge before me–every vital organ electronically visible for the doctors to examine as I walked slowly, then briskly, pacing myself into a jog and then run.

There were others on staff who walked around probing, testing, and working on peculiar sorts of machinery and computers. Always wearing a silvery-grey bodysuit complete with hood and mirrored goggles, they came in and out like footless spirits. It was as if they walked in slow motion, or that their regular motion left this lingering silvery haze behind them, and it only *seemed* that they were moving slowly because in reality, they were about their business and then gone as quickly as they came. I hadn't once heard them enter, and they had never spoken a word to me. I began to wonder if they *could* speak, but I had seen the professor through a window in a laboratory talking with one of them, so I assumed they could communicate in some fashion. One of them walked over to the holographic images in front of us and began tapping at a tablet he was carrying. With each little tap, an organ would illuminate more brightly. The lungs, the stomach, the brain, the heart. I could watch my own heartbeat in front of me, as if I could reach out and hold it in my hands. I was mesmerized every time. I slowly lifted my hand off of the bar of the treadmill, watching the images rise in front of me with my movement.

"Anna?"

"My what? Talents? Um…" I wasn't exactly sure what he was asking.

"You did a musical theater piece or two in college, right? I think I remember you saying that."

"Yes. But what does that matter? I thought we were concerned with physical fitness, not theatre and music skills. I need to get in and get out, Christopher! I don't plan on being in the 1800s long enough for someone to ask if I know how to play the piano!" I insisted.

"The piano, that's right! Perfect. And you've been reading the list of books we gave you?" he continued.

"Yes, but I much more enjoy the ones written *during* that time period and not *about* it, in case you were wondering," I said playfully. I knew he wasn't wondering anything of the sort, but I smiled anyway. The pace started to pick up, and I was beginning to jog.

"So, you have been reading, you already know some French and the mechanics of foreign languages, since luckily your previous studies helped us out there, and you play piano. Perfect."

"What—" I began to ask about how any of that would be relevant, but the treadmill started going faster and faster, and I was in no condition to carry on a conversation at that rate. Christopher stayed next to me, still writing on his tablet.

"You see, Anna, these things could mean the difference between life and death. Someone will find you, or better yet, you will find them. If you are found, our best hope is that they will assume there was a shipwreck. They were all too common back then, and it is a very plausible scenario. If you are lucky, you won't be unconscious for too long, and you will be able to make your way to find someone yourself. That would work in our favor because you can prepare a bit before someone sees you."

The treadmill slowed to a stop, having only gone at a high speed for about thirty seconds, and I grabbed a towel draped over a bar on the side of the machine and hopped off. By the time I looked up again to see how I was faring in the overall tests, the images had vanished and the team was gone.

"You'd think I had already entered a parallel universe with the way these people work..." I scanned the room, looking for where they had gone, but to no avail. I was just the guinea pig and whatever data they needed to gather was, in fact, gathered, and that was that.

Scientists. I chuckled.

"Yes, well," Chris smiled. "Don't let them distract you. Let's get back to how to do this. If you are conscious before someone finds you, there will be time for you to prepare yourself. If you are seen with the space suit, it will be harder to explain away."

The treadmill retracted into the blank white wall, as we walked to an escalator that led us back to the landing where the table of controls was. Chris tapped the surface and images of the equipment began to appear.

"Here, in this small pouch on your back, you will have a linen petticoat that is little more than one of the undergarment layers a lady would have worn back then."

The form of the sleek rubberlike suit floated around me, and the full petticoat–which looked much more like a gown–glowed in a creamy white figure.

"It is the only thing light enough to be compacted tightly into this pouch. It will be sealed and vacuum packed like the other things so it should be dry until you open it. Which will probably prove to be something you will appreciate," he said as he smirked and raised his eyebrows. "So, if you are awake to slip into this, then you will be able to more easily blend in with your surroundings, and your story should most likely be accepted by the kind people of jolly old England," he said mimicking a British accent. It was the first time in a long time I had heard Christopher speak light-heartedly. I smiled.

"And if not?" I asked, tilting my head to one side and raising my eyebrows.

"We hope for the best," he said in a chipper tone.

I chuckled. "Yes, we hope."

His tone turned nearly sympathetic.

"Anna, you will be entering a time in which superstition ruled the actions of many people's everyday lives. The time travel is possible. You already know that. On our first attempt, you must have gotten up there, been seized by the Guardians, and not gotten into the decade we were attempting to enter. Now, if you *do* get past the Guardians, your challenge will be not to get seized by the people who suspect you of evil, of witchcraft, or of whatever other prejudice they might conjure up. It may seem small, but appearance is key here."

"I understand."

We both paused and looked at the suit. Christopher walked over to a small cabinet that stored supplies, and he pulled out a tiny package no larger than a dessert plate, and much lighter.

He tossed it to me. "Here, that's it. The only challenge will be to try to open in without any scissors!"

I held the vacuum-packed petticoat in my hand and looked toward the glowing images before me.

"That is inside of *this*?" I was astonished. It must have been a lot lighter and sheerer than it seemed, because it was hard to believe that so much volume fit into the small, mushy plastic thing I held in my hands.

"It is. And it is actually made up of fabric from the 1800s."

"Cool. So first thing, I remove this from the pouch, find a jagged rock to open this rubbery plastic casing, and then put it on. Seems simple enough! Then what? What do I do with the suits for reentry?"

"You'll have to find a place, Anna. You need to be very aware of your surroundings and store them somewhere until you can return and reenter."

The sand felt so good under my feet. James and Maggie loved the sunshine and sand castles, and everyone seemed to be having such a wonderful time. I walked along the wide beach and didn't even realize that I was humming.

"It's nice to hear you sing again."

I shrugged and grinned. "Mom, that's not singing, it's humming!"

"Close enough, Anna." I knew she was holding back some of her feelings. The worry that I'd never fully be that happy-go-lucky girl they sent off to college with big dreams and bright ambitions was hard for her. But I was changed forever. Somehow I knew I'd be that girl, or that she was at least still part of me. *Somewhere*. But mom couldn't see her in that moment. Being a mom myself, I knew that it hurt her deeply, and for that I was sorry.

Mom smiled at me, and we swung sweet two-year-old James by the little arms as he would hop-step his way between us.

She finally said something. "You spend so much time working at the university, Anna, and I just haven't understood how you would know anything about David's work...but...you finally seem like you may be happy. Or at least content, and I'm glad for that. Maybe having a goal to work toward is the key to getting past this!"

I smiled, swooped little James up into my arms, and kissed my sweet mom on the cheek.

"Maybe it is, Mom."

It was all I could do not to break down and cry right then and there. I had never hidden something so huge from my parents. I had rarely hidden anything at all from them! And there I was about to depend on them to parent my own children for a while in order to achieve the unrealistic goal of finding my husband who was lost in time. And I couldn't say a word.

We continued walking down the long stretch of sandy shore outside the Sturgeons' home. We were nearly out of sight from the large house, and probably on someone else's stretch of private beach.

"We'd best head back," she said. Mom's words snapped my mind back into the reality of the moment. "We left Maggie and Daddy alone back there, and you know how much trouble those two can get into!"

We both giggled, and she gave me one of those mom-hugs. The kind that only moms can get away with no matter how old you are, but it makes you feel like you are a tiny child in the warmest arms ever—and I lingered there for a moment. In that feeling, that embrace. I knew I'd leave it soon.

I struggled to get up the next morning. My head hurt and my thoughts were a bit foggy. I hadn't been sleeping well over the last few nights, and I felt like I wasn't quite prepared. But the time had come. It was the day we had scheduled for my departure, and I had to be ready.

I dressed in my comfortable soft, cotton uniform and light tennis shoes, and went straight to the campus. My nerves hadn't allowed me to eat much over the previous twenty-four hours, and I was feeling famished. I knocked gently on Christopher's office door. I wasn't sure they'd be there yet because I was at least half an hour early.

"Come in, Anna," the professor's greeting was cheerful. "We have breakfast for you. Now, I know you've been queasy lately, but you must eat. You might not survive without the proper fuel for energy."

I knew he was right, so I forced myself to eat slowly, and eat everything. I had lost a considerable amount of weight throughout the whole process. I can't say that I minded. Though I was never completely out of shape, I was never like my fitness friends with rigorous workout routines. At that point, I could have kept up with the best of them.

One last chance. I could walk away and join all of my friends enjoying their youth in that elusive, normal life I should be living. I closed my eyes as I sat silently chewing my food.

I don't remember much of what happened the rest of morning other than being led through the tunnels and cavities of that all-familiar underground warehouse in a practice run-through before our scheduled take off. I was in a dreamlike state until Christopher handed me the suit. I snapped back to reality. It was happening.

"Suit up, Anna. This is it." He held me by the shoulders and bent in close to my face, looking me square in the eyes. "Go bring them back," he said as he gave me a tug, and pulled me in for a goodbye embrace.

"Okay," I uttered the word, but my heart said to run. I started to slip the tight-fitting suit on over my cotton leggings. The breathable cotton would help keep in the warmth, and I knew that I'd need it. I turned my back toward Christopher to have him help me with the long straps that would crisscross and fasten over both of my shoulders.

"Chris?" I stopped.

"If I am captured and return again…I mean, if they let me come back…no matter where I end up in time. Will you promise me something?"

"Of course, Anna."

"Don't let me do this again. Tell me everything from the beginning. I know I'll dig until I find something, just like I did this time...and apparently the time before. But..." my voice trailed off. I couldn't say the words.

Let me let him go.

"I promise. This has *got* to work, Anna. I won't let you go through this again," he promised.

He turned me around and hugged me again tightly. I watched a tear slowly fall down his cheek. The guilt and regret he must have felt was too much even for him to hide. I didn't linger. I thanked him, and then I rode down the long, deep escalator that led to the space pod, leaving Christopher and Professor Trinkton to watch down from the large balcony overhead.

A thick wall of glass, or what looked like glass, but must have been some sort of anti-ballistic material had started to appear from the concrete walls, as they observed me through the heavy veil of protection that separated us. I knew then that I was truly on my own. I stood there in the middle of the luminescent entry pad for the space pod and activated the suit. It began to constrict even more than the already confining rubberlike material, but as it did, a translucent shield began to emerge from it, covering me from neck to toe. It felt warm and suffocating, but in a strange way, comforting. I walked over to the side of the pod to retrieve the large helmet I had to secure onto the suit, and I fastened it in place. I took one last glance at the balcony and lifted my hand toward them, and waved goodbye.

I entered slowly and fastened myself into the capsule that would hold me for the first eighty hours. I kept repeating to myself. "Eighty hours. Capsule release.

Remove helmet. Activate the hood. Exit. Tumble. Extend arms. Twenty seconds."

It was all I could do to stop shaking. I felt scared as the capsule sealed around me, and I took a deep breath. I knew I'd sleep for a lot of the journey because the professor had decided to release a mild sleeping gas in the pod, knowing that my nerves would often get the best of me, and that my body couldn't afford to go on this mission sleep deprived. I kept thinking about setting an alarm so I wouldn't miss my exit. *Silly*.

The pod began to shake, and I clenched my fists. At first, I was almost glad that the entire capsule wasn't transparent. The small window at the top of the pod allowed me to see the tunnel ride I was quickly sucked into. It twisted and turned down a brightly lit path of underground tubing like an amusement park ride. I could feel the force of the speed already. I was counting the minutes. Part of my training was to count in real time. It was ironic, I thought. In order to exit time itself and then reenter requires precision timing. It took only four minutes for me to arrive miles off the coast of the Pacific somewhere and exit the ocean floor in a trajectory into space that could hardly be detected.

I was on my way.

CHAPTER NINE

"Run! Please run, Anna!" I felt a strong, rushing wind as a faint voice shouted at me in the distance. It seemed as if my head weighed a hundred pounds when I tried to lift it, and I started rubbing my eyes to see what was going on.

"*Run where?*" I thought. I could barely feel my feet, and I couldn't see more than grey shadows no matter how hard I tried to focus. The voice kept getting louder and I tried to call back to it, but I was still gasping for air. The wind had somehow been completely knocked out of me and I was starting to panic.

"I–I–can't breathe!" I tried to shout, but it came out as no more than a whisper. I was gasping for air, but to no avail.

"RUN!" I heard it clearly, her voice was louder–she was close, whoever she was.

I began to stand to my feet, frantically reaching out to break my fall until I grabbed what must have been a short branch of a tree or a small bush. I tripped and hit my head on the ground. It was no use. I couldn't stand, much less run. I lay there, face down when suddenly, my hand was being jerked up to pull me to my feet, and I was lifted into this mysterious being's arms, moving at speeds that made my face feel chapped and my hair matted and tangled. I tried to focus. I tried to catch my breath enough to speak.

"This way, Anna. There's a wooden cabin not far from here, and we should find safety there for the time being." She spoke in an accent that was beautiful and mysterious. Her arms were warm and cozy. I felt safe. I started to relax, as my muscles finally stopped constricting enough for me to catch a bit of air.

"Who—who are you? I can't see!" I spoke so softly that I wasn't sure she heard me. The wind was whipping through my hair and clapping at my ears so violently that I thought maybe we had hopped onto some kind of vehicle. But there was no whirring of an engine, and I hadn't left the cradle of her arms.

"Hush, child. Rest your eyes and we will be there soon." Her voice was sweet and melodic. She covered me somehow, as if I were wrapped in a blanket, safely flying through the forest of trees at lightning speed.

I awoke on a hardwood bench lined with a rough mattress of hay. I rubbed my eyes again, able to see a little more clearly, but I still unable to focus well.

"The blindness should be temporary," she said.

I stood slowly, realizing that I had been on a course hay mattress perched atop a window seat. I could feel the warmth of the light pouring in. I traced the outline of the large window with my fingers, trying to soak in the sunshine. I kept blinking my eyes rapidly to see if it would help me focus. Still, everything was murky, shadow-like, and foggy.

"Who *are* you?" I said, as I turned around toward the inside of the room to try to catch a glimpse of the figure who had probably saved my life. I sat back down on the window seat. "Are you a Guardian? Have I been captured again?"

Her tone changed to a perplexed, but scolding manner. "Well, I am not a Guardian who is supposed to capture, Anna. And not the kind of Guardian you think. They are not violent, you know. Not the good ones. They try to guard the ages for your own good! This is not the way it was intended to be, and you have fundamentally tampered with the fabric of your life and time." I could hear a swishing motion from side to side as if she was pacing the room. "And how do you know about last time? Did they not erase all of your memories, Anna?" She paused and the room, which had seemed like it was spinning, came to a standstill. "Fascinating."

"Um...I don't know," I answered. "Not exactly. I mean, I don't remember anything in particular, but I know some type of memory must be there. Because I could feel it, I knew something wasn't right when they told me David was dead. I knew it. They couldn't erase my heart!"

"Mmm..." she stood motionless.

I began to focus slightly, and could make out a slender woman with long hair wearing a flowing white gown. It looked as if her garments glowed, and her movements were sweeping gestures of grandeur, as if she were floating around the small space.

"Please. Who are you? And where am I?"

I began to regain my sight more and more. I think she smiled at me. "Anna," she sounded so loving, so warm and inviting. "I am not *a* Guardian. I am *your* Guardian." I knew it then, I knew she was smiling at me. She stepped closer and I could finally see her face. Her skin was beautifully bronze, her hair pitch-black, reaching long past her elbows, and as she stood facing me with her high, dark eyebrows, full pink lips, and captivating light brown eyes, I nearly gasped. I had never seen a more lovely sight.

"You're beautiful!" I exclaimed. "I…I don't know what to say. You mean, you're my guardian angel?"

She smiled sweetly and took my hand. "If you want to call it that," she said, "My name is Amoriti. I have been charged with providing you protection from harm until your days are expired, Anna."

"Then, if you're always with me, how did you not realize that I already knew that I could be captured and taken back? And why didn't you save me the first time like you did today? That was them after me, wasn't it?"

"I do not haunt you, Anna. I am there when you need me. And…" She paused and stood back up. She seemed to hover over the entire room in her long, white dress. "I didn't exactly get permission to lead you here. I don't have insight into everything in your life. I come and go as sent. I know nothing of what is to come, just what you are doing now, and what you've done in the past. I knew I had to follow you here this time." She paused and stood in the middle of the old cottage that, based on the tools, must have housed a busy woodsman during the peak season. She put her hand to her forehead and swiped it around her face and chin. Until that moment, I had never thought something as perfect as an angel could ever have a care in the world. But I was beginning to understand that her cares of this world were simply of *me*, and *my* life.

"The one chasing you, Anna, was the Guardian of this decade. His name is Mitsraim. He is a good and loving

Guardian, but he protects his borders of time quite well."
She spoke as if she was sad that she had intervened, or at
least sad that she felt she had to.

"What will happen to you, Amoriti? I mean, will you
get in trouble for this?"

She laughed a sweet, melodious sound. "No, child.
I am doing my job. Protecting you, that is all. And I am
happy to do it. You know, it's not the first time nor, I
fear, will it be the last that I have intervened. Only…well,
I come to you in the form you most need at the precise
time you most need it. In this moment, you must see me
for what I am, because it will help you the most. In times
past, you have seen me as other things because that was
what you needed most."

I sat silently for a little while, just trying to completely focus, and see, *really see* everything she was talking
about. See her for who she was. An angel. And that was
the scariest part of all. I could see with my eyes what I
couldn't quite fathom with my heart and mind. I began
to become concerned. I looked down, and I saw that I
was still in my rubbery black space suit. My suit and hood
were deactivated and I thought of how I only had four
days for my mission. *Four days!*

I started to grab at my back to unveil the linen petticoat that had been prepared and packed away in a pouch.
I was instantly in a panic. "How long have I been here?!"
I shouted. I began to rush about the small cabin space
looking for who-knows-what and grabbing at my suit, trying desperately to pull off the tight fabric.

"In earth days? Only two, Anna. Calm yourself, child."

"TWO?! Two *days?!* How am I ever supposed to find
him in two days?"

134

She walked closer to me, and I couldn't help but stop. It's as if she had some special power to soften my reactions and bring a delightful serenity to the air.

"How do you do that?" I asked, bewildered.

"I cannot make you do anything you do not wish to do, Anna. You choose. I just bring a calm to your circumstances and allow you to think clearly. I understand your mission. I have all along."

"It was *you!*" I sat back down, this time on a stack of wood neatly lined and stacked along the wall. "You were the Mongolian woman who brought me out of my suffering! But you looked so…*Mongolian*," I stammered, feeling foolish.

"As I said, Anna, I appear to you in the form you need, as you need it. It *was* me. And I truly believed you would choose to move on after David disappeared, and not risk everything again. So I did my best to get you back to normal, and end your suffering. I never thought that I would have to save you from all of this–again. But here I am, and we shall succeed, Anna; if I can help it, we shall."

I began to cry. My head seemed heavy again, and all I could do was run to the padded window seat, lie down, and weep. "I'm sorry, Amoriti," I sobbed. "I'm so sorry."

"Hush, child." She and her calming presence came over to me, as she began stroking my back. "Now, we will just work from here, right where you are. In the place that you've chosen to come. But you must work on your own for the most part. I am not supposed to be assisting you in this decade, though I do already work some here."

I lifted my head in utter amazement; I was perplexed beyond words. But she somehow knew what my expression was asking without having to say a word. "You see, our jobs last lifetimes, Anna, and one of my people is living not far from here, right in this decade."

She was timeless, eternal. Her presence in my life was just a shadow of what she had done. I envied her. Not really having to make the daily choices that I was faced with, just floating around keeping people out of harm's way. "How many do you have? People, I mean...how do you manage the time, the distance, and..."

She cut me off there. "All answers are not to be revealed to you now, Anna. Time is perpetual, as you have learned and experienced. But please know that my help in this age will be strictly limited, as the Guardians will protect their decades from me as well, should they believe I'm intruding."

I sat up on the coarse hay mattress, which was bound with a thin cotton cloth that allowed the strands to protrude here and there. I stroked the strands softly, picking one out of its sheath and twisting it around in my fingers. "Tell me what to do next, Amoriti."

"I cannot. I can merely tell you where you are and how to get to where you desire to go. I have done my work here."

"Please," I begged, and grabbed her long white dress, "please tell me if I should go to the location that the capsule will be waiting–assuming I can figure out the coordinates–and get out of here while I can, or if I should just forge on ahead with the mission! Is David even here? Surely you know that!"

"Sadly, I do not," she sighed.

"Oh, Amoriti, it's like I can't bring myself to make this decision. I'm so scared. It's...this is all too surreal!"

"Anna, you misunderstand. I am not able to know what is best for your future. My knowledge is limited to your actions. Because you are here in this time and space,

I cannot know if you will succeed in finding David in it, because I only know what you have done thus far in the years you have already lived. I come and go with my mission as needed. These are the things I know. I could go into my list of examples, and I think you know that. Beyond this, I do not know what is best for you, nor am I meant to. That is the beauty of living, Anna. *You* make the decisions!"

I sat silently. Stunned at the recollection of moments my mother had always told me there were angels watching over me. I guess she was right.

"How do I get there? How do I get to David?" I finally said in a whisper. I had come this far. It would be foolish not to try to go forward now.

Amoriti walked to the middle of the room to a small worktable. It appeared to be a place where woodsmen would come to store the chopped wood, eat a meal, and sometimes rest for the night after a long day's work. The whole space couldn't have been more than a hundred square feet, and she seemed to fill most of it. She glided above the table and began circling something with her finger. Over and over her hand would swerve in motion leaving what looked like sawdust in the air. I was still fairly weak from my fall, parachute malfunction, or whatever it was that had landed me there. Or maybe I had been injured and was still on the ground experiencing hallucinations. I blinked. I blinked a few times, then some more. She was still there, and so was I. My situation was unbelievable, yet there I sat. I started to take off my rubbery suit and felt the chill of the air on my bones. The cotton t-shirt and leggings that I still had on underneath the suit were a bit damp from my own sweat, and I began to shiver. I saw the petticoat hanging on a nail near the door, and took a second look. *Amoriti must have removed it when I went into a frenzy; but how could she have?* I batted my eyes again, pinched myself even. She was still at the table; I was seemingly awake, so I convinced myself that I was not imagining things–that it was all real. I dressed myself in the long, flowing vintage linen gown and walked over to the table. The woodshed looked like as good a place as any to hide the suits until I found David.

"Can I leave these here? Maybe over there in that chest?" I asked Amoriti. "Do the woodsmen come here still? Do I need to find a safer spot to hide them?"

"The cabin should not be occupied much this time of year. Come here, child. We shall put them underneath the table." She kicked up a small piece of the wooden floor, took a narrow linen towel that was hanging from the side of the table, wrapped it around my suit, took the suits for David and Laura, and placed them below.

"They should be perfectly safe there," she said as she closed the tiny opening in the floor, "You must return to retrieve them when you are ready, so be aware of your surrounding, Anna," she paused to look at me. "Now, to get you to where you are going!"

Amoriti had etched a perfect sketch of where we were, and what I assumed was the forest that surrounded us, and the villages nearest our location. She then proceeded to gently blow the sawdust up into her hands. The dust swirled and wafted into a single sheet of paper that was a perfect, tiny map of our surroundings. She gently rolled the small map and secured it with a string.

"Hold onto this tightly," she instructed. "One point of entry for the pod is clearly marked. I have seen it–that is as much as I can tell you. It is not far from a large house called Blaise Castle. In fact, it is on part of the vast

138

grounds between that estate and a small church. If you are found there, know that there are two young ladies named Katherine and Winifred who live there. They will help you, I am sure of it. They are giddy and frivolous, but they have good hearts, Anna. The girls are in reputable society, so you shall not be in any danger if you stay in their company. They will protect you when I cannot, I think.

"And, Anna, few have ever been able to see their Guardian for who they are. Most are unaware when they encounter one of us that they are in the presence of angels indeed. You are blessed, loved, and watched over. Never lose sight of that, child."

She vanished. I stood alone in the cabin holding a stiff, tiny scroll, and all I could think was *"run!"*

So I ran.

CHAPTER TEN

"Minnie! Minnie, no!" a girl's voice called from the distance as if she was chasing someone.

"Why ever not, Kitty?"

"Oh, stop calling me that! You know I prefer to be called Katherine, and you are so set on vexing me!"

I heard them giggle.

"Why does it matter what I call you, Sister? For it is Kitty you shall forever be to me, friend of my childhood, and dearest sister in the world." They laughed again.

I lay there, eyes closed, listening to what I thought to be the television. It had been so long since I had rested. I felt comfortable there on my parents' couch listening to my beloved BBC programming, but a wrenching feeling in the pit of my stomach told me I wasn't quite where I supposed myself to be. I could feel myself coming out of deep, un-relaxing sleep, but I felt warm, and the sun felt too bright for me to want to open my eyes. Suddenly, I felt a tugging at my clothes.

"She's not wearing any shoes!"

"And little else, for that matter, Minnie. Good lord!"

I slowly rubbed my eyes, as I realized that it was not the television. I tried to stand to my feet, but stumbled forward. The girls both jumped back, and one of them squealed. We all then stood motionless, staring at one another. I could scarcely open my eyes widely enough to see them well.

"Kitty, you mustn't shout!" One scolded the other. "Father will hear you, and we won't have any adventure if you inconvenience him!"

"She startled me," the one called Kitty said, looking at me as if inspecting me thoroughly, "Father has surely gone back into the house hours ago and that is precisely why we should not be out here with a strange girl, Minnie! He would be quite displeased."

The girl called Minnie tiptoed closer to me, extending a hand and an inquisitive grin. "Don't be afraid, dear. We will help you. What is your name?"

I couldn't speak. I was overcome with fear, and began looking around for a place to run. Woods and trails surrounded me. We stood in a small opening that looked like it led to a more manicured property, and I felt myself begin to panic. I must have gone off in search of Blaise Castle as Amoriti had suggested, but I was still weak. I hadn't made it to my destination. *Or had I? Was this the point of entry for the pod?* I glanced upward. The sun was blinding against the clear, blue sky. I fell to my knees sobbing, as I threw my head into my hands and wept.

"Oh, my dear, you must have been through something dreadful!" She took my hand gently, and stroked my head as she knelt to the ground. "My name is Winifred, but people call me Minnie, and this is my sister,

Katherine," she explained gesturing toward her sister who stood cautiously looking on. "We will help you. Do you speak English?"

I nodded.

"Good! You understand me then?" she smiled in excitement.

I nodded again.

"Did your ship wreck? Have you been washed ashore? Have you been wandering through the woods looking for help?" Her tone became excited as she released my hand and stood. "Or perhaps you were kidnapped by dreadful pirates and you have escaped your captors. Your only hope was to head into the woods!" She gasped, clapping her hand to her cheek as if coming to the realization that she alone had solved the mystery. "You could have died out here in the wilderness, you poor thing!"

"Minnie, really! You mustn't presume such things! Perhaps she is simply lost!" the one called Kitty insisted.

"In her petticoat? With no shoes, Kitty? Honestly!"

I had stopped crying. I looked up at the two girls. They were quintessential beings of every British novel I had ever read about young girls in society, and I smiled with curiosity and hope. They looked at one another, then at me, and we all smiled.

"Let me help you up, dear." Minnie grabbed my arm at the elbow and helped me stand to my feet.

"You haven't told us *your* name." Katherine was the more reserved, sensible one. She needed answers that I would be obligated to give.

"Anna. I'm Anna Wright," I whispered. I considered using my married name, but feared for what it may implicate if David was around and using his real name. Besides, the professor had told me to stick to my lineage since I had studied it, so Anna Wright it was. We began slowly walking toward a hedge that lined the small opening where we had been standing. The grand forest around us was cut away in bits, only to make room for what seemed necessary. It was all thick, lush, and enchanting. As we crossed a small stream, we seemed to suddenly come upon the castle itself, and I began to breathe in the fresh air, regaining my strength. I was feeling more hopeful than ever. *I did it! I'm really here!*

Kitty and Minnie had been chatting about what I was wearing—more particularly what I *wasn't* wearing—and how they would plan to explain my arrival to their mother and father, but when I saw that Blaise Castle was an actual castle, and not just a fancy British title for an elitist's home, I stopped dead in my tracks.

"It's an *actual* castle?" I asked.

"Oh, no, that's only the turrets. Don't let them intimidate you, dear," Minnie said, "the manor is over this way!" She smiled lightheartedly and began to pick up a little speed, skipping with excitement. Kitty was, however, a bit less excited as she was nervous.

"Miss Wright, where do you live? Since you are now capable of speaking, please tell us something about yourself," Katherine insisted. I had a feeling I was going to call her *Katherine* as opposed to *Kitty*.

I hadn't thought of my accent until that moment. I hadn't said much, but I was sure that I hadn't been trying to sound proper by any stretch of the imagination. "I...I am from America."

"Oh! America?" Minnie's eyes were wide and she gasped and clapped her hands together. "How exciting! You *did* suffer shipwreck, didn't you, Anna? Upon my word, you must be terribly frightened if you survived alone! Mustn't she, Kitty?"

"Indeed. She must be," Katherine said skeptically as she looked at me, and I at her. I felt that she wanted to help me, but believed that she should exercise caution in doing so.

"Minnie, stop." Katherine halted us as we had come upon a small bridge, which led across a small stream to a large line of trees. I could see that a meadow lay just beyond the line of woods and assumed the estate to be on the other side. I swallowed hard. I would have to think on my feet and answer their questions, *but what was I to say?* The Professor was right. The real danger was just ahead. I had survived the travel, but now the living part was the true challenge.

I began to assess my situation and study the girls. Katherine was reserved and cautious, not at all like Minnie in her gestures. I could tell that there was a great deal of compassion beneath the surface, but skepticism kept her from acting quite like her expressive sister.

Minnie was a free spirit. I liked her. Though a bit childish and presumptuous, she was so full of life that I couldn't help but be drawn to her. She reminded me of myself—my former self, at least. She had the world on a string, and endless hope, imagination, and naïveté. They complemented each other as sisters, and I was reminded of my sweet sibling, Lyn. I grinned, and listened as Katherine began to drill me with questions.

"What shall we say when we arrive at the house, do you suppose, Miss Anna Wright from America? You have told us very little, and have let Minnie suppose a story that may or may not prove to be the truth. I wish to help you, I do. But I need to know."

"I understand, Katherine, I…"

"You may call me Miss Hartford, Miss Wright," she interrupted, "and I will call you by your Christian name if you wish, but we are not accustomed to being addressed in so informal a manner, no matter what the circumstance of our meeting," she said plainly.

"Oh, Kitty, please. No one cares about that sort of thing anymore! We are not out and about in society, we are out in nature! Look around you! Drink it in!" Minnie spun herself around as if soaking up every ray of sunshine and the fresh, luscious fragrances that surrounded us on that beautiful spring day. I was glad it was spring, but I had hardly noticed the season until that moment. I tilted my head back and breathed a deep breath. "See? Anna understands me, don't you, dear?" Minnie asked, taking my hand and linking my arm to hers. "We shall be the best of friends, Anna, and you do not ever have to call me *Miss* anything!" she said with a tone of sarcasm.

Katherine sighed and shook her head; she was exasperated by Minnie's credulity, and I figured I did owe them some sort of explanation.

"I don't want the two of you to quarrel. Please let me explain now." I turned to look back over the small bridge and took a deep breath. "I did have a shipwreck of sorts. I survived alone. I am not sure how long or far I have come, nor how I survived, but I have. And I beg you to please help me. I truly have nothing left! I came to England in search of family and I have no intention of returning without him–them."

"Returning? You wish to return to America with your family?" Katherine asked.

Minnie just giggled and looked at me with a playful countenance. "How peculiarly you speak, Anna! Do all

Americans speak in such a manner?" she asked, laughing again.

"I suppose." I couldn't pretend very well with the two girls. I was no actress, and though I tried to focus on my most proper speech, I knew my accent betrayed me. "And yes, Kather...Miss Hartford. I do wish to find them and return."

"What relation is he to you that would cause you to not know his whereabouts and to travel all this way on such a treacherous journey to find him, Miss Wright? If he—or they—are all you have left, why not stay here among them instead of wishing to return to America?" Katherine asked curiously with a perplexed countenance. "Though I don't recall any Wrights near here. I think there might be a George Wright in Bristol who keeps a shop on Redcliffe Street. Is he who you are looking for?" she asked.

I froze. *What do I to say now? That my husband abandoned me? That would be far from acceptable for this time period. That I'm from the future and my beloved is lost in their decade?* I didn't remember what story I had been planning to tell.

"My...brother. He left without a word, and without a trace. My ancestors moved to America long before it was even a country. Many years ago, they crossed the seas in search of a new life and have been there ever since," I spoke on the fly. "My brother always said that he wished to return someday to his homeland, and so, after a quarrel with our father, he ran away, never to return. I supposed him to have boarded a ship, and fled to England, but I can't be sure," I said unconvincingly.

"And you've come all this way not knowing whether he is dead or alive? *Alone*?" Kitty asked with an accusatory tone. "Or whether he has even come to England? How do you propose to find him?" She didn't skip a breath. "How long ago did he leave?"

"I...I don't know. What year are we in now?" I said in a whisper.

"Do you not know?" Minnie laughed heartily. "Surely you have not been wandering in the woods that long, silly! It's still eighteen hundred fifty!"

"And one!" added Katherine. "Who's silly now, Minnie? Can *you* not even remember the year?" They both laughed, but the look on my face must have stopped them abruptly.

I was confused, shocked, and frightened. I had no idea if I had come to the right decade. And at the start of one at that! *Was David forced to battle two Guardians from these two decades if he had arrived more than a year ago? Was he even here?* The thought was heavy, and I sighed, shoulders slumped, barely able to stand. I leaned against the side of the small bridge. The sun was starting to get lower, and a chill began to set into the air. Noticing my shivers, Minnie sympathetically took her shawl and draped it over my shoulders. We crossed the small wooden bridge and began to walk for a few moments in silence.

"The house is not far now," Minnie assured me. "Let's get you inside and cleaned up for tea. I'm sure you'll be quite pretty in a proper gown and after a good bath, of course!" We smiled at each other. Somehow the frivolity of looking pretty in a gown sounded important at that point. I had been taught that presentation was key.

The rest of the way we were all quiet. We came upon an extensive lawn just after a large hedge of pines, and there, in its midst, was the grand estate. It was breathtaking. Somehow fresh-looking while still antique. It might

147

have been a hundred years old already, and I wondered at how many more it would live on. It was just the sort of place I loved to visit during my travels with David, and I had a feeling it was going to be just the place I needed to be. Amoriti had guided me, and I was thankful. I smiled at Minnie and finally spoke: "Thank you."

"It will all be well, my dear! It will all be well!" she reassured me.

Even Katherine smiled and the two girls placed an arm around me on either side as they lead me into the house, trying to shield the sight of me in a thin petticoat.

A brash scolding greeted us. "What's this?" A short, stout woman shrilled loudly as we entered the house. "Upon my word, girls! What have you two been up to all this time?" she interrogated, standing in her neatly pressed black dress with her grey locks pulled firmly up under a white cap.

"Dear Nellie, please! Not a word, do you promise? Minnie implored.

"I shall *not* make such a promise!" Nellie protested.

The housekeeper was coming or going along the hallway, which I assumed to be far from the main entryway, just as we were coming in.

"We should not have presumed to come this way had I known you would be here!" Katherine tried to explain.

"I suppose you should not have!" The woman grabbed my arm and looked me sternly in the eyes. "What do you mean, girl? Coming out in your dressing gown and imposing on the ladies of this house?"

Nellie seemed rigid and cruel.

"You mustn't scold her, Nellie, please." Minnie spoke up for me. "She has suffered a great deal and we only wished to help."

"A great deal indeed, has she? Miss, you should take care in dealing with such a girl!" She had not allowed even the slightest explanation from the girls, so I decided to speak up.

"I do apologize, ma'am. I am entirely at fault. I was lost and they only meant to help!" I cried. Tears began to trickle down my face, and the ever-flowing stream of overwhelming emotions would not be suppressed.

"That's quite enough, girl!" Nellie said in surprise. "There's no need for hysterics, surely!" she said with a hint of sympathy. "Get her upstairs, girls. I'll send Sarah up directly."

"Oh, thank you Nellie! All will be well! Did I not say? All will be well, Anna, you shall see!" Minnie was almost jubilant as she bounced and skipped her way down the hall and up the stairs to show me to a room.

"Right this way, Anna. Sarah will draw you a bath presently, and I shall bring you a fresh gown. Supper is at six. I shall come to your room to escort you. Mother cannot be quite upset if we go in together," she smiled.

"Thank you, Minnie, truly. Thank you so much." I squeezed her hand as she left the room, and she nodded and smiled as she drew the heavy door to a close. I took a moment to glance around the tall room. The walls were thick and bright, and the ceiling was lined with etchings along the plaster. Rustic wood encasing accentuated the room's fireplace. It was a bit chilly in the room itself, and I pulled Minnie's shawl tighter around me.

The bed was high and heavy. The shapely wood posts reached far above any regular canopy bed that I had ever seen and the drapes along its sides were thick, in bright green and gold. The whole room was painted in white and pale green, and had a lovely welcome to it that I hadn't expect of such a place. Whenever I had visited castles and manors before, they all seemed to be quite dark, perhaps to protect the antiques from the damaging light of the sun. I was sitting in a place that was real. It was used every day as a person's home. I took another deep breath. *I wonder what the living quarters of Versailles would look like if all the curtains were drawn back and the bright afternoon sunlight shone in.* I thought, as I sat down on the bed. My reverie was interrupted.

"Miss Winifred sent this gown for you, Miss," a young voice with a thick cockney accent startled me.

"Oh, were you knocking? Forgive me, please come in. I was just sitting admiring the room, and…" my voice drifted off as I stood with a hopeless blank stare.

"A'right, Miss. My name is Sarah, and I am here to give you a gown and to show you to the bath. I've drawn it lukewarm if that suits you, Miss," she said with a nod and a curtsey.

"Oh, yes, of course, thank you." I replied with a smile.

The young girl looked to be about twelve or thirteen and had a sweet, genteel disposition. I followed her down a hall into a room that was warm and steamy. I didn't expect a lukewarm bath to warm the room so, but soon realized that there was small stove in the corner behind a room divider with boiling water on its top letting off a pleasant steam.

"If you need anything else, Miss, I'll be in the corridor."

I thanked her kindly, not knowing where "the corridor" was or what I should do for shampoo, soap, or anything else, much less if I'd remember which room it was that I was expected to return to. I was just happy to feel warm again, and tried to wash, dry, and dress as quickly as possible. I didn't even know what time it was or if "supper at six o'clock" was a punctual thing, or if Minnie would return to the room at six, so I rushed.

The gown fit me well. Minnie and I were both around five-foot-six with similar frames, but my long arms protruded three or four inches further than the sleeves themselves. My mom would always joke that I got my dad's long arms, and there was nothing I could do to dispute that fact in my current situation. I smiled at the memory of my parents. I couldn't get the buttons to close over my arms where the sleeves should have lain at my wrists, so I gently rolled them back to my elbows, hoping to keep the dress intact.

I opened the door to the bathroom and peeked my head down the hall. There stood Sarah at a small doorway, ready to be at my aid. "Finished, Miss?"

"Yes, thank you."

"Oh, my, your hair is still dripping wet, Miss," Sarah said, looking a bit surprised, and I realized that my dripping hair had already wet the dress and collar. "I'll help you get out of your gown, and set your hair. There's a housecoat in the room there for you, and we can step into the anteroom to get you ready."

"The corridor. Ah…between the bathroom and the anteroom. Got it. Sorry, Sarah."

"Oh, Miss, no need to apologize to the likes of me," she giggled. "I know you must have been through a great deal. One must have gone through much hardship to forget the routines of dressing," she giggled. "But it's no matter, Miss, that is why I am here to help," she said with an empathetic smile.

Sarah slipped a corset around my waist and pulled tightly. I instantly understood why that was a garment

151

women eventually abandoned, as it squeezed out a cough and a sigh.

"Quite nice, Miss. How well you look."

Sarah was trying to say that she liked the way she "fixed" my figure, I'm sure. But I also knew that I could not respond. I was just concentrating on the breathing part. Was this something I practiced wearing, or did Professor Trinkton and Christopher just forget to prepare me for it? I couldn't remember. *Whew*. I was just practicing my yoga breaths. Slowly. *I can do this.*

Sarah led me to a soft, high-back upholstered chair in front of a vanity. I sat down slowly, still adjusting to having the tight corset around my waist and bosom. I must have nodded off a dozen times while Sarah pulled, brushed, and rubbed my hair dry. It felt relaxing as I had started to feel faint from the trauma of my long journey, wanting to fall asleep in the comfy salon chair. Before I could ask her what her thoughts may be on my excusing myself from the impending meal and meeting of the rest of the family, Sarah turned my head and handed me a mirror to be able to see her handiwork in the reflection of the vanity mirror. It was truly breathtaking. My hair had been twisted, stacked, and braided in a beautiful mound of curls and flower pins. She assisted me with the gown, fastening it in the back where I couldn't reach the delicate ties.

"Lovely," Sarah exclaimed.

"Is it a formal dinner?" I asked with a gasp. I instantly became aware of what I was about to do. Meet the master of the estate, and beg his kindness to help me find my... *brother.* And I felt very out of place. *Were all their dinners so fancy? Did I train for this?* I couldn't quite remember.

"Oh, yes, Miss, I should *say* it is a formal affair. Lord and Lady Watson are to be there, along with their son. It's quite thrilling!" she said excitedly. "Miss Katherine is sure to be engaged to Mr. Edward Watson by summer; I just know it!"

I swallowed. Breathed deeply. Closed my eyes.

"Are you quite all right, Miss?"

"Anna…Please just call me Anna."

"Yes, Miss Anna, are you quite all right? May I fetch you some water?" She hurried to the corner of the room by a washstand and quickly returned with a glass of water.

"Thank you," I said as I sipped it down. "*Of course, Miss Anna,*" I thought. I grinned, tipped my glass to her, and then drank the rest of the water. "I'm much better, thank you."

The irony of the same social propriety of the year *eighteen fifty and one* as well as the formal propriety of the years I spent with Oyoon in Mongolia during the twenty-first century struck me as funny, and I began to chuckle.

What am I doing?

Sarah looked at me, puzzled. "It's only a formal dinner with the family. You seem like a lady who will be able to manage it quite well. And you *do* look well. A little out of sorts, I suppose," she smiled.

"And a little bit insane, maybe? I know *I* think I'm crazy for being here. For doing this." I asked with a more sober tone, "What am I doing? This *is* crazy!"

"You say the most peculiar things, Miss!" a hint of concern hung on her words.

I hadn't realized that I had gotten so serious and my fear had begun to show.

"Oh, Sarah, I'm a mess. You don't have an easy job with me!" I laughed. She looked at me as if she was still trying to figure out what I meant. As I stood face-to-face with a lovely little soul, I took a moment to look into her eyes and smile. I began to laugh, mostly just at myself and how I was ever going to pull off such a mission, but a little bit at the glorious opportunity that I had to meet a soft-spirited girl like Sarah. She looked back at me, and we both began to giggle.

"I think we shall both manage just fine, Miss," she whispered.

She had me stand, turned me around and led me to a long mirror in the corner as she finished buttoning the back of the dress where my long hair had lain in the way before she had it placed well. It was the first time I looked–really looked at the dress I had been given. Layers of draping fabric, lace, and chiffon–a combination that made me feel elegant, giving me the confidence that I might fit in better than I had anticipated.

"Quite pretty, Miss," Sarah said smiling in satisfaction of a job well done. "You do look well," she said, taking a step back. I turned around to see her face without the reflection of the mirror.

"Thank you Sarah," I smiled softly.

Minnie quickly entered the room to announce that she was ready to escort me to dinner, which prompted Sarah to take her leave quickly and scurry down the hallway somewhere in the large house to go back to what I could only suppose was another on her list of duties.

"Did I miss any excitement?" Minnie asked with a laugh.

"I don't think so, Minnie…Miss Hartford?" I was suddenly aware that I must be on my best behavior. I needed to remember the social propriety that we had rehearsed in my training. Christopher, Professor Trinkton, and I had sat around a table practicing proper etiquette for hours. I was beginning to remember, but it was hard to recall everything in that moment. Books, novels, movies…if only I could act like one of the characters I'd seen in those, but a gripping fear was crawling up my spine.

"You mustn't call me 'Miss:' to me you are 'Anna,' and I am 'Minnie,'" she corrected me with a smile. "Let my sister be the particular one, and we two shall be great friends."

"You have a trusting heart, Minnie," I said in relief.

"When you say that, it sounds like a good thing, but I'm afraid that when others do, it sounds like a scolding," she laughed.

"I suppose I do see it as a good thing," I said smiling. "I believe that discretion is needed, of course, but trust is something that you have to be willing to give away sometimes. And I think we both knew that we could trust each other right away, didn't we?"

"Well, in your state, I was not certain straightaway!" Minnie exclaimed with a hearty giggle.

"Fair enough," I conceded.

Minnie led me down the hallway and into a receiving room, inviting me to take a seat. The guests were to arrive soon, and though I had been told that Mr. and Mrs. Hartford were notified of my visit, I was still uncertain of how it was all being portrayed, and if I would meet them before their expected guests arrived. *Would they introduce me to their friends? Was I to introduce myself? What in the world did I practice in preparation for all of this?* Not much, I felt. I remember that I had tried to memorize a story. *What was that story?* I felt myself rocking back and forth in my chair, trying to calm my nerves and recall it all.

My family had left on a ship—the St. Anne—to sail to America in 1623. We had been there for generations, and my accent would be excusable. I had practiced my piano skills. I would pass

155

as an educated woman without suspicion. I hadn't colored my hair or painted my nails, but what was it...how was it that I was to act? The longer I stayed in that room, the more nervous I became. Minnie was talking about something or another–plants, or gardens, maybe the trees. It was a lovely spring, but my mind could only process that I was sitting in another time period, scared out of my mind. *What am I doing? Why have I done this?* were repeating over and over in my mind.

"Miss Wright?" Kitty came in and caught me in my foggy thoughts. I don't know how many times she may have called "Miss Wright" out to me before I responded. I simply looked up.

She had entered the room introducing her father, Lord of the estate–a tall, stately-looking man with a full head of salt-and-pepper hair that looked as if it would eventually all turn a snowy white. His face was pleasant and narrow, and his brow was high and wide. He was a handsome man who looked very reserved, but friendly and kind as well.

"My dear, you must be so fatigued! Your journey was quite the arduous one, I have been told," he said kindly.

"Oh, yes!" I replied. I stood and stretched out my hand, but then quickly and awkwardly retracted it again. I took an embarrassing bow, saying nothing. When I looked up at him, he simply nodded.

"Welcome to our home," he said cordially.

"Thank you. It is so lovely. I do appreciate your hospitality. Your daughters have been so gracious and helpful to me. I will try not to take advantage of your kindness for too long." We all took a seat, pausing in silence for a moment. I began to glance around the room to act like I didn't notice him inspecting me. He didn't look at me in a condescending way, but a cautious and curious one.

"What is it that brought you here to Blaise Castle, Miss Wright? I don't recall hearing of any recent shipwrecks, and Kitty tells me that you were indeed somehow separated from your vessel?" the girls' father asked.

I looked up at him, "I am not sure what happened. All I can tell you is that I awoke with little to call my own, and your daughters brought me here to help. I couldn't be more grateful. I have come to find my family. My…brother, actually." I was the worst liar ever. I always hesitated awkwardly when I said it. "H…he has gone missing, and his last whereabouts were near here, so I came in search of him."

"A young woman? All alone? Quite peculiar," he said in disapproval. "I would scold your father if I knew him," he said with a serious but playful tone. "To allow a young woman as yourself to journey alone on a sea voyage, no less. Most disturbing. So much could have happened, and indeed *did* happen in your case, Miss Wright. Goodness."

I wasn't sure how to respond to that. He was right. This kind of thing would have never been done back then. And the suspicion must have been mounting. I breathed deeply.

"I'm a fairly determined woman, I suppose. It wasn't exactly with my parents' approval that I came on this journey." I was not lying about that.

"I should think not," he said with a raised eyebrow.

Just has he had given another look of disapproval, Mrs. Hartford appeared at the door of the room along with a housekeeper and butler.

"Oh, come in, dear. Meet the girls' newfound acquaintance, Miss Anna Wright."

She whispered a couple of instructions about drinks, the meal, and room set-up, and then turned to look at her husband. She was breathtaking. She was a slender, tall woman of about five foot, seven inches with golden brown hair and natural curls that framed her face. She was wearing one of the most elegant gowns I had ever seen—much like some that you would see in museums—layers of deep blue with a light blue overlay and golden embroidery that cascaded down the edges as it flowed exquisitely. I may have gasped a bit when I saw her face. She had the slightest trace of freckles and natural blonde highlights in her curls that mingled so well with the golden tone of her brown hair, with the greenest eyes that I had ever seen.

She glided across the room in an elegance that made her look regal. Her husband stood and took her hand as she leaned in near his face and he kissed her cheek.

Minnie and Kitty stood as their mother approached them, kissing them on the cheek then took their seats quietly.

"My lovely wife, Miss Wright." I could tell he adored her. And rightly so, I thought.

I stood smiling, taking a slight bow upon our introduction, then returned to my place on the sofa next to Minnie, as Mrs. Hartford nodded and smiled politely, making her way toward her husband on the beautifully upholstered couch. My eyes shifted from person to person waiting for an indication of what to expect until Mrs. Hartford broke the pregnant pause that made me uneasy.

"Welcome," she said with a happy expression, "Winifred tells me that you are in need of some assistance finding your brother, Miss Wright. I do hope that you consider Blaise Castle a comfortable place to stay until you are able to find him. If we can assist in any way, please do let us know. I shall ask our neighbors if they know of any Mr. Wright in our society. Is there any chance he may not want to be found, since you say he has fled after a quarrel? If that is the case, he is less likely to have been seen by anyone we know," Mrs. Hartford stated.

"Beautiful *and* clever!" Mr. Hartford flirted with his wife right in front of us, and I was a little taken aback. He grinned at her with a twinkle in his eye as he took her hand to his lips, kissing it softly. It was refreshing to see their love story lived out before my eyes. It reminded me of home.

"My dear, you are going to give Miss Wright the wrong impression," she smiled playfully. "And you must be on your best behavior for our guests this evening. They are practically family, you know," she chuckled.

Minnie laughed out loud. "We all must behave if we do not wish to get a proper scolding," she said in a sarcastic tone, wagging her head back and forth.

"Mm, yes. The Watsons. We will all have a lovely evening together, shan't we, Katherine?" Mr. Hartford grinned slyly and insinuated his approval of his eldest daughter's romance. Kitty returned the smile to her father, blushing in embarrassment.

"Yes, Father, they shall arrive soon," she nodded.

CHAPTER ELEVEN

The hazy candlelight had a dizzying effect. Maybe it was the warmth of the room after the guests piled in, the servants moved about, and the hot food came and went. Perhaps it was the sips of sweet red wine, or simply the fatigue that I felt after my unbelievable journey. It was most likely a combination of all of the above. Whatever the contributing factors, I felt as if I was in a daze for the majority of the evening. Blaise Castle was spectacular, and I found myself looking around the room to take in the beauty as much as I could. I recalled having visited a castle in Germany once with David that reminded me of such opulence, and as we descended the long staircase together I imagined myself to be in an elegant ball gown and he my escort, so I asked him to slow down, take his time, and let me soak in my moment of imagination. He obliged, smiled, and said that I'd always be his princess, with or without my imagination. Then he kissed my hand.

I glanced down at my hands and grinned. My ring finger was bare, and my heart sank as my smile faded.

"Miss Wright? Do you not think so?"

"I apologize, what was that? I'm sorry. I am having a hard time focusing this evening," I said, excusing myself from not having followed the conversation.

"Why, of course you are," Lord Watson cordially forgave my impoliteness.

"Miss Wright, Lord Watson was revealing how treacherous the waters are this time of year and how something must be done to minimize the unfortunate shipwrecks we seem to experience every year precisely during this time. You must agree, given your current predicament," Lady Watson explained.

"Oh, yes, of course," the young sea captain said. "It is most perplexing why something has not yet been done," Mr. Thomas Hartford, heir to the estate, gave his opinion freely. "I do believe it would be best for all passenger voyages to be abandoned when such storms arise, if one is able to predict it. We have more and more understanding of these things, but we cannot expect to cease all transport at the scare of a storm. It would be impossible to know how severe the weather may be, and we may very well never leave the shore if we are too hesitant," he knowledgably proclaimed.

Mr. Thomas Hartford had been introduced to me shortly before entering the dining room that evening. The girls hadn't mentioned a brother before then, so I was surprised that he was so casually introduced, then sat at my side. He looked much like his father must have looked in his youth. He was tall and broad-shouldered with jet-black hair, wearing a clean-shaven smile even when his face was resting. His mother had briefly stated my name and little else before we sat down for dinner, and the topic of conversation inevitably came to be about what shipwreck anyone might have heard of.

The food kept coming as the servants piled it high on the long, wide table in the great dining hall. We were seated close enough to each other to have side conversations, but we were also able to engage in the whole table's discussion when necessary. Thomas Hartford sat next to me not pressuring me to say a word, though he did remark on my accent when I did. He and Minnie had the gift of lighthearted conversation, and it kept me from having to be put on the spot.

Thomas Hartford was a sea captain by choice, not by approval, which had been clearly revealed by both of his parents since his introduction to me. I had learned over our dinner conversation that Thomas had been at sea for three years and had only returned because of his father's demands to make a gentleman's life for himself and give up the sea altogether. I didn't anticipate that that would soon happen, and to me Thomas' rebellion was endearing. His mother and father, however, were not as impressed with it.

Edward Watson sat on my left, and then Kitty after him. He was said to have an understanding with Kitty, though no engagement had been announced. Edward was everything a young British gentleman of his situation should be. His face was round and young. He was soft-spoken and obliging, caring deeply for his family estate and bloodline in dutiful compliance, and ready to take on the responsibilities that Thomas Harford was reluctant to embrace. Katherine and Edward seemed to be a fitting match.

"But just think of the people we *know*, Mr. Hartford! How many could we name who have been affected by the heartache of shipwreck? The Collinses, who lost their father at sea, the Stebbings, whose cousin was merely voyaging for pleasure–which I shall not quite ever understand," she said casting a disapproving glance. "But dear Thomas, I suppose you share that interest," a stout and boisterous Lady Watson could not help but throw in a hint about her feelings which supported the Hartfords' disapproval of their son's choices, "and think of the Stevenson family who lost poor Mr. Stevenson for more than a decade! It is an outrage that they should allow travel under such conditions."

"It is not as simple as that," Thomas replied. "An act of God may take a turn that can not likely be predicted, and things at sea do not always go as planned."

"Things? You say it so simply, Thomas," she scolded. "But many people's lives hang in the balance," Lady Watson retorted.

She had a pretty way about her, but she lacked the soft elegance that Mrs. Hartford had. She was proper and reserved, but not what I would call graceful. I could tell that she made the rules in the family, and managed the home rather forcefully. But her son seemed to respect her–not just humor her–so I could tell that there was a kindness that lay behind her toughness. I sat back and enjoyed the exchange, trying not to drift off into my own thoughts again.

"What *things* went wrong on your ship, Miss Wright? What was the name of the vessel?" she continued the conversation with a hint of skepticism.

"I don't recall, ma'am," was all that I could think to say.

"Peculiar," Lady Watson said narrowing her eyes. "Very peculiar indeed! Marcy, dearest, has she seen Dr. Andrews yet?" she asked Mrs. Hartford.

"She simply needed a gown and a good washing, Elizabeth. I do not think that there is any urgency for a doctor," said Mrs. Hartford softly.

They spoke about me instead of to me for a few moments, and it was soon decided that I should see the good doctor in the morning. I tried to make sense of where they said his offices were in the town, hoping that I could possibly ride in a carriage with them, and be more likely to pinpoint a location of where the pod might arrive, but they insisted that I needed to stay at the house and that Dr. Andrews would visit me.

"It's settled, then. It is not to be taken lightly that a single young woman who is claiming to be the sole survivor of a ship we have no knowledge of arrives upon one's doorstep, Mr. Hartford," the gentleman continued in dismay.

"Indeed it is not, Lord Watson," he replied.

"It brings to mind young David Stevenson as I mentioned, does it not?" Lady Watson insisted on belaboring the conversation. "And after so many years. What a pity to lose all of that time with one's family. The whole of a young man's childhood, practically. Oh, but how beautifully he does these days. Does he not? Full recovery; such a happy outcome!"

"Mm. Indeed," agreed Mrs. Hartford.

"Ah, yes. Fine gentleman, that. Mr. Stevenson is one of the handsomest, kindest, and most intelligent young gentleman I have ever had the pleasure of being acquainted with. And to think of his hardship! Happy outcome for all!" Lord Watson said. They all tipped their glasses and drank to it.

"And perhaps such will be the case with Miss Wright," Minnie stated from across the table. "All will be well, and she shall find her family. To Miss Anna Wright," she kindly directed the toast to me.

"Thank you. But, if you don't mind my asking," I finally had the courage to voice my curiosity, "what was Mr. Stevenson's circumstance?"

"Oh, sad plight at that, Miss Wright!" Lady Watson was happy to tell the story. "The Stevenson family are of the finest in this county. An earl and countess to be sure, but they sadly lost their only son David when he was a young boy of only ten years. The family had been out to sea, and I believe no one knows the particulars of the incident, but somehow poor young David was separated from the family and was lost in the waters. Some even speculated that he was kidnapped for ransom by pirates, but escaped and roamed the seas from ship to ship until he found his way home—only to be shipwrecked again a full ten years later!" Lady Watson's tone grew with excitement. "He was then found much like you, my dear. In quite a wretched state, and little recollection of what had happened at all!"

"My dear, you mustn't listen to all the idle gossip of the county. Who would believe such a notion?" Lord Watson playfully scolded.

"Is it not true, Edward?" she insisted on corroboration.

"Yes, mother, though I know of no pirates involved. Mr. Stevenson has little recollection of those years, but gets on quite well now. And with such happy news of late. Did you not hear from Countess Stevenson of his engagement?" Edward Watson asked.

"Indeed I did not!" his mother exclaimed loudly as she bounced slightly in her seat.

The room became a buzz about the forthcoming nuptials of Mr. David Stevenson and Miss Jane Bradshaw, and we tipped our glasses once again.

"And perhaps you shall meet the happy couple too, Miss Wright. Shall you join us for the ball Saturday evening? Assuming you will be well enough?" Thomas asked. "You should have a chance to discuss your plight with another who has had such misfortune, but the happiness of a story well ended!"

"Saturday?" I asked. *I didn't even know what today was. Surely my four days would be up by Saturday.*

"Why, of course, Anna, you must join us all! We shall make a lovely party if I may say so myself." Minnie proclaimed.

"Saturday! To celebrate a happy occasion for all." Thomas announced the toast.

"To Saturday!" they proclaimed in unison.

A dizzying air filled the warm room as they tipped their glasses once again, and I knew that I had sipped a bit too much with each toast. We sat, they spoke, and I listened. I endured as much of the evening as I was able to, and soon Minnie and I were excused to the drawing room from which I was able to take my leave.

"Good night, Miss Wright," Thomas Hartford stopped us in the hallway. "I hope you will rest well. Shall I escort you to your rooms?" he asked us both. He had a slender candlestick with two shafts that forked out from the base and held a couple of stubby candles that looked like they were about to burn out completely. The light was hazy and the faint smoke was reaching my eyes. I grimaced, turning my head to the side and swiping the rising vapors from the air.

"I…I'm sorry, but…"

"Don't be silly, Thomas," Minnie interrupted, "I will escort Miss Wright to her room, and you may return to the gentlemen. We will manage well enough," she said as she pushed him aside and smirked.

We headed down the hall and up the main staircase together in silence. When she knew we were far from Thomas' earshot she whispered, "Don't you mind my brother, Anna. He has an eye for pretty girls and has had far too much of the good wine tonight," she laughed.

"He is harmless enough, though his reputation is not a perfect one. People tend to exaggerate–it is a shame that they do–and poor Thomas is merely a victim of giving his heart away to young women who flirt and wink and play games of the heart that should not be taken lightly," she said defending her brother's reputation. "I will warn you that it is for him I voice my concern as I assume you have no fancy of engaging in courtship at all. I suspect that your heart is not readily available to be won–or perhaps, and this is my own opinion, of course–that your heart belongs to another already."

I stopped walking. I wasn't drunk. Just a little foggy and overheated, but I was as sober as anything in that moment.

"Hm, I suspected as much. Don't bother trying to deny it or change the subject to another. I will not force you to speak of him…not tonight anyway," she giggled linking her arm through mine and pulling me along. "Here you are. Sleep well. We shall see each other in the morning. Dr. Andrews will set your mind at ease. He isn't one of those doctors who ails you without cause, though I do suppose that when Mrs. Watson sees him for her nerves, he medicates her more for Mr. Watson than for herself!" she smiled and giggled closing the door to the room behind her.

Minnie spoke without breathing it seemed; she would barely give a chance for another to say a word most of the time. It made her appear ditzy and silly, but if you actually listened to what she was saying, you could tell that she was observant, astute, and intelligent. She could *see* that my heart belonged to David, *but would she help me find him? Can I trust her with the facts of why I am here? Will she be able to understand—and how much truth could I share with the lies I would still have to tell?*

The morning came sooner than I wished it to. I had tossed and turned most of the night, and just as day broke, I fell into a deep sleep.

"Miss Wright, I've been sent to fetch you what you need to prepare for today's journey to Dr. Andrews'." Sarah's tiny, pert face peered through the opening of the door before she stepped foot inside. Her pounding on the door had woken me from a mountaintop dream.

"It's all right, Sarah. Come in."

"Yes, Miss," she said as she entered with a small pail of water and a little towel. She handed the damp towel to me, as I wiped my face. "They sent word to the doctor, and he has asked you to go into town. He was unable to come to the house today as he will spend the morning performing a procedure of some sort. We should get you ready."

I sat up in the bed, swinging my legs over the side. "Thank you, Sarah."

"You were crying, Miss. In your sleep. I don't think I've seen the likes of that before. What were you doing? In the dream, I mean?" she asked with her teenaged charm and acute curiosity.

I grinned at her and sighed. "Just sitting."

"Sitting? Indeed, Miss, it must have been something more, mustn't it? To have been crying…"

"I was sitting alone."

"Aye, Miss. The pain of solitude. You must miss your family frightfully so. I am sorry for you, but you mustn't think of it now, for you have come to find your brother, and all will be well. We shall help you as much as we are able!" her tone turned from pitiful to hopeful. I wasn't sure if she was trying to convince herself or me.

We smiled at each other, and she began to brush out my hair.

"Sarah?"

"Yes, Miss."

"Can you keep a secret?" I asked her quietly.

"Can and will, Miss, if you say it."

"What if I told you that it wasn't my brother that I'm in search of? Would there be much of a scandal?"

"A lover, then, Miss? Aye, it would be more of a scandal, but you should not think that it hasn't been a topic that the family hasn't thought of or discussed. I'm sure that we are all mindful that you may be in search of a lover instead."

"A husband?" I asked.

"A husband, Miss? Oh, that may be more than a scandal the Hartfords wish to be part of, indeed," she said in surprise. "Did he run off on you? With another woman?" She had stopped brushing, and stood motionless, holding a lock of my long hair in one hand and a brush in the other, waiting for my answer. It was a scandal that stopped her in her tracks and let me know just how others may react.

I was sorry that I had opened my mouth. *What could this young girl possibly do to help my situation, and if the household gossip mill were to run, I could be in more trouble than it was worth!*

"Sarah, please," I turned to face her, grasping her dainty hands in mine. "If you were to suggest that he's my

169

husband to anyone, I might not get any help at all. I am not even sure he's alive; the truth is that I am most likely a widow. But the only thing I could think to say when I was asked about why I am here was that I came in search of my brother. It just came out. I didn't know…I don't know…"

"It's all right, Miss. I will keep your secret. Though I suppose Mr. Thomas will be unable to attain your affections now," she laughed.

We both needed to laugh at something. I smiled bashfully at her and looked down.

"I suppose not," I chuckled.

Dr. Andrews was a kind man who assured Mrs. Hartford that I was as healthy as any woman of my age should be, though I lied and said that my age was twenty-four instead of twenty-eight since I assumed it was a bit more respectable for a woman of twenty-four to still be unmarried than a woman of twenty-eight. But I think that Mrs. Hartford was a bit appalled even at my fake age since her dear Thomas was only twenty-six and paid some attention to me. He was surely in need of a wife of twenty or younger who had been untainted by the world, and desirable from a young age. I would not disappoint her, I hoped. I had paid little attention to Thomas, as he insisted on riding into town with us for some errands that he had to run. He chattered on about the town and the sea, how delighted I should be that he planned to introduce me to his friends and acquaintances at the ball on Saturday, and he rarely required my input or reply about anything. He wasn't chatty in a silly way like Minnie, but talkative in a manner that demanded attention. He was a captivating storyteller, and when we left him at his stop, Mrs. Hartford's delight of our separation became my dismay for having been left alone with her. It was of short duration, and we had quickly come and gone from the doctor's office, returning with the carriage to collect Thomas from the tailor's shop.

Kitty and Minnie were back at Blaise Castle with the last fitting of their gowns for the ball on Saturday, and I was to join them only after their mother had taken me into town and gotten clearance from Dr. Andrews that I was healthy—*sane, I'm sure*—and capable of enduring an evening on my feet.

"I am pleased that you are well, Miss Wright. If only in body and not in spirit," Mrs. Hartford spoke softly with the weight of skepticism.

"I am well in both, Mrs. Hartford. I carry the weight of worry about finding my family is all. I appreciate your kindness so much, and I am sorry for any expense you have incurred because of it." I tried to keep a proper manner about me, and a soft-spoken tone that I hoped would ease her apprehension.

"No mention of that is necessary, dear, you are welcome to our home until you are reunited with your family. It is the Christian thing to do, and I would not think of having you thrown out into the street. I simply wish to protect my own family. We know so little about you, and I must now trust that what you say is true, and that you have no ulterior motive."

"I promise that I do not. My one desire is to find him. There has never been another," I was as honest as I could be in the moment.

"Then I must believe you," she nodded.

"Believe what, Mother?" I hadn't noticed that the carriage had stopped, and that we had arrived at the little shop where Thomas was picking up his garments. He hopped into the carriage and swung himself onto the seat with a jolt. He was a handsome young man and his mannerisms were so full of life and happiness that it was hard not to smile at his presence.

"Your mother and I were discussing my recollection—or more specifically, what I cannot recall—of my arrival here. But I assured her that my one purpose in being here is to find my David." I said.

"David, is it? Your brother?" Thomas asked, "David Wright? I don't suppose I know anyone by that name, but we shall inquire nonetheless."

I realized then that I had not mentioned his name before. I wished that I would have begun with that and left out husband, brother, or whatever words I had awkwardly been using until then. But there it was. I was in search of my David, and there was one goal only. To return.

CHAPTER TWELVE

"You look very well in it, Kitty! Please wear it if you wish."
Minnie was standing next to her sister in a dress with
pale pink chiffon and white embroidered flowers as she
took the silver comb she was holding and fastened it in
Kitty's hair. Both of the girls had gotten their mother's
good looks, and were as kind to each other as any sisters
I had ever known. They were stunning in their extravagant
gowns and elegant hairdos.

"You both look beautiful," I said softly.

"Anna, why are you not dressed? Sarah will not have
time to set your hair if you do not make haste!" Minnie
spoke to me as lovingly as she did to anyone. Even when
she scolded, it seemed as if she was happy with me.

"Minnie, I don't think I can go. I am not feeling well,
and I…it's Saturday already. Three full days that I know
of and…"

"Anna, it has only been three days since your arrival
here. You are quite hard on yourself, and you need not

be. You mustn't expect to recall everything at once. A bit of distraction is all that you need. Besides, I need a pleasant companion or else I shall be forced to dance with Mr. McFadden, and will have no excuse to refuse him!" the girls laughed and teased each other.

"I suppose that Sir Edward Watson will keep my sister occupied for most of the evening, and you know how long and dreadful these things can be if one has no one with which to engage in conversation." She grabbed my hand and tried to be demanding. "No, I insist upon it, Anna. You must be this evening's companion for me at the ball or you will be forced to live with the regret of making me suffer a lifetime of pain in one solitary evening," she joked.

"I must insist upon it as well, Miss Wright. I shall not be able to bear the thought of my sister alone all evening–or the victim of a relentless Mr. McFadden–if you do not come!" The girls teased and giggled heartily. They were jovial and playful in anticipation of the elegant soiree.

I wanted to stay home, maybe even explore the grounds to try to gain some new information about my whereabouts and try to see what I could plan in the short time I could, but I knew that I was going to give in and be whisked away to an experience I had only dreamt about. I was fearful that I wouldn't remember the old British dances that went to this music or that. The names of them, the movements, the timing–but the girls' mood became infectious. I smiled and giggled with them as they spoke about boys and clothes and all of the exciting things we may encounter over the course of the evening. It was comforting to know that people are people no matter what time and place I found myself in, and I could relate to these nineteenth century women in a way I would have never expected.

We all dressed in the finest clothes I had ever seen, and Mr. and Mrs. Hartford were continually gracious about my being their guest. I tried not to worry about the mission I was there to achieve, and happily joined the party.

After tonight, I will devote my time to the search and study of finding David. No doctors, social calls, visits or societal obligations with my benevolent hosts. I will be on mission. I have to. Time is running out. But tonight—the ball.

The music beckoned us to enter the grand hall. We had ridden in a carriage for barely twenty minutes or so, but it was long enough to change the mood of excitement I had caught into an uneasiness about my decision to join them. The family had all quickly and eagerly exited the carriage upon our arrival, and as a coachman reached for my hand, I could not move.

"Miss? Are you ill, Miss? May I be of some assistance?"

I tried to snap myself out of it. Dance steps, curtsies, dinner etiquette—it was all swirling around in my head. *Would I remember things right? Surely someone would notice that I was an imposter! What dangers could I face with the Guardians if I stick out like a sore thumb?* I had kept myself fairly hidden in the house until the ball, but I was about to meet a hundred people or more.

"Miss?" he insisted.

"I don't think I…no, I am not well," I said as I sat frozen in the coach. I looked down at my hands. Smooth silk gloves went high above my elbows, and my hands felt slippery inside of them. I clutched my gown and began to trace its embroidery with my fingers. It wasn't until that moment that I had taken a good look at my garments. The pale green silk gown with light grey flowers elegantly embroidered in a beautiful pattern complimented my fair skin tone and brown hair. The exquisite clothes felt even more elegant than I could have imagined they would. My corset was tight and I shifted in my seat. *Perhaps I just need to stand.*

I began to rise off of the bench and heard the music once again. My senses were returning from my reverie as I peered from the small door of the coach where the restless coachman was trying to find a woman to assist me. I breathed in deeply. Just then, Minnie appeared hurrying down the steps of the beautiful entryway.

"Anna! Have you been in the coach all this time? We must be announced, and when I entered the door without my guest by my side, I was mortified! I came back to find you, and well, here you are, but we must be going!" she said without skipping a beat, jerking and tugging at me to leave the coach, and we scurried up the elegant marble steps of the wide porch.

"I believe I will be fine, sir!" I shouted back to the poor coachman who was still among the other guests and servants looking for someone who knew me or could help me.

"Anna, please. You mustn't speak so loudly, not here! What does he care where you are going? You are a funny one sometimes. But I like it," Minnie giggled pulling me along. "We shall have such a lovely evening tonight! I believe you have never been to a ball quite like this one! I must admit that it is the first time I have been to Ashton Court as an honored guest of the earl and countess. I have only met them on two prior occasions, and they are the most dashing couple I have ever seen. Thomas has occasion to visit the estate often, since Mr. Stevenson is his companion, and we shall no doubt be able to meet him and the Miss Bradshaw I have heard so much about. Thomas tells me that she is one of the most beautiful women he has ever set eyes upon!" Minnie was her typical self, prattling on in excitement without stopping.

We entered a large foyer where people were buzzing about with small talk, complimenting their surroundings and lining up to be announced before the Earl and Countess Stevenson. The Hartford family was all gathered to the side of a magnificent staircase while Minnie and I hurried to join them.

"I'm sorry you had to wait for me. I felt a little queasy from the carriage ride," I regretfully explained to Mr. and Mrs. Harford.

"Are you all right now, Miss Wright?" an obliging Mr. Harford asked.

"I am, thank you," I replied sheepishly. I was embarrassed, and I could feel Mrs. Hartford's growing anxiety about my presence.

"Let us proceed, then," he said.

A man in an ornately decorated uniform beckoned us upward, and Minnie interlocked arms with me as we climbed the staircase to a small balcony overlooking the grand hall. At the bottom of the steps stood a lovely couple that I assumed to be the earl and countess. They were greeting and nodding to people as some would nod and others would curtsey and a steady flow of guests was announced.

"Mr. Daniel and Lady Marcia Hartford of Blaise Castle. Mr. Thomas Hartford, Misses Katherine and Winifred Hartford, and guest, Miss Anna Wright," the man in the stately uniform called out as glances were cast upward to see the next coming guests.

It wasn't until then that I saw him. The young man with his back toward the countess engaging in conversation with the crowd around him swiftly turned around to see us.

I curtsied. As if in slow motion, I looked upward. I started down the steps. His glance caught mine.

"David!" I gasped.

I nearly tripped on the steps, clapping my hand to my mouth. I could hardly breathe as I felt tears instantly welling up in my eyes. I was dizzy and suddenly very confused as how to walk in my laborious gown. I could feel my stomach drop and heat rushing to my face. Minnie grabbed my arm.

"Anna, you look as if you've seen a ghost! That carriage ride did not do you well, did it?" She held my elbow as we slowly walked down the steps slowly.

I said nothing. All I wanted to do was run to him. His gaze was locked on mine, and I slowly descended the staircase without breaking my glare. *What would propriety demand? How could I not run into his arms? I found him!* There he stood, and I could do nothing but look at him. He was as handsome as ever, though his hair was much longer than he'd ever grown it out since I had known him. Soft curls bounced a bit around his forehead and the sun must have lightened it, giving him faint natural highlights that surrounded his face. He had it loosely gathered in the back with a black tie, and he wore an elegant coat and high collar. He looked so British, but it was him. *My David.* I had no doubt.

"Miss Wright," Lord Stevenson had greeted everyone by name, and my eyes had not yet been unfixed on David.

"Lord Stevenson, Lady Stevenson," I broke my stare. I remembered enough to at least greet them and fully curtsey

178

as I stood before them. "Mr. Stevenson," my heart leapt into my throat.

"You are very welcome to our home, Miss," the earl graciously spoke.

I lifted my head from my bow, and stood before them. David was silent. His expression was confused, sorry even. I had never seen him look so perplexed and find himself to be at a complete loss for words. He had always known what to say to diffuse any situation. I was the one who was a little irrational and impulsive, and he was as always able to keep an even keel. He was my rock, and without him, my entire world fell apart. Yet there he stood, and I could not lean on him. I was forced to stand on my own. And so we stood. Silently staring at each other for what seemed like an eternity.

"Move along, dear," Mrs. Harford harshly whispered into my ear as she conspicuously nudged my shoulder and broke the awkward silence.

I could feel the pain rushing from my heart to my head as I wiped a tear off my cheek that had finally spilled its way from my eye, slowly turning away from the love of my life, and into the enormous ballroom. Minnie, Kitty, and Thomas were just a few steps in front of me joining the busy crowd who had taken their places around the room. Everyone was engaging in conversation, laughing, mingling, and sipping on their drinks.

"Shall I fetch you a drink, Miss Wright?" Thomas cordially attempted to soothe my nerves. "I must say that you look a bit weary already, and the evening is just begun! Surely we haven't had enough excitement to wear on your stamina already, have we?" Thomas Hartford joked.

"No, I am fine. I just had a bit of a shock. How do you know the Stevenson family again, Mr. Hartford?"

179

"Oh, the family has always been a friend to ours. Father and the Earl were comrades as young children, and their fathers before them were close as well. But it wasn't until Edward Watson and I were at King's College for a time that I remember Stevenson's extraordinary rescue from the sea. What an exciting thing for us all. It was quite the reunion. With his sister being the only child of the family to inherit the whole of the estate after Mr. Stevenson vanished, there was such concern that Ashton Court would cease to be as it is. Of course the Miss Stevenson would not be able to secure a family namesake..." he paused to make his gender prejudice seem less heartless. "Well, it was a happy reunion indeed, I'd dare say."

"But did you know him as a child?" I probed. "Surely you had to wonder if it was the same David who was lost at sea so many years earlier."

"Of course. There were many who doubted. Even Lord and Lady Stevenson had their doubts for a time. It was a rainy day in August when a young stable boy came upon poor David lost in the woods on these very grounds here at Ashton Court. He was roaming the thicket with little recollection of anything but his Christian name, 'David' and no surname to supply. But, just look at him. The family resemblance is remarkable. What other explanation could there be? But why do you ask, Miss Wright? Are you one to try a man's word?" Thomas lifted his eyebrow and leaned toward me as he teased.

"I simply wondered what you knew of him. The family resemblance is astonishing. He looks very much like Lord Stevenson." I pointed as discretely as I could, "and that woman there near him. That must be his sister you spoke of?"

"That woman there in the blue gown? Oh, no, that is his fiancée, Miss Jane Bradshaw. The other one over there to the left in the gold and white gown is his sister, Miss Mary Stevenson. She is but a few years his junior and suffered the greatest loss when David disappeared."

David disappeared. Those words rang in my ears. He had disappeared, and yet, there he was. I was staring again.

"Naturally, you would have a keen interest in the story, Miss Wright. Perhaps we shall have a chance to get better acquainted with the whole company," Thomas assured.

The whole company meant his fiancée–oh how that word pierced my heart! David had obviously given up on me, and had decided to make a life for himself there in the nineteenth century. Or maybe that had been his intention all along–to leave the kids and me behind in search of a fascinating life as heir to a British fortune and bloodline. My insides were hurting. I felt a burn from the pit of my stomach rising up to my temples and I reminded Thomas of the drink he had offered.

The music had gone from being introductory and ritualistic to light and familiar. Everyone started to dance in traditional British elegance. I had promised a Mr. Corbyn that I would dance two dances with him, and Thomas had insisted on a couple of dances himself, so I had enough distraction to keep me from standing out like a sore thumb and thinking of nothing more than how to be alone with David.

"Anna, dear, join me for dinner, will you?" Minnie grabbed my elbow and pulled me closer to her. "I must have an exciting partner to dine with!"

"And your Mr. Holman won't keep you entranced enough to be a fine dinner partner, Minnie?" Thomas poked.

"Yes, Minnie. It seems that you vanished for most of the evening and left me to be the possible victim of your frightful Mr. McFadden!" I said, joining in the fun.

"Oh, dear, I have not yet seen the likes of Mr. McFadden. Perhaps we have all been spared this evening!" she scanned the room to be sure he wasn't lurking somewhere. "Mr. Holman has been kind to show me some attention tonight, and I must say that I have enjoyed the dancing, but Anna and I have an agreement that I must honor," she smiled gaily and kept the mood light. I was enjoying the evening and for a few moments was able to concentrate on something other than my pain. Soon, it was announced that we were all called into the dining rooms.

Long, ornate tables were covered in soft, yellow tablecloths and large vases with billowing greenery held red and yellow roses. Deep silver bowls of fruit, salads, cold meats, and nuts lined the middle of the tables and each place was set with fine china and silver cutlery. Tall candles began to set a romantic mood in the rooms as the sun set. We all walked in and began to take seats around the tables with the Stevenson family at a large head table that seemed to join the two L-shaped rooms in harmony.

"I thank you for joining our happy celebration this evening," Lord Stevenson addressed the rooms. "For indeed many of you joined the celebration just eight years ago when our beloved young David was returned to us, and it is with great joy that we ask you to celebrate another happy day in our lives because of the felicity that our son has brought in bringing Miss Jane Bradshaw to soon be joined to the Stevenson family. It is a union that will surely bring honor to both families, and has certainly brought a great deal of happiness to us. To Miss Bradshaw and my son, Mr. David Stevenson!" he beckoned the room to a toast.

I could not raise my glass.

Eight years? Had it truly been eight years that David had spent in the past? How can I hold him to blame if he had waited for that long and he was just now moving on with his life? He must have thought that I'd never come, and that he'd been lost in time forever. I want to hold him. To console him. To tell him that I am sorry that it has taken me so long to find him—even though for me it hadn't been more than a few months. I need to get close to him.

I could barely see David and Miss Bradshaw since the head tables were set in a way to have the earl and countess to be seen by the majority of their guests at once, and the Bradshaw family was set a bit off to the side. David and his sister, Mary, had been placed toward the far left end, and David was obligated to join his fiancée since this was, in fact, a celebration of their love.

But did he love her?

My mind was whirling. The dinner conversation was aflutter, and I was able to drift away in thought for the most part. I simply had to raise my glass on occasion, smile, agree, and laugh when everyone else did. It wasn't that difficult to pretend with so many people around to share stories and jokes for the merriment of the whole party. We soon began to stand, greet and be introduced to some of the acquaintances that a few had and others had not yet made.

"Charming young girl, Miss Winifred. You must bring her to call on me next Tuesday when you join me for tea," a rigid older woman dressed in all black said as she looked me up and down.

"Miss Wright, this is Lady Jones, the earl's sister and my tutor in Latin and French."

"Pleased to meet you, Lady Jones," I curtsied.

"And I you, Miss Wright. We must become better acquainted. I suspect your experience will be an account that I wish to hear, and I trust that I will be quite diverted by your stories. I need some diversion in my life as an old woman," she said lightheartedly, but there was coldness in her voice that gave me the chills. She didn't look that old, and I remarked something as odd since it was reserved only for people in mourning to be dressed in all black. I assumed that she must be a widow since she did not bear the Stevenson name still, and I most likely looked at her as inquisitively as she did at me.

"I am not a very good storyteller, ma'am I assure you. I recall little of my experience at all." I tried to dissuade her mistrust and act casually.

"Mm. But you do know your purpose here. You are in search of your young brother. His name is David, I believe?" her eyes narrowed and her glare was fixed on my reaction.

"Yes. I see news of my circumstance has already reached your ears, ma'am, so I doubt that I could tell it any better than what you have already heard."

"Ha," she grunted, "I suppose. Nonetheless, I will expect you at four o'clock, Miss Winifred?" she said as she turned away.

"That was strange," Minnie said, "I don't recall Lady Jones ever speaking with quite that tone before. She doesn't take an immediate liking to people in general, but she did seem to clearly dislike you, didn't she? Yes, well, we shall be forced to prove your trustworthiness to her!" Minnie laughed.

You would think that nothing was ever of a serious nature with Minnie. Even when she was concerned about something, she would move along in her typical happy way. The people kept shifting in and out, round and round, introducing themselves, and sharing pleasantries as we stood and sat, up then down, getting to know the population who joined the festivities.

"Miss Bradshaw, Miss Anna Wright." Thomas Hartford introduced us.

"Pleased to meet you, Miss Wright. My fiancé has told me that he heard of your arrival to our country and that he shares a similar circumstance."

Your fiancé? I wanted to slap Miss Jane Bradshaw with my bare hands. I could hardly breathe. David was only a few steps behind her.

"And Mr. Stevenson, this is Miss Anna Wright," Minnie continued the formal introduction.

"It is a pleasure, Miss Wright," David said as he slightly bowed his head toward me. I curtsied, pouring all of my energy into keeping my shaking controlled and my face neutral.

"Do tell her, David dear, of how your shipwreck at sea must have been. I am quite sure Miss Wright will find consolation in your happy tales," Miss Bradshaw spoke lovingly to him. With each moment that passed I was finding it harder and harder to stand.

"I would enjoy spending some time acquainting myself with Miss Wright and her situation, but surely it would be agreeable to not have such an audience. Miss Wright and I must be allowed to share our stories with some privacy, do you not think?" David asked.

He sounded so British. I was mesmerized with his voice, his face, his demeanor, and his British self, standing before me. He was obviously an expert in his new role, and had everyone convinced that he was who he claimed himself to be.

"Of course you wish to have some time to yourselves to share in the similarities and the differences of your plights," an understanding Jane Bradshaw complied, "Shall you take a stroll in the garden this evening?"

"Indeed. Good thought, dear Jane. We shall take a turn along the path, and we will rejoin the party again shortly."

As quickly as that, David had motioned to a terrace that led out to the vast gardens of the estate. A few torches dimly lit the way along the garden paths to allow guests to leave the party for a breath of fresh air when the ballroom and dining rooms became too overheated.

We said nothing as we walked down the steps and onto a narrow walkway that turned up a path that led to a fountain by large rows of shrubbery.

"There's a bench by the fountain that we may wish to sit upon," David instructed. His voice lowered to a whisper. "The flow of the water will prevent the likelihood of our being overheard."

"You sound just like them, David."

"Shh. Not yet," he warned.

I walked to the marble bench and sat down as properly as I could. I tried to keep my gestures effortless and relaxed when all I really wanted to do was to cause a scene by throwing myself into his arms.

"I never thought you'd come, Anna," he began. He looked at me. His eyes were fixed on mine, and the moonlight coupled with dim flickers of the torchlight flames danced on his face.

"Oh, David. I am so sorry. I...I don't know what to say. I came as soon as I could." I could feel a tear falling down my cheek again.

"Please do not cry. I cannot bear it. I was just about to abandon all hope. I…I am engaged, Anna. And yet…I am married?" he said, almost as if he was asking permission for it not to be true.

"Only if you want to be. I will attempt to go back alone if you want." I tried not to become hysterical, but I was crying steadily by then.

"*Want?* Anna, very little of this was ever about anything I wanted."

"David, you can't be serious," anger began to overtake my sadness. "You risked everything that we had, and for what? Was this your plan all along? To create a legacy of British heritage and become someone you rightfully are not? These poor people! How did you manage to get them to believe that you are their son?"

"It was not difficult," he confessed, looking down. "If people want to believe something, the discrepancies of the facts are of little importance to them. And I do now love them all dearly as if they were my own family," he paused to allow us both to soak in the gravity of his words. "I was alone. In danger, Anna. Even now, I believe that Lady Jones is an agent of the Guardians who has had her eyes on me for these eight years. My own *aunt*. Well, practically my aunt. You know what I mean to say," he said as he shrugged his shoulders.

"Yes. Oddly enough. I do. It doesn't surprise me about her. She gave me a feeling that she couldn't be trusted," I said turning my knees toward him and scooting in closer. "But what do we do now, David? And whatever happened to Laura? Is she here? Was that her? Is she actually Miss Bradshaw?" I asked, not sure if I wanted to hear the answer.

"No, Anna. I discovered Laura fairly quickly in the year 1977. It was my first successful journey. I had found her in London at the University of Greenwich with a Professor Maxwell who studied the same travels we do. She had confided in him; she was…not lost," he said slowly lowering his head. "She had stopped leaving codes and clues because she did not wish to return. She had fallen in love and had made a very happy life there."

"What?" I was shocked. "And you still went after her?"

"Yes, we had feared that something had gone terribly wrong. Initially, I was angry with her when I arrived. I thought that she should have at the very least left us clues of her wellbeing or of her desire to stay. She could have married the professor, which would have provided us with a marriage record that we would eventually come across," he shook his head.

"But, I saw them together, Anna. I worked with both of them a bit, leaving some clues behind for those in the future to know that I had found her, and that we were all well. Then I set out alone on my journey home, but I miscalculated the pattern–very dreadfully so," he explained, lifting his gaze to look into my eyes.

"You certainly did." I sat motionless. There was nothing that could have prepared me for sitting across from my husband trying to process the facts of his other life.

"Yes, well, that led me to this life for the past eight years." We both sat in a few more moments of silence.

"But, do you love her? Do you love Miss Jane Bradshaw?" *I have to know.*

"I am very fond of her, Anna."

He wouldn't just deny it straight out. I knew that I was being unreasonable. Of course if I would have followed everyone's advice back home and moved on with my life after David's disappearance, I would have most likely grown *fond* of someone over the course of eight years. But I couldn't help myself. I was so jealous that I couldn't see straight. For me, it had only been months. I stood up and started to angrily walk away.

"Anna, don't," he pleaded.

I headed back toward him so I could look him square in the eyes. "*Don't?* Don't what, David?" I simply threw my hands in the air then walked toward the dark line of tall bushes that led into an unlit walkway. David followed.

"Anna, stop. Let me explain, please," he begged. It is not what it seems to be."

I turned to look at him. He grabbed for my hand, and I felt his skin touch my gloved arm. I looked down at our hands in the moonlight, and plunged myself forward into his embrace. As we backed up into the tall bushes out of the line of sight of the house, I leaned in and kissed him like I had rarely kissed him before.

He pulled me in close wrapping his arms around my waist. I gripped his coat tightly, but he suddenly stopped and pulled away from me.

"Anna," he whispered, "We mustn't."

"Mustn't we, David?" I insisted. "I am your *wife!*"

"I have not been unfaithful to you, Anna. I have as much as kissed Miss Bradshaw's hand, and no more," he stated plainly.

I backed away a little. I knew he was telling the truth. I looked at him perplexed. He was not just acting like Mr. David Stevenson. He had *become* him. The proper, rule-embracing British gentleman. His accent never faded and his heart was obviously determined not to let his new family down.

"And what was your plan for our marriage, David?" I said with a hint of confusion coupled with accusation.

He bowed his head and spoke softly, "I had no plans, Anna. I have scarcely made any personal plans myself since I have come here. Father...um, Lord Stevenson was keen on the Bradshaws as a fitting match for the family, and I could hardly disappoint him when I knew that I was not getting any younger, while the hopes of returning home to you and our children were becoming less likely to happen with every passing day. Though it's not as if I haven't tried, Anna," he insisted.

"Tried? *Really?*" I doubted him. "Did you get more than four days for your journey then? Because my four days have more than likely expired, David. So now what?"

There were voices in the distance that began to sound closer and closer to us. I backed further away from him, as he led me toward the fountain in a whisper.

"We may still have time, Anna," was all that he said.

"There you are, Miss Wright! Mr. Stevenson, one would think that you did not have a house full of guests to entertain with how you have abandoned us all!" Thomas playfully scolded. "I escorted Miss Bradshaw out this way in search of you," he said, as Jane Bradshaw walked toward David's side with a grin.

"I am sorry, Thomas. Dear Jane. Forgive me," David said. "We must have lost track of time. There is so much to discuss. Perhaps we can continue our dialogue another time, Miss Wright?"

All I could think to say was, "Yes."

Time? Did we still have time? I stood in shock, unable to move.

David and Jane Bradshaw walked the path back toward the house together as a couple, and I remained frozen in stunned dismay, watching as their shadowy silhouettes neared the estate. Thomas lingered with me gazing at me, a little puzzled.

"Miss Wright?" he said with concern.

"Yes, Thomas…I mean Mr. Hartford."

"I don't mind if you call me by my Christian name," he approved with a smile. "But I'm not sure what others would say," he laughed.

I smiled and looked down at my feet. I didn't recall those rules of propriety at the most importune times, and I felt embarrassed that he would think that I was flirting with him simply by calling him Thomas.

"Shall I escort you back to the house, Miss Wright?" he asked, offering his elbow. "Truly, you do look flushed. I would have hoped that the fresh air would be a welcome relief from the airless indoors!" Thomas said as he accompanied me toward the house.

"Yes, it was a relief, thank you." I held his elbow, trying to make use of all the most proper practice and mannerisms that I had been training to perfect. I let out a long sigh and attempted to keep my composure.

"What is it that you and Stevenson have in common, then, Miss Wright?" Thomas asked, not suspecting that it could be more than he would ever imagine.

My immediate response was "Everything."

"Indeed? *Everything?*" Thomas laughed with a tone of incredulity. "I have not yet known another to have been separated by tragedy at sea as a child and then reunited with family so many years on!"

"Not that. I just…I know what he's gone through in a way. And I think he understands me as well. I will be happy to meet him again." I tried to play it off as nonchalantly as Thomas seemed to be while asking me his questions.

"Perhaps you will be able to continue your conversation soon, then. Perhaps when you return to the manner for tea with Lady Jones?" I looked at him with a questioning gaze. "Stevenson and I may be able to join you soon after tea. We have a little project that we work on together, and we shall be returning to Ashton Court on Tuesday. That is, if Lady Jones doesn't forbid our intrusion. She is a rather temperamental woman," he laughed.

"Is she?" I smirked. "I cannot say that that surprises me."

"No, I assumed it would not. Minnie told me of your cold introduction, and I surmised that Stevenson and I should soften the visit if at all possible," he chuckled.

"So you've already been plotting, have you? Well, I can't say that I don't appreciate the sympathy. I would be happy to have you both around to diffuse some of the tension that I'm sure will be present when I don't have the answers that Lady Jones expects," I admitted.

"Ha! Then I am at your service, Miss Wright!" he exclaimed with a cordial nod.

We had reached the house again, and certainly didn't seem to be missed by anyone. David had already made his way back into the large rooms and must have been moving about here and there to make sure that his absence was not felt, and that all guests had been welcomed.

We remained until after midnight, maybe even past one or two in the morning. It was so hard for me to keep track of time without my digital devices. Minutes seemed like hours, but then the moments of time with David a mere flash of seconds. However long it was, it took everything I had in me to endure the long evening. I was in the best shape of my life physically, but the emotional drain I felt was almost more than I could bear.

We left the house sleepily as a coach was called for Thomas, Minnie, Kitty, and me. Mr. and Mrs. Hartford had taken their leave earlier, as was acceptable for the young people to engage in dancing and merriment for longer than their older counterparts. I would have happily returned home with them earlier, but Christopher and the professor had warned me not to raise any suspicion of being an outsider. I figured that playing the "American" should be reserved for extreme situations, so I tried to force myself to appreciate the moments of the experience that I could.

At least I was leaving the ball with something I had not come with. *I had found him.*

CHAPTER THIRTEEN

I could not get out of going to church on Sunday, no matter how hard I had tried. I didn't want to be a disgrace to the family, or whatever other guilt-laden words they were throwing at me, so I found myself scurrying to make myself presentable. It was a wonder to me that they could dance and eat all evening and well into the night, but then be ready for an eleven o'clock Sunday morning service, as if it was the norm.

"You look a bit weary!" Minnie tugged at my arm and giggled. "Not to fear, though. Reverend Cooper will not think that it is out of the ordinary for one to have drifted to sleep during his sermon. I dare say it will neither be the first nor the last time he shall witness it!" Minnie and I both laughed.

"I am surprised that there would be such an extravagant ball on a Saturday if everyone intended to go to church on Sunday!" I admitted. "Poor Reverend Cooper!"

"It *is* customary to have such a ball on a Friday, isn't it? Now that you say so, I don't know that I've been to many such balls on a Saturday. Country dances never last so long, and they are the only diversion on a Saturday evening one can hope for in the summer!" she pondered. "But I must tell you, Anna, that I do believe it was the fault of Thomas and Mr. Stevenson." She leaned in and whispered. "They are in some sort of business with Captain Bradshaw. 'A project' is what they say it is, though I am not sure what they may mean by it, but I would tell you that if Mother and Father knew of all the time Thomas spent on the shores and in the groves with Captain Bradshaw and Mr. Stevenson, they might not be so keen to allow Thomas to continue such a close friendship with Mr. Stevenson."

"Allow him? Would they really tell your brother what friends he could and could not have?" I asked.

"Of course, silly. But no one would deny the Stevenson family anything, I'm afraid. They are in a position to befriend anyone they wish to without question," she stated confidently.

"I don't understand. What does David have to do with anything?" Minnie looked at me a little stunned. The ease with which I threw out my beloved's first name seemed to startle her. Or at least make her curious. "I mean, Mr. Stevenson, your brother…and who is Captain Bradshaw?"

"Miss Jane Bradshaw's father, Captain William Bradshaw. He is the sea captain with whom Thomas sailed for a time, and the reason that Miss Bradshaw and Mr. Stevenson met, in fact. The three of them have a jolly time together, and work on such things I do not understand.

They speak of harnessing power of the waters and great machines of the future together. It is all rather tedious to try to comprehend," she said, shaking her head. "I never listen much. But Thomas' interest in the sea would not be so great if he wasn't so fond Cpt. Bradshaw, I believe– and I am sure that Mr. Stevenson quite encourages him! Our parents believe that Thomas will stay at home for some time at least, but if he is not back on the decks of a ship within a month, I shall be astonished!" Minnie said with wide eyes.

"But why would that make a Saturday ball instead of another night?"

"Oh, Thomas and his 'great mission' on Friday was with Mr. Stevenson, and I believe that I saw Cpt. Bradshaw there once as well!"

"You *saw* them?" I was hungry for as much information as I could gather.

"Well, no, not this last time, but once, when Thomas and Cpt. Bradshaw had returned from the sea, he and Mr. Stevenson were so secretive about their plans that it put me in mind to follow them. *You mustn't tell!*" without taking a breath, she gestured with her hand as if to shush me. "They would be quite put out if they knew!" she exclaimed. "Thomas thinks I'm too silly as it is, but I do not know why they act so mysterious. I followed them into the woods to an old mill. I do not know what they think they were hiding!" she giggled. "Everyone knows that Harper's Mill has been sitting in those woods unused for years since the old brook dried up!" Minnie smiled in her typical way while she lightheartedly shared the news as she saw it. She and I had been the last out of the house, and it was nice to have a chance to listen to her chatter while I tried to keep myself alert as we strolled down the path.

We arrived at the church on foot. It was a small parish with stone walls, a beautifully ornate wooden altar, and long, oak pews. Lady Hartford gave the two of us a disapproving look for having dilly-dallied that morning and not having arrived a few minutes earlier with the entire group. As Rev. Cooper continued his opening remarks and began to introduce a hymn, we slinked into the family pew, taking our seats silently. They were straight and stiff, and I quickly realized that I was not at risk of falling asleep, as Minnie had suggested. People filled the small sanctuary, and an organ piped out somber music. I began to scan the crowd as best as I could without looking too conspicuous.

I leaned to Minnie, "The Stevenson family doesn't attend?" I whispered.

"Not this parish, no. Though I am sure the hosts of the grand ball would be allowed a Sunday off," she whispered back smiling.

Thomas nudged his sister's shoulder in a brotherly scold, and we both straightened our backs and directed our attention forward.

The songs were slow and melodic. I was surprised at some of the hymns which were familiar to me from the times my grandfather would take out his old hymnal to play and sing for us. I enjoyed soaking in the moments of wonder as I imagined how many generations had most likely sung those songs before they reached the voice of my grandfather and my young ears. I was happy to be there in that moment, and I began to empathize with David. He must have been able to take in so many of those occasions. The allurement of yesteryear had to be so appealing to him. A quieter, simpler life was his for the taking, and he took it. *Could I blame him?*

I heard little if none of the sermon that morning as I was lost in thought. Torn between anger at David for what he knew he was risking with leaving us for this mission, and yet, understanding him completely. I too had risked abandoning my poor children to be parentless in order to go in search of him, so who was I to judge?

But how does this all work? My days are up. Four days. What were we thinking? This was an impossible mission. I didn't have a clue of what to do next, except to find a way to talk to David. To get him alone. He had said that there was hope. *But what did he mean? Is there hope for us to be together in this day and age? Is there a chance that we could return to our own time? And if we were stuck together in 1851, did our children even exist?* I had no way of knowing the answers to any of the facts that he had devoted years of study and research to. And then there was everything that Minnie had just shared. It was significant in some way. I knew that it had to be.

"I must get to David," I whispered to myself.

"I'm sorry? Was that a yes?"

I looked up at Thomas who was reaching for my hand to escort me out of the church. I had no idea what he had just said. I looked around and saw that most of the parishioners had exited the sanctuary, and I sat alone in my thought.

"A yes? I don't think so..." I stammered, "What was the question?"

Thomas smiled and took my hand as I stood up to exit the church with the rest of the crowd.

"For dinner. Stevenson and I have arranged it."

"Mr. Stevenson? Today?" I asked in surprise.

Thomas stopped in the middle of the aisle, looked at me and laughed. "You truly have not heard a word that Minnie or I have said to you, have you?"

"I believe I haven't. I'm so sorry. I was lost in thought," I quietly admitted.

"Indeed you were; quite lost! Mr. Stevenson came to me early this morning. In fact, I do not believe that he must have slept at all!" Thomas exclaimed. "Stevenson wanted to convince me that I need to help you find your family, and that he wishes to continue your conversation about your experience. He thinks he might have an idea of who may know something about your brother. You, Minnie, and I will have dinner together now in town, and then Mr. Stevenson will escort you to the groves near Ashton, where there is plenty of privacy for the two of you to speak. Minnie and I will not be far behind. It is… delicate, you see. I am not aware of how the rules of propriety are dictated in America, but I am sure that a betrothed young man and a single young lady would not be expected to be completely alone. Mr. Stevenson must protect Miss Bradshaw as well as himself," he explained, "but he does insist that the two of you be able to share your hardships without any prying eyes. That, I suppose, I do understand." As we stood in the aisle together, he took my hand up to his face and kissed it gently. "I do hope that you know that you can have true friends here, free of suspicion, Anna."

I clenched my hand and swiftly drew it back away from him. "I…"

"Forgive me, Miss Wright. I did not mean to…"

"No, It's fine, Thomas. Mr. Hartford…or…ugh, whatever," I trailed off.

I was flustered and walked toward the rear of the church where the last of the crowd was leaving. The Reverend Cooper was standing at the entrance as people left, and I awkwardly nodded to him as I briskly brushed passed him and out the door.

"Please do not be angry," Thomas followed.

"Angry? Why would you be angry, Anna? Surely the sermon was not that difficult to bear!" laughed Minnie.

"I am not angry, Minnie…Mr. Hartford." I curtsied toward both of them then tried to set some distance between us just so I could shake the awkward feeling of his flirtations, and still figure out how to accept his help. I kept finding myself being drawn to the Hartford family and yet the familiarity to me that meant nothing more than normality, to them meant either impropriety or overt flirtation.

"Miss Wright, Thomas and Winifred tell me that you have business in town?" Mr. Hartford approached me as the family headed toward the path that led past the church and around the bend to Blaise Castle. Their coach awaited as Thomas and Minnie stood wide-eyed behind their father as to give me a *please-play-along* look. I couldn't help but snicker a little under my breath.

"I do, yes."

"I see," he nodded. "Then you must have an escort. They will be free to join you. We shall send the coach around for you again momentarily, but I would ask that you try to refrain from planning such business in town on Sundays, Miss Wright. It is quite irregular. Though I suppose meeting someone to help one find one's family is an urgent enough circumstance to require business even on a Sunday, is it not?" he winked, leaned in and then whispered. "But I must do my duty and remind you of such things!"

"It is urgent, thank you, Mr. Hartford," I smiled and curtsied.

"No need," he smiled sweetly waving his hand, "no need, my dear."

The rest of the family moved toward the coach while Minnie and Thomas skittered closer to me.

"I knew father would understand!" proclaimed Minnie. "He is always good about such things."

"*Always?*" Thomas contended. "And do you always plot and scheme to do things without Father's knowledge?"

"Plot and scheme?" she said defensively. "Is that what we are carrying out here, Thomas? A scheme? I believe we are behaving exactly as we told Father we are doing. We are helping Miss Wright find her family, are we not? And who are you to scold about keeping secrets? Who knows what you are always up to?" She smiled as if she knew he was teasing her, but that he shouldn't take it too far because she knew things about him that she could use as blackmail.

"Why do you think I spend my time at sea?" he joked. "But you will have Miss Wright believe that I am a charlatan, sister!"

"Do you, indeed, Miss Wright?" Minnie asked turning her head toward me with raised eyebrows. "Think my brother to be a charlatan?" She grinned and carried on the little game.

"I do not," I smiled and played along.

"But I do not suppose you think him to be a saint?" she smirked.

"I do not," I admitted, "but I know no saints. Who among us could claim that?" I said.

The three of us stood without a response, knowing that we could understand each other, even if we weren't revealing all of our cards at once. Minnie was the type of person to give the impression that she always revealed her entire hand, but I was finding that she still had a few tricks up her sleeve.

The coach arrived and carried us through the bumpy cobblestone roads of town to a small inn. There was little movement in the streets. Minnie had told me that most people would be in their homes resting on *the Lord's Day*, and that the inn would be the only place where we could eat a small meal before meeting David. As we stepped out of the coach onto the rocky street, and into the quaint room where a table was set with cold meats, cheeses, and fruits, David stood up from a window seat in the corner.

"Stevenson! I did not expect you to meet us until after two o'clock as we had discussed," Thomas said in surprise.

"I am sorry, Hartford. I...I am...eager to help Miss Wright, and I was able to get away a little earlier than I had planned," David said.

He was eager to see *me*. Perhaps he hadn't slept a wink at all like Thomas had suggested. *David was eager to see me.* My heart swelled within my chest, and I felt a tear well up in my eye. I nervously brushed my right cheek to try to hide my emotion, quickly stepping closer to a table where David had moved to pull out a chair for Minnie, and then for me.

"Thank you," I whispered. I could barely speak.

"Well, we shall all dine together, then. How lovely!" Minnie said happily.

"Yes, Stevenson. Lovely of you to join us. But shall you be able to stay away for long? What are your intentions for the day, and how may we assist Miss Wright in her conquest?" Thomas asked.

"I would like to hear more of Miss Wright's experience. There were a few things that helped me overcome some of the trauma and the...gaps...I had in my memory. But I will need...I would very much enjoy hearing Miss Wright's account of her experience before I may fully understand how I might be able to aid her in her quest," David explained nervously. It wasn't like him to be flustered, and I hoped that Minnie and Thomas wouldn't dig any deeper.

"But has she not shared that with us all? How her recollection is minimal, Mr. Stevenson? I do not know that you need privacy for that!" Minnie said in her typical lightsome manner.

"Oh, I do know that I cannot make her recall anything that she is unable to do herself, but I have found that in my case it was helpful to speak with others who had suffered great loss and could somewhat relate to what I had been through," David said, empathetically casting his glance toward me from across the table. "I also wish to hear of Miss Wright's family, and how we may help reunite them. Surely with our connections we must know someone who will be able to help," David responded convincingly.

"Yes, indeed, we must do all that we can to help Miss Wright, I quite agree," Thomas affirmed.

Minnie looked at me inquisitively and tilted her head to one side. "And do you wish to continue your conversations in private with Mr. Stevenson, Anna?"

"I do," I said softly, nodding my head in approval.

"All right, then. Thomas and I will be happy to help you," she smiled.

"Thank you," I mumbled.

"Yes, thank you," David said as his voice cracked a little.

I looked down and felt a tear hit the top of my arm. I rubbed my cheeks with my napkin and lifted my head. They were all looking at me.

"It's been quite the journey," I said casually, trying to shake my head and stop the tears from flowing.

"Shall we head to the groves now, Miss Wright?" David stood and motioned to the door.

"Surely, Stevenson, we…you must mean to stay here a little longer? We haven't yet eaten!" Thomas insisted. "Minnie and I can take a walk around the town up to the shops and back. That will give you half an hour at least, then we can dine together," he said. "Do stay here and let Miss Wright rest a bit."

"No, Thomas, I am quite sure that we must go to the groves…" his concerned voice trailed off.

"But David…" Thomas said apprehensively as he stood, narrowing his gaze on David.

I was unsure of what to do. There was something that the two of them weren't saying that was causing tension. Thomas rested his palm on the table leaning toward David, who stood next to him, waiting for a response from me. I hadn't yet gotten up from my side of the table, and Minnie and I looked up at them in surprise at their exchange.

"Oh, what does it matter, Thomas? Miss Wright cares nothing of your secret adventures to old Harper's Mill. That's the only thing in the groves anyway. Nothing exciting and certainly nothing to hide," Minnie said, breaking the quiet of a tense moment.

I raised my eyebrows and bit my bottom lip as I looked at the bewilderment on the faces of the two young men astonished at Minnie's revelation.

"What do you know of it, Minnie?" Thomas said in reproach.

"Know of *what*? Of your silly escapades into the groves at Harper's Mill? Just that. What is there to hide or fear? Are you secretly in the business of clandestine milling?" she mocked. "Let us all simply enjoy a nice bit of tea!"

I was tempted to laugh, but David and Thomas were not amused, so I waited for a reaction from them, holding my breath.

Thomas sighed and shook his head. "Don't be a simpleton, Minnie. You know nothing."

"We must go, Hartford. Please trust me," David said as he extended his hand.

"Very well," Thomas returned the gesture, and the two shook hands and afterward, embraced. "Be careful, Stevenson," he whispered.

I then realized that there was something more to their relationship than a formal or even casual familial obligation. They were confidants, colleagues, friends, and each other's trusted advisors. I had understood Edward Watson to be David Stevenson's closest friend, but it was actually Thomas who held the title. I presumed it was to cover for the fact that David and Cpt. Bradshaw were the influences that kept Thomas at sea, but quickly surmised that I still had so much more to uncover.

David came to my chair, helping me to rise from the table, and I took his hand as he led me out the door. I wanted to hold on for dear life and never let go. Just being able to hold his hand made my heart nearly leap out of my chest. His eyes met mine, and he quickly glanced toward the door. I felt myself getting warm, and I looked down, embarrassed at what I was thinking.

We walked to the door, out of the inn, and into the fresh, cool air of spring. As we strolled silently next to each other along the cobblestone street, I began to notice the odd shapes of the stones as the soles of my feet clicked along them. It's funny the things that you notice when you find yourself in situations that you never imagined could possibly happen. Since no words were being said, the click-clack of our shoes along the road became my focus, trying to allow the cadence to calm my anxiety. We continued along without saying a word–the peace of discomfort is often better than the conflict of confrontation. At least, in nineteenth century England it was. David was searching for the right words.

"How long of a walk is it through the town? It is quiet today…" I finally broke the awkward silence.

"Yes, quite. It is Sunday; there is but little commotion. Precisely why I concluded that it might be best for us to meet as early as today in order to…"

"Not be seen or heard? Propriety and all," I said cynically.

"Anna, take care. Someone could hear you while we are still in town. It is a short walk, not above ten minutes," he said. And we walked in more silence.

CHAPTER FOURTEEN

"Run, Anna!" David grabbed my hand while we tumbled down a long incline in the terrain. My legs wouldn't move as fast or far as his. I was out of breath, and my arm hurt from his tugging me along the grove. We spiraled down to the bottom of the slope in seconds, and he rolled me over on top of him to cover us both with the long branches of shrubbery that we had landed in.

"Don't move a muscle," he whispered.

I buried my head deep into his chest, trying to catch my breath. Rustling of branches and soft billows of wind swirled around us. It was as if I listened to the music of the woods in slow motion, trying to drink in the moment of being in David's arms. Flecks of light danced between the swishing leaves and the verdant woods enveloped us in its romance. David held me tightly while I closed my eyes and began to softly kiss his neck. It was covered with a proper high collar, but I was close as I could possibly get to him, and I could feel him tighten his embrace as he rubbed his cheek against my hair. I didn't care what dangers lay outside of that bush, if only I could have a precious moment with my beloved. I began to cry softly, and I tried to keep myself from making a sound.

Suddenly, a large gust of wind rushed past us, followed by a whirring of chattering voices which moved so quickly that I couldn't identify what it was, or what was being said. I moved my head enough to have my eyes meet David's. I had to at least question him with my gaze. I was scared for both of us. His eyes told me not to budge and he clutched my dress a little tighter.

Closing my eyes again, I tried to listen to the sound of his beating heart. So many were the moments that I had taken for granted when I was able to lay my head on his chest and hear his heartbeat that I swore to myself then and there that I would never again take those moments as anything less than a divine blessing, and cherish each one. I would never let him go. *But do I have that option now?* Whatever the price, I determined to never miss the opportunity to appreciate each second of our existence together.

Almost as quickly as it began, the swirling sounds ended, and a hush fell over the grove.

Seconds later, Davis whispered, "I think they're gone." He held me close and quiet for a few more seconds. I clutched his shoulders, pulling myself to his face to kiss him. He kissed me back and rolled me over onto the ground before he stopped and began to stand. I was not ready to release him from my embrace, as I lay on the cool ground, surprised and motionless.

"I did not bring you here for this, Anna," he said abruptly.

"David, I just want to hold you!" I begged as I began to sit upright.

"Anna, there is nothing more in this world that I want than to be with you again," he said as he knelt next to me and stroked my face with his hand. I gently caressed his strong arm and placed my hand on his. "But we don't have much time. We must be prudent," he said standing and pulling me to my feet.

I smirked at his proper speech and laser-focused attention no matter when or where. There were some things that never did change at all. I could barely ever distract him when he was on a mission. Before, it used to annoy me, but this time, it made me grin.

I held on to his arm and asked, "Who were we running from? Clearly Minnie isn't the only one who knows about your old mill, David. But why is it so important?"

David smiled and kissed my hand. He did not reply, he just continued moving forward, deeper into the forest.

"What is it David? Please tell me. Are we still in danger?"

"Shh…you shall see."

We hurriedly walked along the grove as I held his hand tightly. There was a narrowing of the trees and an overgrown path that we headed toward.

"I feel like we are moving into the haunted forest, and I should be chanting 'lions and tigers and bears, oh my!' This is a little scary!" He laughed, pulling my arm closer into his chest.

"You know, I'm the only person on this planet who would possibly understand what you just said!" and he laughed again.

"No surprise there," I snickered. "You're the only person who's ever really understood me, David Sturgeon!" I leaned my head on his shoulder and stroked his fingers as we walked along.

He stopped. I didn't think of what it may mean for him to hear the sound of his former name. "Oh, I have missed you, Anna, my dear," he whispered, kissing my hand, then stifling some of his emotion with a gulp, and moving along the path again.

It was strange to hear him call me *my dear*, referring to me in such a formal way and speaking in an accent, but it was all that my heart longed for. His voice, his presence, his touch.

"I have missed you too, David." I attempted to hold back tears again.

We stopped at an overgrown portion of the path, where he climbed over a fallen tree, grabbing me at the waist to hoist me over. He lowered me gently to the ground and our faces met once again.

"Anna, please know that my love is and always has been for you. For our children…" his voice cracked. He couldn't go on, and I gripped his arms as tightly as I could, holding him as he let out a cry.

I had never really seen him weep. Not fully. He had gotten teary a few times and been upset before, but this was different. The steady man of steel was crippled with grief in my embrace. I could do nothing but fall on my knees to the ground with him and share his pain. He didn't let go of me, and we stayed there for a few minutes in each other's arms. I kissed his hands and wiped tears from his eyes and mine. David leaned over and kissed my cheek. My eyes closed as I felt the touch of his lips on my skin.

"We should keep moving, Anna," he finally whispered as he kissed my face again and again. "We've lost so much time."

"I could get lost in this moment forever, David. It's all the time I need!"

He smiled sweetly, rubbed his face with a handkerchief and pulled us both to our feet. We both took a deep breath.

"Let's move on, shall we? I must not let the grief overwhelm me, I now have cause to rejoice, to go forward…now that you are here, my sweet Anna!" he kissed my hand again and then turned to walk on.

We moved toward the small mill that sat on a hill at the end of the path. There was a brook that ran along the side of it, from what I could tell.

"I thought that Minnie said the brook had dried up." I said in surprise.

"It had when the mill was abandoned. But that was nearly six years ago, and it has been running nicely since the day we unclogged a dam that had diverted its flow some years ago. It is a rather powerful steam. You shall see when we approach it more closely."

"You said *we*. You and Thomas unclogged it?"

"Yes, and Captain Bradshaw. He has been keen to learn more of our findings in electricity and stored energy."

My heart dropped; the name Bradshaw shook me back to reality. We had been alone together in the woods for a while, and I didn't want to think of anyone or anything outside of the groves.

"But you still haven't told me what the secrecy is all about. What are you hiding, David? What were those people chasing us for if there's nothing but a revived brook and an old mill here?"

"Let's talk about it more when we get inside. I don't want to speak about it here in the open," he said, as he looked around checking for intruders before he led me upward.

We reached the top of the hill after a short climb, and David led me into the wooden structure after reaching under a large beam to retrieve a key, unlocking the door that had been secured with an iron padlock.

"It should be safe to speak in here," he waved his hand, motioning for me to come inside.

I quickly scanned the room in skepticism. There was nothing spectacular about the space. It was a dingy, old cabin that smelled musty and worn down. I could hear the stream of water underneath, and it sounded more powerful than I had expected.

"What are you hiding that anyone would be chasing you for? There's nothing here!" I incredulously proclaimed.

"Come this way," he motioned for me to join him at the back of the room, where a small lift looked like it could be lowered to a level that reached the water.

We entered the cage-like carrier as he pulled on the ropes that lowered us. The sound of the water got louder, and as it jerked, I reached for the sides of the metal structure that held the wooden base.

"Do not fret, my love, it is safe," David grabbed my arm and I thrust myself into his chest, wrapping my arms around his neck.

"Okay," I said in disbelief burying my face into his chest, "How far down are we going?"

"There's a cave about a hundred feet down where we'll get off. You will see, Anna," he said, as he tugged gently to slow the descent of the lift.

As we reached the cave, the lift jolted to a stop, when David pulled the metal door to the side and slid it back for us to exit. It was dark and damp. I could see nothing but directly above my head, some one hundred feet in the air, where a faint glimmer of the hole in the floor of the cabin let in a grayish-blue light from the sunlight that peeked in from the cabin. David stepped off the lift, and it swung a bit with his exit.

"I can't see you, David!" I was terrified that I would plummet to the river and be washed away, or that I would slip off of the side of whatever it was that David was standing on and meet my death. I stood frozen.

"Reach your hand out, and I will take it, Anna. Watch your step, it's safe, but slippery—nothing to fear, my love. There's an entire landing here at the door, which will lead you to the cave. Trust me."

I reached out my hand to find his in the blackness. *Trust.* I had trusted him since the day I had met him. He called me *my love*, words I hadn't heard in what seemed like forever. The months that had separated me from him…the years that it had been for him, were rushing through my mind like a fast-forward dream sequence. The little things that I remembered in those few seconds of blackness and fear were bizarre, but comforting. I grasped his hand in trust as he pulled me onto the slippery landing.

"Come with me," he said, his voice full of excitement.

I grasped his hand tightly. I couldn't see where I was or how I'd get anywhere without him. We walked only a few seconds in darkness. The rushing waters still echoed against the stone walls, but the sound grew a little fainter.

"Are we in the cave?" I asked, assuming that the river was now behind us.

"We are." And in a split second, I heard the sound of a large metal switch, as David and I stood in the light of a fully operational electric glow.

"David!" I gasped; I was stunned. I looked around the room at large metal containers and wires strung in webs of black and copper. "What is this place?"

"It is my escape home, Anna," David stood, gazing around the room in delight.

"Home?" my eyes welled up again with tears, and I realized that he had not abandoned me. He had always intended to return.

I threw myself into his arms and kissed him. I could only whisper the words *thank you* again and again. My moment of joy was brief. I stopped abruptly. I realized that he had been working on it for eight full years and had not yet been successful.

"Have you been working on this the whole time, David?" I whispered, not knowing if I wanted to hear the answer. I knew that I sounded defeated when I asked him.

"No, not the whole time," he began to explain. "I had to catch my bearings at the beginning. It was almost immediately that the Stevensons took me in as their own, and I knew that I had not made it to the right century, much less the right decade to return home, so I quickly tried to form the acquaintances I needed to make in order to start my project. It took me about a year. We were studying at university, and it was only natural for us as scientists to branch out and try new things. Thomas and Edward became interested in the study, but Thomas has been the one to really delve into the work and help me. Captain Bradshaw began to fund some of our experiments and show a strong interest in our studies and family." David paused.

He probably didn't want to explain the Bradshaw's connection any further. It made us both uncomfortable to find ourselves in such a predicament.

"Who was it who helped you come to me, Anna? Professor Trinkton?" he asked, changing the subject.

I nodded, "And Christopher." I said.

214

"Oh…how is Christopher…and Rebecca?" he asked pensively.

"They are both well, David. He wants you back. We all do…but Rebecca doesn't know anything of the secret lives the two of you lead. That life we knew seems so surreal right now, and I've only been gone for a little while," I said. "Though Christopher and the professor told me that I had tried to reach you once before. I guess that could explain why it took me eight years to get to you. Or not. I still don't know how this all works, David." I shrugged my shoulders. I was confused and tired of the perplexity of the puzzle we had to solve.

"We talk of conjecture and speculation on some parts and on others have formulaic answers, Anna. The science of this may not have ever been intended for us to discover, and yet…here we are," David said with a sigh and a long pause. "No one can know all of the details, Anna. Not truly. Did you have a run-in with the Guardians?" he asked.

"I must have; I think they sent me back to the time where we were together and made me suffer your loss all over again," I said with a quivering voice. "Do you think that my depression and illness was a punishment from the Guardians then? To live and lose you all over again?"

"I cannot say that I know the answer to that, my love. Life is full of ups and downs—illness and grief, as well as joy and elation. If the Guardians let you survive, it was for a reason. It may be possible that we had both been captured and sent back. I did have one attempt to find Laura that failed…right before you had that bout of sickness. So much of this is still a mystery, Anna. It is why I study, why I so enjoy being a student of the sciences. It is what drives me to take the risks that I do—and you risk so much now as well—we must beware of your movement here," he said cautioning me. "It may be safest to keep you indoors with the Hartford girls as much as possible." He smiled and nodded. "That might not be too difficult to do. They have formal social gatherings to attend, and not much else."

"Okay, I'll do what you want me to, David," I said in agreement. "So, you think you have been captured before too?" I asked. My heart ached at the thought of all he had suffered.

"Possibly," he whispered.

"But you are still in danger? That was a Guardian after us in the woods, wasn't it?"

"More than one, I think. I've been eluding the Guardians for a while. I have passed into this decade from the last under great suspicion," he explained.

"But who are they? Angels? I mean, surely if they are spirits they can know what we are down here right now and can see everything that you are hiding!" I said hopelessly.

"They may. But they are not here right now, or at least I do not believe that they are listening. They take on forms–like superhuman people sometimes, and normal people other times, or they certainly look like people–and they have the ability to travel in a supernatural way, yet I have found that they are limited to certain borders. Something greater than them dictates their movement." He swept his hand upward. "But take a look around, Anna, what could any one of the Guardians protest? A student of science trying to lead his country in the electricity movement of the nineteenth century? Anna, it's only a few short years before Thomas Edison invents his incandescent bulb, and even then it's only an improvement from what already exists. Electricity is present, it's simply not accessible to most." David enthusiastically shared his love for invention and the history of his craft.

"And you can only use what resources and technologies are available in the decade in which you find yourself," I said, remembering what Professor Trinkton had told me.

"Precisely," he smiled. "The professor has taught you well."

I took a good look around the room, noticing that there were wires that held small, dim bulbs that hung in draping strands all across the space. Other wires, thin and thick, black and copper, formed an enormous web that was attached to each of the large black metal boxes sitting in a row in the middle of the room. I walked toward the center where the largest chest stood.

"Don't touch them, Anna. They are live conductors," David warned.

"But what are you doing with them, David?"

"Storing energy. Do you still have the suits?" he asked, now in problem-solving mode.

"I do."

"Good, what about the coordinates?"

It was almost fun to see him in action again. The little annoyances that I had of his scientific mind were a thing of the past. I knew that his focus, drive, and intelligence were going to be our ticket home. Back to our kids. Back to our normal.

We talked about my training, my journey home from Mongolia, out to California, back to Illinois, and then the return to the university to take on the mission of time travel. I had not brought any notes, nor did I have the small map that Amoriti had made me, but I had started to recall many of the details that I had been drilled with during my training. There were numbers swirling repetitively in my mind, and I began to recite them. I didn't know what they all meant, but I hoped that some of the other numbers I could recall would help David find where else we could possibly catch our ride home. He walked over to a small desk in the corner and jotted down whatever information he needed. He had always been a numbers guy. He could remember the numbers from any given credit card that we had used online having to enter the numbers only once before being able to recall the entire sequence. I smiled as I watched him scribble data on the page.

"So, what would happen if the Guardians saw this place? And what does Thomas make of it?" I asked.

"As I mentioned, I believe that they indeed may have seen something. But it is only suspicious to the point that we are storing energy in a way that no one is currently doing–harnessing the power of the deep waters here and using the materials we have to contain it. As for Hartford, he is a student of science. He is thrilled to be part of such innovation. He has not shown any signs of suspicion… not yet," David said pausing to look up at me.

"That's good. Did you guys do all of this together?"

"Yes. He is actually the one who found this location. We had been discussing energy, electricity, and the future of technology when he said that he knew of this abandoned mill where we might be able to study and experiment. We worked quite well together from the start, and it was surprising how much we were able to find here."

"I can imagine! I didn't realize that the hill was as tall as it is…to have a cave and all this underneath. I mean, this place is a little primitive for the twenty-first century, but for the nineteenth, it's pretty impressive!" I said nodding my head with a smile.

"Yes, Hartford gets rather elated about what the future may hold, and I cannot blame him. It is an exciting time to be part of history."

"And yet…you plan to leave this all behind…" I was conscious of the loss he would have to bear.

"Are you asking me, Anna?" He looked at me intensely and with every ounce of seriousness he could express. "Because you need not wonder if I know my place in time. I do. I have not forgotten my responsibilities as a husband and a father."

"It's all so complicated, David," I whispered, unable to keep myself from shedding another tear.

"It is." He looked down at the paper again.

We stood silently for a few minutes until he began to copy down more notes. I peered over his shoulder a couple of times but couldn't make out more than a few numbers and symbols.

"You still leave a lot of this stuff in code," I smiled, attempting to lighten the atmosphere.

"I'm glad that you found me, Anna." He knew that I had seen his notes and codes before and had to try to decipher things that I would never have known without the help of Christopher and Professor Trinkton. And those efforts led me to him.

There was still an underlying silence to our conversations. David would change the subject so he would not get too distracted by his emotions. He had let his guard down completely in the woods, and had shown me the true state of his heart in those moments of vulnerability, but he could not continue to be so expressive and still be able to keep us safe. He had eight years of fine English training to stifle his sentiments. I had to come to grips with the fact that he was and is David Sturgeon and at the same time The Honourable Mr. David Stevenson, son of Lord Stevenson of Ashton Court. And he had to reconcile the fact that he left on a mission from which he knew he might not return, and his wife was also now risking everything to help him. He had been trying to come back to us, all the while in danger of being revealed as a fraud to his new family and friends, or being caught by the Guardians. He could have put all of his efforts into getting home regardless of the risk, or the only other option that he had was that he could simply move on with life, marry, and live as English nobility. It seemed that I had come just before his decision was final, and his destiny could have become something he was never intended to live. It was too painful to linger in my analytic thought, so I followed David's lead, and silenced my own feelings in order to focus on the task.

"So, according to your calculations…do we have enough energy to power up the suits and meet the pod at the coordinates in a few days?" I asked.

"I think that we should take a few weeks to monitor the pattern, Anna. It may even take a few months. We must not waste the energy. I believe we only have enough stored energy to make one attempt to reach the pod. There are four locations, correct? And they alternate every eight days? We must see if we can be at one location every day until we see the pod appear. After that time, we will be able to know that we have between eight days and thirty-two days before it returns to that location."

"But do we power up the suits up on the first eight days or wait?" I asked impatiently.

"That is what I was attempting to explain, Anna. We have to monitor the pattern first. Perhaps the space pod is released every eight days to different locations and they alternate the locations, or maybe it goes in the same order, appearing in one location on a day, two days later appearing in another, and so on. If you could be at one location, and I at another, that doubles our chances. And if Hartford would be willing to help..."

"And tell him? Tell him the *truth* of who we are?" I asked looking at the two of us in our nineteenth century clothing, talking pod reentry and stored energy, and completely understanding each other, but I couldn't fathom how a person like Thomas Hartford would react to anything remotely close to the truth.

"Possibly. He has been the reason—the one person who gave me hope to come back to you, Anna," he said compassionately.

"But it's all been a lie, David," a tinge of accusation hung in my tone.

"Not all," he hesitated in protest. "My feelings for him as a gentleman and dear friend are not fabricated."

"I know, David...I didn't mean to accuse you, I just don't know how we are going to navigate this whole thing. I'm sorry," I replied softly.

"Let me worry about Thomas Hartford." His face changed a bit, as he seemed to realize that we had been gone for quite a while. "Let's head back. It is surely near dusk outside, and we mustn't get lost in the groves."

David held my hand as he led me back out the entrance of the cave just around the corner from the small room we had been standing in. It looked so different in the light, and it wasn't as scary as I had imagined it. The little wooden platform stood at the edge of a narrow cavern that housed

221

the river below. A small part of the cabin floor was visible high above my ahead and the ropes to move the lift swayed softly as they reached from where we stood all the way to the wooden floor above. We entered the lift and David closed the chain link doors while sliding a small lock to secure it.

"The lights," I said, "you didn't turn them off."

David smiled. "They will burn out soon enough. The next time the lever is switched, it will catch a different strand of lights and activate."

"You've thought of everything, I guess," I nodded and smiled. It didn't surprise me.

The lift was slow and smooth, as David pulled the ropes gently to ascend, and I took the opportunity to lay my head on his shoulder as I tried to soak in the few moments we had to be together as ourselves before I sent him back to his *pretend* family. It felt so strange. Before, I had lost him to the abyss; now it was as if I was sending him away in acceptance. It was nice to be down in the cave away from the world that lay above if only for a short while.

We reached the top, closed up the small house, and headed into the woods.

"It is almost dusk. We must hurry," David said.

I followed behind him as quickly as I could. He began to worry that we were being followed and started to walk faster and faster. I tried to keep up with his tall, long legs, but in my cumbersome skirt, there was little I could do to keep the pace he did. A soft rustling sound started to resonate through the air, and I turned around to see what was behind us.

"Amoriti!" I gasped. I was startled—even frightened a little—but immediately felt a strong sense of calm and peace rush over me.

I could see the flow of her white gown appear to span the width of the forest opening, and I paused to gaze at the sight of the angelic figure approaching us. The rushing of the wind got louder and soon I was caught up in an intense speed. I couldn't make out the sights around me because everything began to move so quickly that it made my eyes burn, so I closed them tightly and held on to Amoriti's tender arms. Within seconds I was at the edge of town. I looked around for David.

"Where is he?" my calm turned into panic.

"He is safe," she said as she stood before me in what now looked like normal human form and size.

"You will see him again soon."

And she was gone.

CHAPTER FIFTEEN

"Afternoon tea with Lady Jones is most enjoyable when one has another kind soul with which to engage in conversation, Mother."

Katherine was not as fond of Lady Jones as Minnie was. It was implied that Minnie had always been a favorite, a better student of the languages, and the jolly agreeable type that educated women prefer to the more stoic personality that Kitty exuded. The girls were both expected to attend Lady Jones' luncheon, and Mrs. Hartford couldn't see why she was preferred to attend as well.

"I will be there to divert any unfavorable attentions to myself, I assure you, Mrs. Hartford," I said in my most proper fashion.

Minnie and Mrs. Hartford could not stifle a laugh.

"Yes, that is true, Kitty, you shall be ignored altogether!" Minnie exclaimed.

"Minnie!" Mrs. Hartford tried to scold her without laughing at the outburst.

"No, it is true Mrs. Hartford. I can accept it. Lady Jones made it rather clear of her disliking me from the moment she laid eyes on me," I admitted.

"You see, Mother? Miss Wright quite understands the situation, though I am rather perplexed as to why Lady Jones gave you such a harsh greeting and then invited you to tea at once, Anna!" Minnie was unfamiliar with being unkind to anyone, so I presume it caught her off guard a bit.

I concluded that I wasn't the first to be the victim of Lady Jones' brash disapproval, so I was more apt to brush it off than Minnie would have been. I didn't care for her either, and I was sure that she knew the feeling was mutual. It did make me nervous that David had said that he had never been in her good graces and even suspected her of having something to do with the Guardians that were keeping an eye on him.

Mrs. Hartford disliked Minnie's honest assessment and instructed her daughter lovingly, "Winifred, it is not right that one question another's motives. Perhaps you misjudged the coldness of her greeting toward Miss Wright. Nevertheless, you all have been invited, and I have not, so it should be quite improper for me to join the party," she said decidedly.

"Been invited to what, Mother? Tea? Oh, do come along. It is nothing so formal as that!" Thomas entered the room mid-conversation, jumping right in.

"What do you mean, Thomas?" Kitty asked with excitement. "Are you to join us as well?"

"Yes, of course. Stevenson and I will be there to make the afternoon most delightful!" he joked.

"Mr. Stevenson?" I was elated. Thomas had done what he said he would, and arranged for David to join us. My heart fluttered at the thought of being able to see him again.

"Yes, of course. We cannot leave you ladies to have all the fun. Besides, he told me that he wishes to discuss more of his knowledge of your brother's whereabouts, and since you ladies had already been invited, we agreed that we should abandon our other plans and accompany you at luncheon."

"Indeed?" Kitty asked, "Will his aunt approve, Thomas? One can assume that her dislike of Miss Wright was founded on the improprieties of the past few days." Katherine's disapproval went from a lighthearted teasing to pointed accusation.

"Katherine, please," Mrs. Hartford scolded Kitty incredulously.

"What, Mother? Is it not so?" Katherine insisted on implicating me in some sort of impropriety. "Miss Wright, the way that you could not keep your gaze away from an engaged man on Saturday at the ball…and do not think that all of town was not gossiping at the *business* you had in town on Sunday. Thomas, tell me, where was Mr. Stevenson that afternoon? I dare say that you would not keep a secret from your very own sister though Minnie insists upon it!" she said, casting a glare at her sister.

"Katherine!" Mrs. Hartford was clearly disturbed at Katherine's boldness and spoke as firmly as any of the three children had ever heard from what I gathered by their reactions to it. "I will not have the assumption of the gossip mill be presented as truth in my own home! Thomas and Winifred have helped Miss Wright in a most innocent way, and you will not accuse your own brother and sister as doing anything less than what is respectable," she insisted. "What has gotten into you, Katherine?"

"I'm so sorry, Mrs. Hartford. I truly didn't mean to cause any problems," I said apologizing through my unsuppressed tears.

"Miss Wright, you would share the truth of your dealings here if you had more to tell, would you not?" she said.

"I am here only to find my family." I lowered my head as I looked down at the floor.

"There, Katherine. And Thomas...Winifred...what have you to say on your behalf?" their mother insisted.

"Nothing, Mother," Minnie replied self-consciously.

"Mother, if you must know, Miss Wright did meet with Mr. Stevenson. It was only to see if he could help. You do understand that the situation of Miss Wright and Mr. Stevenson is similar, and he has a far wider circle of acquaintances than I. He might have known, or at the very least heard of the Mr. Wright that Miss Wright has been searching for," Thomas explained. "We offered them privacy, yes, but we were there as well. How is this to be misconstrued as improper by anyone in town? We must have been seen at luncheon together—all four of us."

"Indeed you were, Thomas," Kitty was still insistent on digging deeper.

"I will not be charged with any wrongdoing by my own sister, Kitty. And you will kindly do me the courtesy of accepting my word," Thomas angrily retorted.

"It is not you whom I accuse, Thomas," Katherine lifted her eyebrows and stared at me.

"That is quite enough!" Mrs. Hartford scolded again, and I could no longer sit among them.

I hurried out of the room into a corridor where an attendant was standing. I began to let my tears flow, and looked around me for a tissue. It made me laugh. I realized how ludicrous the thought was, as I stood there cry-laughing. The attendant approached, handed me a handkerchief, and then quickly exited the room. I wasn't sure if I had scared him off, or if he had just wanted to offer me a moment of privacy to gather myself. Whichever it was, my solitude didn't last long. Thomas entered the room and approached me.

"I *am* sorry, Mr. Hartford," I began.

"It is I who should apologize to you, Miss Wright. My sister should have never been so unkind. I believe that she fears her Mr. Watson—or in fact, his mother, *Mrs. Watson*—will not approve of any girl associated with scandal. She wishes only to protect herself. I do not think that she truly dislikes you," he groped for excuses.

I stood, silently wiping my tears, trying to find the words to say. I didn't care if Kitty liked me or not. Thomas had known—had been a part of my meeting with David alone. He had been flirting with me all along, so I couldn't imagine that he would suspect that there was a romantic connection between David and me, but at the same time, he did facilitate what would have been viewed as an improper meeting of the two of us. I took a long, deep breath.

"Why did you do it?" I asked. "Why did you take me to meet him?"

"Mr. Stevenson and I are close, Miss Wright. He and I have our secrets, as you now know, and I trust him completely. If he tells me that he needs you to see our old mill, that it may somehow lead you to your brother, then I trust his inclinations. I think he suspects that your brother, Mr. Wright, is a fellow scientist from university who may have been working on the advancement of electricity as well. I am not quite sure what the secrecy and competition is all about. I think it is an exciting thing to be able to share our studies with one another."

Thomas seemed so innocent and credulous at times. It was no wonder that he gave his heart away so easily. I did think it ironic that it was the cause of his tainted reputation with the ladies. He was simply a kind, loving, and sometimes-gullible soul.

"It is the movement of the future, Miss Wright!" he continued. "Whole cities, even now, are exploring the use of electric lights, machines, and motors for streetcars. I believe that we are within twenty years of greater strides in science than we have ever seen before!" He spoke with the excitement that David had when he talked about his work.

I grinned at him, "I believe you're right."

"You think I'm silly," he said, shaking his head.

"No, I promise, I do not think you are silly. I truly believe that you are right, and I thank you for understanding Mr. Stevenson's reasons for taking me there." I nodded and smiled at him.

"I must confess I do not fully understand them, but Stevenson would never do anything improper to hurt Miss Bradshaw."

"No," I said shaking my head, "David would never do something that would intentionally hurt anyone. Not if he could help it," I said.

My heart sank. My happiness meant the sorrow of so many others. If the studies that David and Christopher had done were correct about time's perpetual and simultaneous existence, it meant that our children were potentially orphaned. Grieving the loss of their parents. Suffering. Yet if we left, Miss Bradshaw would suffer the heartbreak of abandonment. The Stevensons would lose their only son again. *Would their grief be bearable to endure a second time?* Thomas, who stood before me, would lose the friend that he considered his closest confidant. I could not let myself think of others in that moment.

"Please, Miss Wright, you mustn't speak of him so informally, or you shall give my mother ample reason to mistrust you, no matter how Minnie and I insist upon your innocence."

"I am sorry, Thomas...ugh, Mr. Hartford. I...it is just more acceptable in America to address someone by their Christian name than it is here in England." I had done it again. My emotions had caused me to forget my training, and I was showing my true self.

"Hmmm, I'm not quite sure that I would understand the culture in your country, but I do think it intriguing. Mother calls it 'savage,'" he laughed, "but I would very much like to see it with my own eyes, to be my own judge." Thomas said with a hopeful smile. "Perhaps we shall find your brother, Mr. Wright, and all journey across the sea together."

I tilted my head back and rolled my eyes. "Your parents would be mortified!"

"Indeed, but I do imagine they suspect that they will lose me to the sea again one day," he said with a light-hearted smirk.

"I think they do," I responded in agreement.

Thomas' attitude lightened my mood, and I went to meet Minnie and Kitty in the foyer for us be driven to Ashton Court for tea with Lady Jones. It had been decided that Mrs. Hartford would join us, and I think everyone was pleased that she would be there, hoping to provide a buffer between me, Lady Jones, Kitty, and more particularly, David. I let out a heavy sigh as we jostled along in the coach. Thomas gave me a raised eyebrow and a side-smile. I cleared my throat and Minnie cleared hers. The tension was nearly unbearable. It was a full twenty-minute ride of complete silence.

"Well, then, here we are!" Mrs. Hartford finally broke the quiet with a happy declaration, and we all breathed a little more lightly as we got out.

Lady Jones and her attendants met us at the entrance. "Welcome to our home," she greeted us with a cold, dry tone and nodded to Mrs. Hartford.

It was the first time that I had seen a proper British woman look slightly awkward since I had been there. Mrs. Hartford was stunning and graceful, but there at the entrance of the great estate, she seemed uncomfortable as she tilted her head to the side and coyly smiled. She only spoke the words "Thank you."

Lady Jones greeted everyone by name, and the attendants took our light overcoats. It was a beautiful spring day, but *one always travels with a cloak for the journey* I had been told, so I trusted sweet Sarah and dressed in the proper layers I was prompted to.

"Miss Wright," said Lady Jones coming to my turn for the greeting, "and I believe you've met my nephew, Mr. Stevenson."

"Thank you, yes. Lady Jones, Mr. Stevenson." I curtsied and joined the others to the side of our hosts.

David stood in the entrance and nodded in gentlemanly appearance. I was so nervous already, hoping that Lord and Lady Stevenson were not to join the occasion, and was delighted to hear him apologize that his parents were unable to receive us that day, as they had been traveling to visit a family member of Lady Stevenson's in Devonshire and would not return for some weeks.

We all then followed Lady Jones to the dining area.

"I should've enjoyed tea on the terrace this afternoon, but Mrs. Burch assures me that it shall rain today and refuses to serve us outdoors. I shall never understand the employ of such a brazen women, but it is my brother and Mrs. Stevenson who must make these decisions, is it not?" Lady Jones scoffed. She chuckled in a way that made me even more nervous than I had been. Her passive-aggressive behavior was something that I could barely tolerate without a reaction at least in my facial expressions. *It's going to be a long luncheon.*

David caught my eye and gave me a nod as we entered the elaborate dining room. It was a room that we had not had access to at the ball. It must have been closer to the kitchen, and the dining room where the family ate their everyday meals. The thick, white curtains with golden embroidery draped from ceiling to floor, and were drawn with massive shimmering gold rope tassels to expose the grand windows and doors, which led out to an expansive terrace and continued into a vast garden. It looked like it was the rearmost part of the same garden that David and I had walked through during the dance. He had not removed his eyes off of me, and I returned his gaze and gave him an inquisitive look. He nodded again, gesturing for me to sit between Kitty and Minnie. I met him at the chair he had pulled out and sat down. Thomas had pulled a chair out for his sister Kitty and before he could sit on the other side of me, David had seated Minnie to my left.

"There we are," he stated. "Mr. Hartford and I will be able to converse with each of you this way!" David sat directly across from me after seating his Aunt to his left and Thomas and Mrs. Hartford to his right.

"Yes, of course," Thomas complied.

"But we mustn't test propriety and inspect our fair friends the entire afternoon, Mr. Stevenson," his aunt insisted.

"Inspect them? No, ma'am. I meant to engage them in conversation," David assured her.

"Indeed. To conversation," Thomas said loudly and evasively lifted his glass.

No wine had been poured, but we all slowly lifted the small glasses of water that had been set before us, and tipped them awkwardly. *To conversation!*

I grinned slightly. It was astonishing to me that I could have so many silent thoughts. I was used to speaking my mind at will, but found myself swallowing most of my thinking and observing each moment for what it was worth. I imagined that that's what most of the people around me were doing as well, and hoped that I could use it to my advantage. Thomas winked at me and put his glass down. I bit my lip and tried not to smile. The games people played to keep up perception were amusing me, and I was finding it less intimidating and more entertaining.

Lady Jones chitchatted about the food, the wine, the selection of tableware, and much else that I cannot remember while most of us nodded, agreed and listened. Mrs. Hartford would occasionally chime in about the weather, recent goings-on in town, what was happening with people's children; but for the most part, Lady Jones did the talking and we did the sitting. She did have a way of asking a question she did not want you to fully answer since she would tell you what she thought before you could get out a full sentence. She had asked Kitty about Mr. Edward Watson, and before Kitty could reply with much of anything, proceeded to give her full account of the Watson family, her dealings with them, and how they were of *fine society*. I could see the relief on Kitty's face when Lady Jones approved of her choice, and understood why she wanted to be able to have a friend to join her for a side conversation through one of Lady Jones' diatribes.

"Aunt, have you heard anything of your friend Dr. Bennett recently?" David had the courage to bring up a new subject, and trespass on his aunt's supremacy.

"Dr. Bennett? Funny you should mention him, David. Indeed I have," Lady Jones responded with delight.

My ears perked up at Dr. Bennett's name, knowing that it was the same name of a man who was whom they believed to instigate the entire scheme of time travel.

"He has suffered a great deal, I am afraid." She began to tell the story to the rest of the group since none of us were familiar with what had happened. Except perhaps Thomas. I was beginning to think that David had told him more than he let on.

"Dr. Bennett is no real doctor, you see," Lady Jones continued. "Not a medical one, in fact. He is a rather strange man, but my brother is quite taken with him. They are both fascinated with such sciences of horticulture and biology, and Dr. Bennett insists upon studying different plants' effects on human life, medicine and the sort, though—I must be clear—he's never treated any patient at all that I am aware."

David kept glancing at me. I assumed that he was trying to pick up on whether or not I was following along and putting two and two together. I was trying, but I was coming up with anything but *four*. I attempted to concentrate more on what Lady Jones was saying.

"Nonetheless, he was whisked away to New Zealand in search of a flower or a plant of some sort that is said to be indigenous to that area, and wouldn't you know? He's been caught up in the Maori Wars. Disappeared into thin air, they said, but we all assume that he has been captured and forced to take the British stance of arms, though I know him to be passionate about nothing more than science and plants, and naught of politics!" she exclaimed.

"But you see, there was no word from him for months, and now…dear Mr. Gibbons, whom you know, my dear Mrs. Hartford, has gone in search of his colleague. I was sure that he would end up dead as well, just as we all supposed Dr. Bennett had, but there has been word from Mr. Gibbons that they are both alive, and indeed Dr. Bennett is quite ill. He has not said what ailment he has suffered—only that his life is threatened and they wish to return to England as soon as Dr. Bennett is well enough to travel. I suppose that he wished to spare us women the gory details of war, and included no more minutia of the adventure. And there you have it—that is all of the account that I can faithfully relay."

"Indeed, Aunt? Was there any mention of the coordinates where he had found the mosses he had been studying?" David asked casually.

"*Mosses*? He certainly did not mention such things, Nephew," Lady Jones responded in exasperation. "It is not likely that he would send word of coordinates for moss, honestly," she said impatiently.

"But I do think that Father would like to know," David said.

I understood then that he had mentioned the word coordinates for a reason. I just had to pray that he was not suggesting that our coordinates had been so poorly measured that we had to run off to New Zealand to find our way home. That seemed like another impossible mission.

"Of course your father would wish to discuss his silly infatuation of greenery with Dr. Bennett, and I'm sure when Mr. Gibbons and he return that my brother will have occasion to do so, but you should hardly expect someone to send news of these mundane things when a man's life is in danger," she said brashly.

"Perhaps not, Aunt, but a man's work is nearly as important as his life, is it not?" David insisted.

"Indeed, Sir," Thomas agreed.

The women around the table said nothing, probably finding it a little difficult to relate. I bit my tongue. I wasn't sure if David was trying to communicate to me how strongly he felt about his studies and why he took the journey through time in the first place, or if he was getting at something more. Whatever it was, I was finding it hard to understand his point.

"I do believe that Father's interest lies in the fact that similar coordinates are right here in England, Aunt," David continued the subject.

My eyes widened.

"Here? Do you mean the coordinates are here?" I asked.

"Oh this very property," David confirmed as he pointed downward with his finger, tapping the table.

I understood then what he was saying. I did not know the connection between his own studies, his *father* Lord Stevenson, and the Dr. Bennett that had been lost, but what I did know was that he was trying to tell me that the pod entry point for us was located somewhere on the grounds of his own residence.

"Coordinates? Nonsense!" his aunt protested, "you speak as if you were out to sea on a voyage of some sort. Mr. Hartford, have you ever heard such a thing?" Lady Jones' patience seemed to be wearing thin.

"Coordinates? Yes, ma'am, but not for plants. I admit that mosses and biology of horticulture are not my specialty. I know more of kinetics and electromagnetism," Thomas replied.

"Gibberish!" Lady Jones gestured in disapproval, "Complete nonsense. I do not know a soul who could comprehend what you gentlemen find fascinating about such things that one can neither prove nor see."

David sat and grinned at the exchange between his aunt and Thomas, all the while with his eyes locked on me. I could feel Mrs. Hartford staring down the side of my neck so I glanced at her and grinned, keeping myself from looking back up at David. I hoped he could tell that I had understood what he meant about the coordinates of the pod. He kept moving his chair in and out of the table slightly and fidgeting with his hands. It was clear to me why he had come to the luncheon and insisted on joining a ladies' afternoon social affair. He had to tell me. I tried so hard to breathe normally. It was all I could do not to grab him by the arm, run into the gardens, and hold him as he told me everything that he knew, assuring me of our successful return. As I sat there, imagining the happy scene in my mind, I looked down, folded my hands in my lap and twiddled my thumbs. I don't recall having ever done that in my life before, but it seemed like the perfect occasion to start the habit.

"Miss Wright, are you not entertained by the thought of such notions of futuristic events? You have become more interested in looking down at your fingers than you first seemed about coordinates!" Lady Jones laughed.

"I do share Mr. Hartford's and Mr. Stevenson's interest in the sciences. But I am afraid that I am more a student of literature and music than of kinetics and electromagnetism," I replied.

She raised one eyebrow at me and leaned forward.

"Hmph! Gibberish," she said coldly.

"Well done, Miss Wright, perfect pronunciation," Thomas interjected, "you shall be welcome to join us at any time to study the subjects further. I would be pleased to discuss the matters of other types of energy, electricity, and even chemistry. Have you heard about the studies of Sir Robert Boyle of the past century?"

I let out a surprised laugh, and tried to retract my previous statements.

"I have heard of him…but truly, I am not a student of science and certainly not of chemistry! It was my worst subject for sure."

"Worst subject? Miss Wright you speak so oddly at times. The accent I can tolerate, but some of the things you say, Miss, really," Lady Jones shook her head, Lady Hartford repeated the gesture and I am sure she shared the sentiment, though she did not voice it.

"Shall we take a turn around the gardens, Lady Jones? It is such a lovely time of year. Everything is blossoming so beautifully!" Minnie tried to divert the attention of their disapproval knowing that a change of scenery would benefit us all.

Each of us left the room without speaking to one another. The large terrace spanned the entire side of the long room and led to marble steps that were outlined with shapely pillars and thick banisters, which led to a second patio around it. Once we were outdoors, chatter began among the girls, and Lady Jones and Lady Hartford walked ahead into the gardens speaking about the hedges and flowers that were blooming and those yet to bloom. Everyone had taken a breath of fresh air and seemed to have relaxed. The men walked to the right side of the porch, down the steps, and onto a small landing where they stopped to converse, while Kitty and Minnie followed them.

I walked over to the ledge of the banister overlooking the steps into the garden to take a deep breath.

"When can I see you again, Anna?" David had come up behind me.

"David...I thought you had gone into the gardens with everyone."

"I had begun to go, but you didn't join us," he said with concern as he leaned his elbows on the banister next to me.

"No, I didn't. I just needed to breathe. To think. Won't they become angry again if they see us talking alone?" I asked nervously.

"*Angry?* Have they been angry with you, have they been unkind?" he asked in concern. "Did they offend you in some way?"

My heart swelled at the thought of him standing up for me, but I remained worried about appearances. "They... there has been talk already, David. I am so scared about having things blow up in our faces before we even get a chance to try to get out of here!"

David smirked. I knew he was not used to hearing phrases like "blow up in our faces," and he couldn't help but smile at my use of twenty-first century jargon. I was sure that it was almost as amusing for him to hear me speak as it was for the rest of the people I encountered.

"You must stay calm. We have time, Anna," he stood straight again, trying to reassure me with his confidence.

"*Time?* How can you say that, David?" I insisted. "That is the one thing that we do not have! We must return to our children before it is too late. How long can we stay here? It's already been eight years for you; eight years in which you've aged and changed. What will happen when we do go back?" My mind began to contemplate the what-ifs.

"Anna, please."

"No, David. Tell me. What will it be like if we don't act soon? And we must be so precise. To not miss a week—a month—a year of our children's lives? If you've been able to stay here for eight years, while for me, it was a matter of months, who's to say that we will not miscalculate and miss our destination—miss our children completely?" I spoke desperately.

"Anna, we cannot discuss this here," he warned.

"No, not at the precise location of our departure, can we? That won't be difficult to pull off at all," I said cynically as I moved to another banister to avoid being too close to the edge where Thomas, his sisters and the two elder ladies explored the gardens below.

David followed my movement, and continued to encourage me. "I know that it will be difficult, Anna. But we will manage. Allow me the time to prepare our exit for the journey ahead, will you? We have two hundred days from the time of your arrival, do we not? The pod should be powered enough to give us that much at least. Do you know how many days you've been here for certain?" he asked."

I turned to look at him, "No. Not really. Amoriti...she helped me at first, and it had been two days. Then I ran into the woods where Kitty and Minnie found me. I must have collapsed there in exhaustion, but I don't know how much time had passed. I thought I had longer, but I don't know if I've been right about anything," I said in confusion.

"Is that who took you when we were in the woods? This Amoriti?" he asked.

"Yes! Did you see her? How did you even get out of the woods that day? I almost forgot that I had been led out of the groves and that you had gone off on your own or something."

"I did not go off on my own. I hid when I heard the sound of the Guardians again, and I did see her through the trees. I tried to follow the bright figure when I saw that you had been taken. I thought that perhaps you had been captured again...for them to send you to be with

240

our children, hoping that they would have mercy on you… praying that you would survive once again. Those were my thoughts until Thomas came to discuss our meeting today and assured me that you had arrived to the town unscathed and were resting at home," he explained.

"She told me that you'd be fine," I said smiling. "That I'd see you again! I don't really know why she'd take me and not you, but I knew it. She helped me again!"

David furrowed his brow at my excited outburst. "How do you know…*her?*" he asked suspiciously.

"She is my guardian angel!" I exclaimed. I realized that it sounded unbelievable, but I was sure of it. Whoever the other Guardians were, was something I was not positive about, but Amoriti, I knew was on my side.

"You must beware, Anna," he admonished, "I am not sure that you can trust her."

"I am," I said stubbornly in protest. "You must believe me, David. She is not the one who sent me back. She is the one who led me to you!"

"I know that I can trust *you*, Anna, and that will have to suffice for the time being, but we must be on mission from this time onward. No suspicion will arise if you do as I tell you. I will monitor the skies daily from where I am, but you must go to where the next coordinates are. Thomas will be able to help you. I have told him that you will be carrying out a task for me. You will both go to the field near the church each day. It is not more than a ten minute walk from Blaise Castle; perhaps you may have a picnic with the Misses Harford. Whatever the excuse, Thomas will aid you in finding a way to get there daily. I have told him that there are possibilities of storms, lightning, and sky activity there that you will be recording for me. That will explain the sighting of the pod if it is able to make its entrance where I believe it may. You will need to monitor the skies from the exact location for the next eight days, and we shall meet and discuss our findings sometime afterward, all right? We shouldn't discuss this any further here. Let's go into the gardens with the others. I do not want to raise suspicion."

He offered me his arm. I was so glad to be able to hold him if only for a brief time as we walked down the steps of the grand terrace and into the garden. It was entirely proper for me to take a gentleman's arm while descending the steps, but once we reached the bottom, it took every ounce of strength I had to release my vice-like grip.

I paused at the bottom of the steps, still holding on. We stood face-to-face for a moment and I lingered to stare into his beautiful golden-green eyes. Hazel wasn't a good enough word to describe them. There were flecks of green and gold that glimmered when the light would hit them, and a bright tawny shade that encircled his iris. I heard the music of my heart sing the sweetest song I could imagine, as I longed to utter words of affection, knowing that I couldn't. The strings of violins would crescendo in my mind's ears with sad confirmation that my heart was about to be torn in two, and as if in slow motion, beckoned me to loosen my grip from my true love, and let him go once again. He walked away toward the long labyrinth of the garden.

CHAPTER SIXTEEN

The days were long and quiet. Kitty and Minnie would plan events and outings, but other than our picnics and long, lingering walks to and from the church, we had little excitement. They were surprised at my lack of sewing or painting skills, but were pleased that I knew some classical pieces to entertain them on the piano. Both of the girls played as well, but were rather rigid in their movements, and lacked the practice that I had been forced to endure throughout my childhood and teen years. In college, with a music minor, practicing piano seemed more like study than the brutality it seemed as a child, so it helped me enjoy taking the time to perfect my skills.

The unanimous favorite of my memorized repertoire was *Clair de Lune*, although I was unsure if it was a more modern piece than the time I discovered myself in. I tried to avoid suspicious actions, but the music of *Clair de Lune* had been a consolation to my anxiety for as long as I could remember, and clearly spoke to the two girls who had become my dear friends. They would tell me to play "the French one" since I choked on my words when they asked the name, the composer, and the year of its transcription. Minnie was sure that she had heard it before, and Kitty had not. I, however, was fearful that I would be caught in a lie about the smallest things, and had wished that I had paid more attention to music history in college than I did. My delight was to sit and play the pieces that spoke to my soul, and the study of music history and theory bored me. I later regretted that I didn't find it more useful when I had had the time to study. When pressed, I only admitted to it being *French*, and that I couldn't recall who wrote it or when.

I sat on the piano stool as the afternoon sun shone through the imposing windows of the parlor caressing the keys as I was swaying to my favorite tune. The domed ceiling made the melancholy ballad resound in an almost haunting way, and I imagined it carrying my sorrows away as it echoed off of the thick walls.

"It's lovely," Thomas remarked.

I stopped abruptly and turned around.

"I have startled you. I apologize, do continue, Miss Wright," he said softly.

"Oh, no thank you. I didn't mean to disturb anyone. I thought everyone had gone to watch the cricket match."

"It is not a disturbance to hear such a lovely sound, Miss Wright. And they have indeed all gone. All but I and a few of the servants. I was about to head that way myself. Shan't you join us?" he extended his hand to help me stand.

"I prefer to stay here, I think. Thank you, Mr. Hartford."

"No hope of sighting any energetic sky activity today?" he cheerfully prodded.

"I don't know." I sighed and shrugged my shoulders. I was sad, lingering in my thoughts, and trying to find some comfort in my solitude.

"Nothing of note for the past number of weeks that I have observed either. But maybe there shall be something to see today. The cricket match is being played over by the very field where we've been going, you know."

I didn't know. What I had been told previously was that every year there was a break right before summer was in full swing, for all of the people in the community to come together and play a match of cricket–a match of wits as well, some would say. The noble gentleman of the county would come together to challenge each other in a game. All of the servants and workers would take off work, serve only cold meats, vegetables, and fruits at the outing, and all would gather to cheer on their household's teams. I knew little of the game, other than the fact that it could last for days, but I was more concerned that, with the whole town around, I might raise suspicion or question again, and I was in no mood to handle any of it.

"I did not realize that it was in the same location. But I really don't have a mind to go, Mr. Hartford. If you see anything, you'll let me know, won't you?" I asked.

"I dare say anyone will be able to report today's weather to you since the whole of the county will be there!" he laughed.

"I suppose you're right," I smiled in agreement.

He knelt beside the piano and took my hand. "Miss Wright, I admit that I stayed behind for a reason when I saw that you had not left with the others. Anna, please allow me to…"

"Please, don't." I stood in objection to his affection. "I cannot accept your desire to express romantic sentiment. Mr.

245

Hartford, please do not mistake my familiarity with impropriety. I do call you Thomas at times only because you remind me of my own dear brother and it is hard for me to remember all of the societal obligations of etiquette that I have not been accustomed to practicing in America–I *am* trying! I have certainly meant nothing by them other than my fondness for you as a friend," I said as I paced the room a bit.

Thomas moved toward the luxurious alabaster fireplace that sat on the left of the room and rested his elbows on the mantel. "And your heart has been broken by another?" he turned his head to look at me with a hint of pity. "It is all right. I have loved before as well, Miss Wright. Loved and lost–and I am told that one who has once loved is likely to love again. I believe it to be true. Such could be the happy case for us."

"It's not that. I mean, yes, I have loved. And suffered great loss; you are not wrong there…" my thoughts drifted off to the acute pain of those first moments of grief that I had suffered at David's disappearance.

"And so our lives must go on, Miss Wright," he reassured.

I had moved to the opposite side of the room as I began to lean upon one of the great marble pillars that towered above me. Thomas walked away from the fireplace and toward me without saying a word.

He came to a halt mid-room and sighed.

"Miss Wright, I only ask one thing. Please do not set your heart upon Mr. Stevenson. It is no good. He is the most faithful and disciplined gentleman that I have ever been acquainted with. When other men–even myself, I am ashamed to admit it–were partaking in some of the pleasures of a frivolous youth, he was faithful to his study, his family, his friends, and now to his fiancée."

I had no doubt of it. By the time he had arrived in 1843, he had the maturity of a thirty-year-old man in what everyone believed to be a twenty-year-old body. But even when I met him as his true twenty-two-year-old self, David was one of the most dignified people I had ever encountered. He was oblivious when it came to his looks. He would turn every head in the room as his tall imposing figure would enter, and people would nearly gasp at his presence. He would notice them, would be kind, cordial, and friendly, but never think that he was the object of anyone's desire. It intimidated most people. It surely intimidated me at first. I had thought that he was just another pretty-boy player, especially since he had kissed me after having known me for only a few hours. I of course thought that our moment in that airport terminal would likely be our first and last encounter. But he was different. As perfect of a man as I could have imagined. *How could I not love him when he had pledged his love for me in return?* But that was in the twenty-first century, not the nineteenth; my doubts of his love in the century in which we found ourselves were growing.

"Mr. Hartford, I do not wish to cause hurt or scandal for anyone. I only mean to rely on Mr. Stevenson's aid in my quest. He has been so helpful and..." I could not hide my true feelings completely. My heart and soul belonged to David Sturgeon, and in this century, to Mr. David Stevenson. No matter the time, age, decade or year, I knew that my soulmate existed in the one person my heart cried out for. I could speak no longer. I turned my head to avoid eye contact with Mr. Hartford, pushing myself away from the pillar and toward the door.

Thomas had heard the silent cries of my heart for David no matter how hard I struggled to stifle them. I knew that it raised suspicion on both of us. Maybe that was why David had avoided returning as quickly as he had said that he would. My pining for him was not helping the situation at all, and I was becoming anxious about the whole thing.

Thomas followed me to the side of the room and hurried to block the doorway with his arm. "Mr. Stevenson is my closest friend, Miss Wright. I do not wish to think ill of him. Indeed, I do not believe that I am capable of it, but if you tell me that he has declared his love to you, I will be forced to believe that his marriage proposal to Miss Bradshaw was born of familial obligation and not of love. Though it would be most unlike him to act dishonorably and declare it to be so before breaking his engagement to a respectable young lady."

"He has been the perfect gentleman," I said decidedly as I pushed his shoulder to pass him and exit the room. I wanted to be left alone. To cry myself to sleep. *Oh, sleep, how I wish it would wash away the pain of my life!*

David had been gone for nine weeks. I had seen no activity in the location that we had been frequenting. Not one single sign of the pod—or anything else for that matter. It had rained on only one of the afternoons, and everyone was enjoying the longest bout of sunshine without interruption of rain that most people could remember in a lifetime of English summers. Minnie, Kitty, and I had spent hours almost every afternoon roaming the grounds of Blaise Castle and beyond, playing, laughing together, and becoming real friends. Kitty's suspicion of me had subsided, and I was happily allowed to call them by their first names while we were together in private. It felt as if I was starting to do what David had done—to build a life there. It made me angry, sad, confused, but also comforted in my loneliness.

I had double-checked the site of the place marked on Amoriti's map a hundred times. I was beginning to think that it was all a farce—the idea that we could return. It was hard for me to believe that we had actually traveled through time in the first place. And I was silly enough to believe that we would be able to make it back? *Ridiculous. I just need to sleep it off.*

"Miss Wright, I do not mean to upset you," Thomas followed me as I walked through the long corridor.

"Please, Mr. Hartford. I do not wish to be followed," I politely insisted.

"Anna…dear, sweet Anna…" his voice lovingly pleaded with me. He touched my elbow, grasping it tightly enough that I couldn't easily get away. I turned to look at him for a moment, and when he had let go of my arm, I quickly started to walk again toward the residential wing.

He continued his plea as he followed me down the long hallway. "I request that you would allow me to declare my admiration for you. I only desire to protect you from harm, Miss Wright. Mr. Stevenson has not returned to the estate these two months at least, and has written that it may be another fortnight or longer before he and his parents return from Devonshire. He has entrusted the resolution of your predicament to me, and I am happy to help. Indeed, I am honored that I could be of service to you, and would hope that if your journey has not brought you success in finding your brother, at least it may have brought you success in securing my love." He spoke quickly as he kept up the brisk pace behind me.

I stopped and brusquely turned toward him.

"Your *love?*" I was angry. "After a couple months of knowing me you are certain that I am a woman worthy of your love and devotion? You know nothing of the sort! You don't know *me* at all," I shouted.

I did care for Thomas. I did not mean to hurt him, but the way in which he easily declared his love for a woman he hardly knew offended me to my core. And I didn't even know what to think of David.

It was true. David had left. He simply confided in a note that we would not be able to see each other for a time. His writing was very formal. He had apologized for his inability to continue helping me in my search for my brother for the time being and asked that I would forgive his absence.

Thomas stood in the hallway in stunned silence.

A few moments passed as he glanced from side to side, struggling to find words. I bit my lips in embarrassment. I could feel heat rising to my cheeks as I tried to swallow down my pain. I looked up at him. His face was long and sad; his brows wrinkled in thought.

"I…I am sorry for the outburst, Mr. Hartford. I did not mean to be unkind to you. Please believe me if you will. I am not capable of accepting your addresses. You are right about my heart belonging to another. I have suffered loss, but not as you imagine. I am still quite committed to the man to whom my heart belongs. I must complete my search, and return home to him. That is all that I can say on the subject. Please do not ask me to mention it again!"

I covered my face with my hands and ran down the remainder of the corridor to the east wing of the estate. I found my bedroom and threw myself onto the bed.

"If you please, Miss? Shall I come in?" Sarah peered her face around the edge of the heavy door as she had done so often when she desired to come into the room.

I sat up on the bed, rubbing my eyes. "Oh, yes, Sarah. Do come in."

"Oh, dear, Miss. You must've fallen asleep in your day clothes. You have quite wrinkled them, and your hair is not properly set any longer."

I grimaced at the thought of having her pull at my hair again to make it presentable. "Then you have come at just the right time, Sarah," I said as I pushed myself to the end of the bed and swung my legs over the side, trying to behave cheerfully.

"I will have you looking acceptable in no time, Miss!" she smiled and approached the bed to help me.

I laughed at the thought of being acceptable, and Sarah realized that her choice of words was a bit comical.

"Not, *acceptable*, Miss. Quite agreeable. Pretty and elegant as you know you are," she stammered.

"Don't worry yourself over silly words, Sarah. Believe me, I have not only been the victim of a careless slight, but also the aggressor without intention at times, I'm afraid," I said as I stood moving toward the vanity chair.

"You are very much the empathetic type, Miss. To understand one's counterpart and not take offense easily is to me one of the most admirable characteristics anyone could possess." She began to brush out the stray strands of my unruly hair.

"Thank you, Sarah. I am very fond of you as well," I grinned.

She chuckled under her breath. "And I am fond of you, Miss." She pulled and tugged at my hair trying not to undo it completely so she could set it faster.

"You missed quite the excitement in town, Miss. Today was the end of the noble cricket match, but what do you know? The servants of the households who lost the match have challenged the servants of the winning team. And they have accepted! It was a potential brawl that Lord Milton was set to diffuse when the parties of the winning households meant to refuse the losing house's challenge stating that they were *'not fit to be a match for such skills.'* And quickly hence, there was an announcement that it would be a respectable thing for the peasants to participate, and that was that! There shall be a cricket match between the men, and the Lord and Lady of Gloucestershire have approved another day of leisure for the whole of the county!"

"Can they do that?" I asked in surprise. "Call a holiday like that for everyone?"

"Of course, Miss. And why not? It is a noble thing to do. To allow the peasantry some of the privilege only the upper class may enjoy. Ha! To see the lords and ladies look on at the common folk. What a sight it will be to behold!" she paused her task of pinning the last bits of my hair. "I didn't mean, Miss…I apologize for speaking out of turn."

I patted her little hand, and took the last bobby pin from the vanity to push it into the remaining lock of wayward hair as I piled it on my head myself, turning to face her.

"Do not fret," I said as I leaned in and pulled her hands toward me causing her young face to be right in front of mine. "I am much more like you than you may imagine, Sarah," I whispered.

"Thank you, Miss. We, both of us, have to look out for one another I suppose," she chuckled.

"We do," I said smiling. She was alluding to the secret of my brother really being my husband, and she had told no one. I did feel like I owed her a great debt. Much greater than forgiving her from speaking out about her feelings of the distinction between the classes. Little did she know that in another century I would champion her cause right alongside her, given the chance.

"Do you believe that you are closer to finding him, Miss?" she asked.

"I can only hope, Sarah."

"Well, we shall hope and pray for it, Miss. But for now, you look lovely enough to join the queen for tea!" she exclaimed.

I stood, twirled around, and curtsied in front of her with a low bow and a swoop of my arm. We both laughed and I thanked her for her help as I made my way out of the room and down the hallway to the main wing of the estate.

The family was to have a meal in the candlelight after which we would probably read a few passages from the plays of Shakespeare or poems from the more modern poets of the time like Lord Tennyson and Lewis Carroll. We were soon to begin a work by an American author— no doubt for my benefit—and our evenings were spent in the same reticence that made the days drag on. Thomas was an entertaining narrator, and Minnie—when she would insist on taking a turn—provided such animation that we were sure to have a long laugh. It reminded me of the evenings in Illinois with my parents and siblings. People, times, customs and traditions come and go, but somehow the essentials of relationships in life never change. It made me fonder of my time there, and of the family that had been so kind to help me along my journey.

"Good evening, Miss Wright." Lord Hartford greeted me with a kind salutation, and was genuinely concerned for my plight. "Any word of your brother?"

"Good evening, sir. No word that I know of."

"Sorry to hear it. But we must keep in mind that it takes the post a few days at least to reach certain destinations. And if the distance is great, then we can only speculate as to how long it may take! I know that Mr. Stevenson has sent word to his friends and acquaintances far and wide. We mustn't be dejected, Miss Wright. No, no! Head up!" he encouraged me with a smile.

"Thank you, sir." I smiled toward him as I took a seat at the table.

Everyone was excessively cordial and kind. I was no longer sensing that I raised much suspicion within the family and circle of acquaintances. I was falling into my role with greater ease, speaking properly, and no one seemed to comment when I would tag along with them to our teas with Lady Jones that had become a twice-a-week habit. I wanted to be around Ashton Court as often as I could to see if perhaps David would return with the Stevensons. Even Lady Jones had warmed up to me a little, I thought, and I found myself more comfortable in her presence.

As we had begun our first course, Mr. Hartford received an interruption from his meal via messenger. The butler presented a small note to him, and as he read it, he gave me a quick glance that made me blush. The only news that we had heard about David had come by post, and I assumed the message had something to do with me by the look Mr. Hartford had given me.

"Miss Wright? I suppose you know nothing of Lady Jones' intention?" he asked.

"Intention, sir?" I unquestionably knew nothing of Lady Jones or why the two of us would be linked in a letter.

"Lady Jones has sent word that she will join us this very evening, and wishes not to trespass on our habitude, but must speak with you as soon as is possible," he stated with an inquisitive tone.

"I know nothing of her intensions, sir. Perhaps she has had word from Mr. Stevenson regarding my brother and wishes to tell me in person?" I speculated.

"Ah, yes, Father. Such happy news must be divulged while in one's presence and not simply through a note!" Thomas was quick to reply. "Indeed, that must be it. Good news!"

"Perhaps." Lord Hartford was not convinced, but I could not think of any other reason myself.

We had not yet finished our meal when Lady Jones was announced at the dining room door.

"This is highly irregular, Lady Jones!" Mrs. Harford exclaimed. "You should have at least joined us for a fine meal if you insist upon making the journey from Ashton Court so late in the evening!"

"I am well and fed, Mrs. Hartford, and I do beg your absolution for my offense, but I must speak with Miss Wright this very evening." Lady Jones' tone and mannerisms were cold and abrupt.

"Indeed? It is most urgent then, Lady Jones?" Lord Hartford asked, standing to greet his guest.

My heart leapt and my stomach sank. I wasn't sure if I should be elated and hopeful or if I should prepare myself for devastation.

"It is. Be not alarmed, Mr. Hartford. I do not bear ill tidings, but those of a time-sensitive nature. Miss Wright must be allowed to travel back to Ashton Court with me on this very night—at once, in fact. I would much like to discuss the details in private in order to explain what I have to say and the instruction which I must relay. You do understand, Sir? Lady Hartford, Misses Katherine and Winifred, Mr. Hartford," she properly greeted every person by name and nodded to each one.

"Veritably, Lady Jones," Thomas answered for the entire family. "Of course you wish to aid Miss Wright, but do allow me to escort you along your journey. You mustn't travel alone."

"No, Mr. Hartford. I insist that I must speak with Miss Wright immediately. Shall we go into the garden?" she motioned to the door for us to leave.

"The garden? It is profoundly dark out and you will scarcely be able to see a thing. Do use the library," Mrs. Hartford urged.

"No, indeed, I think we shall be exceedingly content with the luminosity from the rooms that emit sufficient enough a glow for us to be able to converse," Lady Jones insisted.

I had sat motionless since she had walked in the door. I could not fathom what it was that she would have to say to me that she hadn't shared earlier that week at one of our teas. In the few moments during the dialogue before me, I had convinced myself that there was no good to come of the visit, but I had no way of knowing if I didn't go with Lady Jones and hear the news for myself. I pushed my chair back from the table and stood.

"I will be happy to join you in the gardens, Lady Jones." She nodded to the family and turned to lead me out of the dining room, down the hall to a small patio and onto the grounds of a stone pathway near a row of rose bushes. The lights from the house offered little aid, but the moon was as bright as I had ever seen it. Still, Lady Jones was difficult to see in her long black garb that covered nearly every inch of her skin. Her steps were so quick that I followed breathlessly behind her until she abruptly turned to face me, as she neared a line of towering bushes.

"Wait here," she raised her hand to motion for me to stop.

"Wait? What do you mean *wait*? You aren't leaving me here, are you?" I breathed in belabored discomfort, standing in the dark courtyard.

"It's all right, child," Amoriti's slight glow appeared from behind the hedges and startled me enough to knock me to my knees.

"Well if you intended on showing yourself here, Ami, you should as much as told me so!" Lady Jones scolded.

I was on the ground in shock, but quickly leapt to my feet to run closer to Amoriti.

"What is going on, Amoriti?" I asked in a panic, trying to hide myself behind her billowing gown. "You two know each other?" I began to back further into the hedges. "Are you here to hurt me, Lady Jones?" Amoriti scooted closer to me and I could feel the warmth of her calm.

"Shh, child. All is well. Shall you explain, Judith?"

"*Shall I?* I am but a messenger for David. No more, Ami. I am accursed already. If they find out…it is no good. I shall be forced to tidy up the catastrophe that all of you will leave behind. As if I have not suffered punishment enough for my wrongdoings," Lady Jones brashly chided. "Now, I have delivered her here as David has wished. Please, leave me to be as miserable as I ever was before the day I set eyes upon Miss Anna Wright," she pleaded.

I hadn't thought that Lady Jones was capable of emotions other than, perhaps, disdain, but she was clearly suffering great pain about something, and I began to feel sorry for her.

"You have done a good thing here, Judith. Live in peace now, won't you?" Amoriti implored, her empathy almost palpable.

"Peace?" Lady Jones said harshly. "My body lives in peace, but my heart shall ever live in torrid despair, Ami. It is the curse upon me. Let my circumstance forever haunt your thoughts should you ever consider making the dreadful choice I have."

My eyes were wide in disbelief. These two women shared a past that I could not understand, but curiosity prevailed as I dared to ask.

"What are you talking about, Lady Jones? How do you two know each other and what is Amoriti referring to? Have you somehow arranged a way for me to..." I was afraid to say it. *Does she know who I really am...who David really is? Has she found a way for us to return home?*

"You wish to know, Miss Wright?" she said abruptly. "Then I shall tell you. I suspected something to have been awry since David's return to us. But never did I expect to find myself in a place where I would tempt fate this way again. To aid one in defiance of the natural course of life is not a task that goes unpunished. You shall see. But, perhaps that shall be my consolation. To know that you too must suffer."

"You don't mean the cruel things that you say, Judith," Amoriti lovingly reminded.

"Don't I, Ami? You would believe that I mean them, wouldn't you, Miss Wright?" she threw her head back and laughed angrily. "Though your friend here would have you believe me to be sentimental and kind, those days are long behind me. But, yes, I shall enlighten you as to why.

"You see, Miss Wright, I was once as Amoriti is. A messenger, a Guardian, commonly known to some as an angel. During that time, I had a young man in my care who was the kindest soul that I had ever encountered in my duties. He was gentle, well-mannered and as empathetic to all people as I have ever seen. I was sent one autumn afternoon to guard him from a possible death by stray bullet where gentlemen were moving about with a hunting party on the grounds near Ashton Court. I was granted permission to reveal myself in human form for the deliverance. I was to give an excuse as to why he must stay away from the spot where he would have been killed had he been alone. He was only seventeen," she paused. "Sir Anthony Jones."

She reflected on the memories for a silent moment. It was as if she cherished the simple action of uttering his name.

"I presented myself as a young lady of sixteen, Miss Judith Wickham," she continued, "and we walked and talked for hours that day. I truly knew not a man so kind and gentle. He was the son of a duke, Lord Jeffery Jones, who had come to visit and hunt with Lord George Stevenson, but Anthony did not join them because he took little interest in the sport.

"I was spotted on that day as Anthony and I walked upon the property of Ashton Court, and it was brought to the attention of Lady Stevenson that her guest, Sir Anthony, was seen alone with a young woman. She avoided all possible scandal by saying that a young lady who was put in her charge by a distant relative, who had recently passed, was visiting her that day. And so the story remained.

"I became the ward of Lord and Lady George Stevenson. I had vanished that day as we often do, but I later began to secretly return in order to see Anthony as often as I could in human form. One day, I revealed myself to Lady Stevenson, and begged for her help. I never again returned in spirit form to the other world. I chose to remain here in this world, frightful place that it is," she explained as she had begun pacing. "I am what most would call the *fallen* kind. Fallen angels is what one may whisper not knowing how far the plummet to be." She paused and hung her head.

"Lady Stevenson was tender-hearted and believed my story to be true. That I was an orphan who could easily be the very girl she had told her friends was in her care from a distant relative. I pleaded with her to give me a life there and not to release me back to the orphanage from which I had escaped. It was our secret. Not even my father knew the truth of where she had found me–in the brush behind the estate trying to catch a glimpse of Anthony on one of his visits to the manor. I never truly intended for it to happen…for me to be found, to choose to stay. But I did make the choice, Miss Wright…the choice not to return. There *is* such a thing as the point of no return."

Lady Jones looked around at the moonlit garden and then at me. I had crouched back into the large hedges and taken a seat on the ground with my back resting on the tall bush. I was intently listening to the unfathomable story. Amoriti was near me the whole time. I could not tell if she was in human form at times, or at a place in between. Lady Jones continued to pace the small portion of the garden walkway that we had stopped in, and stepped in rhythm before us, unveiling her story.

"I spent nearly five glorious years in the care of the Stevenson family as one of their own. Even my name was immediately shared with both family and acquaintances as Miss Judith Stevenson. I adored my parents. I did not know the joy that the bond of family brings until those days.

They of course approved of Sir Anthony's addresses to me and encouraged the match. It was decided that we should be married just before my twenty-first birthday.

"It was the happiest of occasions. Ashton Court is the finest estate in all of town, but that day it must have been the envy of the world. Banners, flowers, pennants, and plants, the likes of which one had rarely seen were brought in to dress the gardens for our blessed union. And so we did, Miss Wright–pledge our undying love and devotion for one another. We were united as one."

She looked at me sternly. I got a chill from her harsh stare and waited for her to continue with the story. She paused, tilting her head back with a slight scoff.

"Undying love only lasts when one is alive, Miss Wright. Have you ever pondered that thought? No immortal would declare undying love to be so. It is mortals who think it possible." And she laughed a gloomy snort, pausing again.

I gasped. *"He died?"* I whispered in disbelief.

"Indeed. The very week of our wedding. I was not there to protect him–to keep him from harm or guard him from the stray bullet, which got him in the end regardless. As if we had tempted fate. And so it is I who am accursed to live with my undying love while his love is dead and gone; and all I have to console myself with is the happiness of bearing his name until the day that I meet death myself." She stopped moving and nodded. "At least I have that with which to comfort myself. I shall soon die and my heart will be at peace. But to think that I could have saved him! I could have guarded him all of his long days and watched the happiness of his love–even if it was for another! I could have chosen to protect him instead of love him!" she said pacing again and swinging her arms in frustration.

"Yes, I have made my choice as one of the fallen, Miss Wright. Love I have known—and I now know that David has found his true love in you. To deny him of the joy I myself may have had in life would be a greater sin than that of choosing my own demise, I think," she said pensively.

She huffed a bit and took a moment to reflect on her actions.

"I had always suspected David's peculiar entrance back into our lives after such a horrific tragedy to be something he had not admitted to. I considered his arrival to be something similar to my own some forty years before him. But it was not until I encountered Amoriti again last week that I discovered David not to be whom he had pretended to be all these years. He has, I admit, grown as dear to me as any nephew could be and has brought my brother and sister such great joy. The pain that they must suffer again be upon your shoulders, Miss Wright," she blamed.

She stopped once again to look at me, glaring at first, but her expression soon changed to resemble pity.

"Amoriti has assured me that you and David must try to return to your proper place in time and reset your course of actions against the universe. But I shall repeat myself, Miss Wright; it will not go without consequence. You must prepare for the effect of your actions."

With that, she stopped and turned toward the house.

"Let us go and have you say your goodbyes," she stated as she began to walk away while I sat numb, trying to process the information that had been shared.

"Go, child." Amoriti nudged me as I stood and speechlessly followed Lady Jones back toward the house.

CHAPTER SEVENTEEN

The air was filled with a night chill, and I was happy to have my summer cloak with me. I was not sure of how far we had gone, but my eyes had grown heavy while the coach trudged along the dark roads with only its lanterns aglow. I attempted to shake off the fatigue by asking Lady Jones about David's involvement and location.

"Miss Wright, do not concern yourself with the details of our adventure at this time. You must rest for the journey ahead," was her only reply. She preferred to ride along in silence, and I supposed her to be sleepy herself, as she closed her eyes, trying to avoid conversation as much as possible.

I felt as if I was in a dream, sitting in the coach while the events of the past few hours played vividly in my head. We had said goodbye to the Hartford family with the assurance that Mr. Stevenson had a solid lead on my brother's whereabouts. Lady Jones gave the family no promise of my return, and I had said little other than *thank you* again and again. I had truly grown to love the Hartford family as dear friends, and would always count them as being part of some of the fondest memories I would ever have. It's funny how painful trials are often coupled with such happy moments because they are spent with people you love.

Thomas repeatedly insisted that he escort us along the nighttime escapade, and everyone else voiced their opinion on how the capricious event was highly displeasing to the entire family, but Lady Jones prevailed in the end. She had convinced the Hartfords that it would not be unseemly for us ladies to travel by night without Thomas because she had brought the footman along to accompany her, and since it was the family's coach and not a public transport, it should be most acceptable for us to travel with the servant escort. Everyone complied, but not without speaking his or her unfavorable impressions on the matter.

I tried to gather as little as possible. Everything that I called mine was, in fact, borrowed from the generous family since my being there, but the girls had insisted that I take a small trunk, at least. Lady Jones prompted me to comply, so I had packed a gown, petticoat, and a bonnet, and then headed out to the coach.

The family was chattering, and a few servants were bustling about preparing some things for our furtive trip. Thomas took one last opportunity to offer his admiration and assistance as he took my hand to help me into the coach. He whispered that he would wait for me to rejoin the family and that his hopes of proving his feelings to be a good choice for me as well as for him would be accept-able to me by the time of my return.

I had a feeling that I would not return to them, knowing that Lady Jones had mentioned nothing of our plans to the family. I knew that her evasion of the questions about our reappearance was an admission of either her not knowing that we would ever return, or her keen insight about what may lie ahead. I simply followed along in submission.

My head was against the back wall of the coach, bobbling along in the agitating commute. After the emotional exhaustion of the past few hours, the perpetual motion almost lulled me to sleep.

"Miss Wright, we must exit here," Lady Jones said as the coach abruptly came to a stop.

She opened the door to the coach, motioning that I get out, but I was startled from my daze and didn't quickly react.

"Make haste, Miss Wright," she scolded. "We've not a moment to lose," she said hurriedly.

I shook myself into complete awareness and nearly jumped out of the coach. The door instantly closed behind me. Lady Jones leaned her head out of the window and instructed, "Wait here. It is safe."

I didn't see how I had a choice. The coach quickly started to depart as I heard bickering between the footman, coachman, and Lady Jones. It slowed, stopped, and started again a few times in the distance. The men were obviously uneasy about abandoning a young woman in the street, but by that point, I didn't even care. I was willing to meet any ill that may have been lurking. I sincerely wanted it all to be over.

I walked a few steps in the blackness and sat on a boulder, watching the glowing lanterns of the coach fade into the distance. It had begun to rain lightly, and I pulled my overcoat shut, and covered my head with the hood. Then, I waited.

"Wake up, Anna!" I felt my shoulder being rattled and I opened my eyes.

"David!" I clasped his hand as he pulled me upward and I jumped into his arms. I could see his face in the misty dawn light of the morning. "I can't believe it's you!"

"We must hurry, my love." He kissed me, took my hand and led me to the edge of the road to a line of trees.

"Where are we? This looks like…" my voice trailed off.

"The cottage?" David asked. "It was Amoriti who led me here. The suits have been placed under a board in the house, she said. Isn't it so?"

"Yes, but the cottage—it couldn't be here, could it? I thought it was so close to where I was running toward the girls near the castle the day they found me…"

"The distance is hard to judge when you travel with a Guardian, Anna. I believe this is it. Does it not look familiar?"

"It does. I just am not sure…how did you get here?" I asked, trying to figure out how we had found ourselves together again.

"We will have all the time in the world to discuss the events of the past few years, Anna. For now, let us move on with the objective at hand." He continued to speak as Mr. Stevenson, and I was concerned that he could not be certain of his choice to reunite with me, but I determined that my fears would not dictate my actions.

"All right," I said.

I recognized the path that led to the woodsman's cottage, and we soon came up to its quaint door. David, during our brisk ten-minute walk toward the cottage door, revealed the events of the previous weeks to me.

He had gone to Devonshire to meet the Stevenson family. He had confessed to them about not truly being the David that they had hoped him to be, and they refused to believe him. The family insisted that his memories of those years apart from them had been compromised and that he had been fooled by the wiles of a temptress. He did not declare his love for me, simply that he loved another, could not marry Miss Bradshaw, and that he could not bring himself to continue living the lie that he had been living. Hoping to avoid scandal and heartbreak, they coerced him into staying with them in Devonshire to reconsider.

David truly did love the Stevensons; he had spent the past few years being doted on as their only son, and felt as if he owed them a great debt as his rescuers. When his sense of obligation dwindled and his heart's desire to return to his rightful family were more than he could bear, he understood that the heartbreak of one family he loved must take place for him to be reunited with the other. My doubts began to subside.

"Did you finally tell them that it was me? That you wouldn't come back to them because of me? That we were leaving together forever?"

"In a way..." his voice was low and melancholy.

We had arrived at the cabin and entered cautiously. I quickly recognized the floor space where Amoriti had placed the suits.

"What do you mean, *in a way*?" I asked as I moved toward the table.

"Anna, I did not wish to hurt them, not more than I had to. Had they known it was you–that they may have had a chance to stop you from what they perceived you were doing, stealing their son–they would have done everything in their power to separate us. I could not risk that. They will endure enough anguish without having to know everything," he said through his own pain.

We had taken the suits out of the floor space, and returned the wooden slats. David unwrapped them slowly, stroking the rubbery fabric in thought.

"Our ship to America will not exactly be what anyone assumed it to be, will it?" David pondered.

"I guess not." I smiled at him and took his hand. "But how did Lady Jones get involved? And Amoriti? Did you see her? I told you that she would help us!" I said.

"Yes, it was she who saved my parents–uh…the Stevensons–from more disappointment," he assured me.

He kept referring to the Stevenson family as his own. I didn't mind by that point; I could feel his kindness melting into an agony of loss. I knew that he couldn't help it. I realized that it would be a while before the two Davids became one whole man again.

"What do you mean?" I didn't understand how Amoriti and Lady Jones could have schemed to allow us to be together.

"Amoriti came to visit our family in Devonshire. She was quite convincing, in fact. She claimed to be the wife of Professor Bennett, come to beg my assistance. It was a wonder my father hadn't realized that Dr. Bennett never introduced us to a Mrs. Bennett, and he even remarked on the fact that he had long wished to make her acquaintance. Furthermore, she had claimed a friendship with my aunt whom she said would arrive the following day to visit us. It was surprising, since my aunt has never enjoyed accompanying us on family travels, but when she did arrive, we could not help but believe Mrs. Bennett.

"Once my aunt arrived, she attested to the fact that Mrs. Bennett and she had once been colleagues and dear friends. Father then quickly consented to release me to help with aiding the search for Dr. Bennett, and my aunt abruptly returned home. It was all rather puzzling, and my parents were so upset with me for breaking my engagement that I believe they wanted to be rid of me anyway."

"Your aunt then came and got me from Blaise Castle last night!" I started to see how the puzzle connected.

"Did she indeed?"

"Yes, Lady Jones just brought me by coach and left me by the side of the road," I stated with an accusatory tone.

"I am sorry for that. I believe she was only doing as Amoriti had instructed her. She has some kind of power of persuasion that needed little explanation. Even now, my parents believe that we are to journey to America–not to New Zealand as had once been miscommunicated–in order to accompany Dr. Bennett home."

"But they will soon realize that I will be gone as well. And your aunt...Lady Jones...what will happen to her? Surely they will realize that she helped me run away with you." I had begun to feel pity for her.

"Possibly not. My aunt will simply tell them that I have left for America with Mrs. Bennett *and* you. Questionable, possibly, but not entirely scandalous. You will return to your family there, hoping to find your brother arrived at home before you, a probable student of Dr. Bennett who may have been accompanying him in his studies, and I will be doing the noble thing of aiding the doctor in his time of need."

"And never return..." my voice drifted off.

"No, not if we are successful, but they do not understand that now. They shall find out soon enough," he sighed.

I inhaled deeply. We had been standing in the cabin talking instead of preparing for our escape.

"Will they all be okay?" my empathetic nature kicked in, and we were both feeling anxious.

"We mustn't think of that now, dear Anna." He kissed my forehead and handed me the suit he had been holding. "We need to get to Harper's Mill."

269

"Harper's Mill?" I was surprised to think that we had to travel so far after everyone acted like we had no time to lose.

"Yes, the suits have to be repowered. It's the only place we can do it. This is what I've been preparing for, Anna. And it's finally happening!" We looked into each other's eyes and realized that it truly was a happy occasion. We were putting the past behind us. I smiled at him as he grabbed me by the waist, lifted me up and twirled me around with a kiss.

"Thank you, David. Thank you for always believing you would return to me." I hadn't thought that this would be our fate. When I was refusing to move on because people thought I was living in the past, unable to cope with the loss of my true love, I could have never imagined that we would be reunited—and yet there we were.

"But David…" I remembered my own lack of success, "I haven't seen the pod once. Did you find it?"

"I think so. Let's hurry now. Amoriti will lead us to the right path, Anna," he confidently assured me.

I knew that Amoriti could be punished for her actions. She could be doomed to live a miserable existence like Lady Jones if she were found out. Or maybe worse. But for whatever reason she was helping us mortals, and I could only be grateful.

David and I, with the suits in hand, walked through the woods to an opening by the edge of a tall hill. I heard the rustling of the trees and a gentle wind begin to sound louder. I knew it was her. It was calm, warm, and peaceful.

"No others are with her, are they? It doesn't seem like chasing this time, it's just calm." I said.

"The Guardians must not be interfering at all. Even if they do know, it will be satisfactory for us to return to our own time. All will be well, my love," David reassured me.

I sank into the words every time he said them. *My love.*

"Come, now. We must be on our way," Amoriti's pleasant voice beckoned us toward her. Her arms reached out long and wide as she scooped us up to carry us through the fields and forests until we came upon the groves that I recognized from before. We were near Ashton.

I felt my stomach drop a little. We were so close to making it back home to the twenty-first century. But we hadn't made it yet. We were standing near the place that David Stevenson had called home. All I could do was hope that his decision to leave with me was one that he wasn't doubting. If someone were to see us, there was a chance that we would be unsuccessful and be stuck in the nineteenth century forever. *Would he choose to really run away with me to America and start a new life with nothing but our love to live on? Or would he abandon me and go back to his 'family' if we were forced to remain?* I couldn't allow myself to dwell on my dark, inner thoughts.

"Here you are, my dears. I must go no further. You have all that you need now," Amoriti said, and with that, she was gone.

"David?" I whispered.

"Yes, my love."

"Let's get home to our kids, okay?"

He smiled at me, grabbed my hand, and kissed it. "Yes," he whispered. "We need to get down to the cave in order to charge these. After that, we will go to Ashton Court. The pod reappeared right around ten o'clock in the morning, so we must be quick about it, okay? It is at least a three-mile walk from here."

We ran to the old mill cabin, descended into the cave, and got to the electric boxes as quickly as possible. There was a small cable that looked a little archaic, but was fit to insert into the small opening of the suits' battery skins.

"This should take about fourteen minutes according to my calculations," he stated matter-of-factly.

"But will we be able to wear them? I mean, I feel like we are going to be electrocuted."

David smiled at me and huffed under his breath. "No. The wiring here may be primitive, but the suit's outer casing will be ample protection from electrocution."

"Okay. Just checking," I said doubtfully, and then laughed.

David pulled me close to him and chuckled. "I suppose that you should trust your husband by this point."

My husband. It felt so good to hear those words again.

"Hmm, I seem to recall the fact that it was my husband who got me into this bit of mess," I teased and kissed him.

"For which I beg forgiveness, and for which I will attempt to make amends for the rest of my days, Anna," he slowly and solemnly said.

I sighed, knowing that I would truly have to work through the emotion of the impossible events we had lived. "David, my one desire is to be with you. I was only teasing. Kind of," I smirked, and kissed him again.

The fourteen minutes expired quickly as a spark and smell of burning rubber filled the air. I was startled and jumped back.

"Don't be uneasy, dear. It is a good sign. I don't think the suits can hold any more energy. We must leave. Take your suit, and I'll disconnect mine. Don't touch the wires," he went about his business quickly.

He had a long, wide wooden fork that he was using to maneuver some of the wires, disconnect the suits, and push the metal cases around.

"Go over to the lift, Anna. It will take a few minutes for me to reconnect some of the wires and get things set up properly. Get your suit on. We must move quickly in order to be ready," he continued to scurry around the room.

"Okay," I said it almost as if it were a question. I was getting nervous watching him hurriedly manipulate the things around him, whispering to himself about this-or-that procedure, and then speaking to me without looking up. I backed out of the room and rounded the corner where the lift sat.

All that I had on underneath my heavy dress and corset was a thin petticoat like the one the professor had given me before my arrival. When David and I were back at the woodsman's cottage, I hadn't thought to look for the cotton leggings and t-shirt that I had traveled in. It was difficult to manage the rubbery fabric of the suit, but I was able to stuff the petticoat in and cover my skin as much as possible so I would not have the material brush uncomfortably against me.

David soon came out of the cave entrance suited up while I was still trying to clasp the tight straps that crossed the shoulders and up to the front of my chest.

"I'll get that," he said as he walked closer to me.

I hadn't seen him out of his old English clothes, and I was surprised at how different he looked. I smiled at him.

"Thank you," I said as I turned around, moving my long hair that had fallen out of its proper up-do so that he could reach straps.

David gently kissed my neck, and I found myself in disbelief. I had dreamt of that moment for so long it had seemed, and there I was, standing in his embrace preparing to go home.

"Are you ready for this?" I asked.

"I have never been more ready," he replied and smiled. "Now let's move on. We have little more than an hour to go, and only if we hurry. We should arrive right when the pod is to appear. We mustn't be seen before then."

"What happens if we get there, and our suits don't activate, or if they do, we get into the pod, and our helmets don't?" I asked.

So many things could go wrong, and even though I had David with me, somehow I had lost some of the complete faith I had put in him before. I was always the skeptic with others, and he now had to experience some of that himself. I don't think he was used to it.

"Oh, I believe it will all be well. But if it is not, then we either will be forced to remain in this century, or we shall not survive. Are you willing to take the chance with me?" he asked as he reached out his hand, leading me to the lift.

I took his hand and conceded. "Yes, I am willing to do whatever it takes to be with you."

The lift went up and we came to the cabin where David walked over to a small fireplace, taking a match to light a torch.

"What do we need that for?" I questioned.

"Just be ready to run, Anna," he said, not missing a breath.

He threw the torch down the shaft and started to rush out the door, grabbing my hand and leading me as quickly as my legs would move.

"What are we doing? What's going to happen to…" I couldn't finish my sentence before a loud boom was heard.

We kept running for a few minutes until we had made it down the hill and far enough away to look back and watch the sparks fly upward and consume the old mill. The immense waterwheel that reached from the stream nearly to the edge of a small landing attached to the little building, tumbled in flames into the river.

"It looks so strange. How does it stay on fire when it's so soaked in water?" I asked.

"It was just the intensity of the heat. We must have stored more energy in those crates than we had calculated. It won't stay aflame. They will most likely find the wheel intact downstream."

"But why did you have to destroy it all? Won't Thomas be so disappointed?" I empathetically asked.

"He will. But we mustn't leave any evidence of our existence in this century other than the clues I left behind for the professor and Christopher to know where I was. Dr. Bennett was part of that, but Thomas need not be implicated. He will advance in his studies without having to have the use of old Harper's Mill," David said. He had done his homework.

We moved on quickly, and after almost an hour, came to the outskirts of the grounds at Ashton Court according to David's calculations. I was always amazed at his ability to track time well. It shouldn't have surprised me that he had such a fascination with the study of time since he always seemed to be so well in-tune with it.

'The pod should be arriving in about ten minutes," he assured me.

The sun had fully risen and the cool morning air had replaced the dewy mist of dawn. We looked strange in our space suits, standing near the meadow that lay between us and the manor itself. The strings of my heart played a slow, portentous, and melodic song as we stood silently saying our goodbyes to the impressive estate preparing to embark on a fantastic journey. I was scared to approach the open field. I knew that if we were seen in the light of day and we missed the pod, if it didn't come—or worse—it did come and our suits malfunctioned, that we would be in more trouble than we could manage to get out of if we remained in the nineteenth century.

"It will be all be well, Anna," David said as he took my hand and led me toward the opening.

I breathed in and out heavily. "Let's do it."

We approached the field and lay flat on our backs to conceal the activated suits' glow. It was a bright, sunny day, giving us the advantage of hiding in plain sight. David held my hand and started to whisper numbers in what I could only assume was a countdown. The warmth of the sun felt comforting, and my heavy eyes shut in fatigue. I was happy. Content. Ready for whatever was ahead.

CHAPTER EIGHTEEN

It's difficult to describe the feeling of weightlessness. I have no recollection of how I left the warmth of the field at Ashton Court that day, but when I awoke, I was weightless, covered in a thick fabric, with a large space helmet secured to my head. It was completely black, and I began feeling around, trying to reach out for something to grasp. I realized that David must have remained conscious when we were being lifted into the space pod and had put the heavy jacket and helmet on me before we reached the point of the atmosphere when one becomes weightless. I tried not to panic.

"David!" I shouted. My efforts were futile. I could see nothing, and terror began to set in.

"Anna? Anna, you're awake? I'm here. I can hear you! The microphones on the helmets are functional." It was strange to hear his proper British voice through the tiny speakers by my ears.

I wondered what the plan was. When we would arrive home the David our children knew…the David my family loved…the David his family cherished…was simply different. *Recognizably different.*

"David, I'm scared," I whispered through my tears.

"I am here. See if you can move yourself toward me. I'll try to come near you as well."

We weightlessly grasped for tangible objects to clasp and push off of, trying to find each other in the small pod. It seemed bigger than when I had come. I hadn't remembered that much space, but it was hard to tell in the pitch black.

I felt a hand touch the lightweight boots that I was wearing. "That's me! You grabbed my foot," I said, trying to lean my body upward and take David's hand.

"I turned off the illumination of the craft to preserve energy. I don't know how much power we need to reach the portal," he said.

"Well, that explains the complete darkness. How long have we been in here?"

"I don't know. I have slept for quite a long while, I believe," he sighed a long breath of relief. "I was afraid that the shock was too much for you, Anna. I tried to get you to wake up after I activated our suits for entry. You gave me such a fright. I was not sure that you survived," David said as his voice shook.

"I just can't believe that we made it. We're here. Headed home. I just want to kiss you!" I cried out. I felt another tear leave my eye. I went from terror to emotions of complete elation.

"I could have only hoped for this day, Anna. I had nearly given up…" David's voice drifted off apologetically. "Can you ever forgive me for all that I have caused you to endure? Love me again as you did before?" he asked.

"Oh, David. I am bound to your heart in a way that I cannot explain. I have never stopped loving you," I proclaimed through my tears, then paused for a breath. "Yes, maybe it is in a different way. Our lives will be forever changed. Stronger maybe. Knowing that neither time nor distance is powerful enough to separate us from our destiny. I will forever be yours, my love!" I spoke the words I had longed to declare since I had found him.

I could hear a soft sniffling through the headpiece. His grip on my arm became tighter.

"I love you, Anna," was all he could mutter.

We held each other as closely as we could manage to.

"Isn't there enough oxygen in this pod for us to remove the helmets?" I asked. I longed to feel his lips against mine.

"We mustn't risk it. I believe that we should simply watch for the light to appear, activate our hoods, and tumble out according to procedure. With any luck, we'll get back as easily as we came."

"*Easy?* I wouldn't call it that!" I insisted with a sigh.

"Yes, I suppose that easy is relative to its circumstance," he sighed.

We began to feel more at ease while we talked for hours. David had much more to tell than I had, since I could only recall a window of a few months from the time of his disappearance to the time I left on the mission to find him. I had been desperate to recover him for less than a year, but he had suffered the agony of loss for nearly a decade.

He had a new college experience to tell me of, a new family dynamic to explain, a culture and custom of another century to describe, and a whole different man to teach me about. I wanted to know everything. How this had made him different, and how much he had remained the same. He was the same in demeanor, kindness, and elegance. His reserved mannerisms and his intelligence made him the perfect candidate to take on the role with ease, but there were some things that made me wonder.

"You speak even now with the accent, David. How did you become so good at it?" I asked.

"I've been well-trained. I spent years in instruction and exercise. I shifted into the accent with ease. The colloquialisms came with some time, but I managed fairly well because of the extensive research and training."

"But if you knew you were going to the 1970s, then why prepare so rigorously for the accent and mannerisms of Old England? I mean, I get it, 1977 was different than the twenty-first century, but there would have been no suspicion about an American guy coming to London to find a university student back then," I said.

"Indeed there would not have been. But we do train for a plethora of scenarios. I can speak Italian, French, and a little bit of Mandarin and Khalkha, as you know. Our six years in Mongolia were partially spent in exploration of the proper departure site, and proportionately spent in education of many languages, cultures, and history."

I could feel myself breathing more heavily as my heart began to beat faster and my mind started to race.

"All that time…" I whispered. My heart sank. I began to think that ignorance in fact was bliss, and that I would spare myself some hurt knowing that the secrets that David had from me were strictly professional. At least that's what I kept telling myself.

"I am so sorry, Anna. Please forgive me. Can you understand that to tell you the truth of what I was doing would have meant risking not only my own studies, but also centuries of research in time travel that must be protected for us to be successful? I never meant to hurt you or anyone else."

"But I know the secrets now," was all that I could think to say.

"Indeed you do, and you have become one of us. A time traveler, Anna," he said with a tinge of enthusiasm. "Can we sacrifice the good of the whole for our own satisfaction by revealing anything to those who are not proven trustworthy? No, I believe that we cannot," he left no room for response. "We must protect this legacy of our scientific forefathers and carry on the mission with rectitude."

"David, I certainly don't share the passion that you do for all of this, but I can understand your position. I am happy to know the truth, even though it meant so many lies before this," I replied softly.

We were both silent for a while.

"Do you plan to continue when we return?" I finally asked.

"Not without your approval."

"*Approval?*" I laughed. "When has that ever been the way we do things? I mean, I want to know what you're doing, David, but you can't put that on me as if I'm your mother allowing you to go out on a Saturday night!" I retorted, a bit annoyed at his answer.

"I just mean to say that I shall not be inclined to go anywhere without your consent. I intended to resign after this mission. I had told Professor Trinkton as much. But now...well, you are here...we have been successful thus far, and if our return home is successful indeed, that could open so many doors for improvement," he paused, seemingly trying to find the right words to continue. "Yes, I do admit that I wish to continue my studies, Anna, but if I am not the one to travel to a different time and place, I will not be dissatisfied. I will have the joy of knowing that our journey has advanced the cause," he explained.

"I won't tell you what to do, David. Can we just get back to our children first and then think about making a life-threatening choice again?" I was probably annoyed at myself as much as with him in that moment. We had both consciously taken on a mission with full knowledge of the dangerous implications.

I could hear David sigh deeply.

"I imagine that once our family is whole again, I shall never wish to put any of us in peril, Anna. I will abandon my work forever if it means gaining the priceless treasures that I have in you and the children."

There it was. What I had wanted all along. *Choose me over your stupid job.* But this is what it took. All this time, effort, and risk. In that moment, I had to come to peace with knowing that we are all such complex creatures. That total devotion to the love of your life does not mean giving up a part of yourself, it means sharing it. And sharing it fully.

"David, I love you. Every part of you. I don't want you to deny who you are as a scientist. I prefer that you don't ever leave my side again and chance the uncertainty of your return. But all I ask is that you never conceal your decisions from me again. Ever."

He did not reply.

I'm not sure if he was overcome with emotion, shock, or if he simply could not find the right words to say, but I could hear him breathing in the absolute stillness of the dark. He clutched my hand tightly. We had never let go of each other's arms once we had found one another in the black pod. I suddenly began to faintly make out the shape of his helmet.

"There's a light!" David exclaimed.

We looked upward through the triangular-shaped window of the pod, and there it was. We were probably less than an hour from the band. Soon, it would be too bright to open our eyes, and I began to tug at my hood to make sure that I had everything in place.

"Are you ready for this?" I asked him, trembling.

"Anna, I have never been more ready for anything in my life," he said, sounding a bit like his old self.

I could feel a wave of contentment wash over me, and I smiled. The moments before we exited the pod were spent in discussion about our approach to evacuating, rehearsal of precise counting of the seconds, and reassuring each other that everything would all be all right. We decided that we would, if at all possible, hold each other's hand the entire time, ensuring that we would land together.

We tried.

I awoke feeling myself drifting—floating along in the dark. *Where is David?*

I was searching the dark skies for David's parachute. The dizziness I felt made me queasy, but I hadn't lost my sight like I had when I landed in the past. I was mid-air, floating to the ground, and drifting toward a few blinking lights that I could see in the distance. It was foggy, damp, and dim. In a matter of minutes, I reached the ground with a thump, ripping of my hood and mask.

"David! David! Oh, please, David, be here with me!" I shouted and ran around in a panic. I couldn't get far, as I tried to disentangle myself from the large black parachute.

I detached the clip that tethered me to the chute, and looked around.

I was in an open field near an airport. The lights of a runway dimly lit the field, and I immediately began to fear that David and I may have been detected on a radar or been seen by someone in the control tower, and that he could have been apprehended already. I stopped shouting and began to crawl, searching through the wet field for any sign of him.

"Anna? Anna!" I heard a harsh whispering sound and made out a figure on the ground a few feet away from me. I crawled over to him, laid myself in his arms and wept.

"We did it!" he kept whispering and kissing my forehead as I cried.

I could not bring myself to think about anything. I had to let out everything that I was feeling in a good, long sob. David sat stroking my hair while reassuring me that we had been successful. He allowed me all the time that I needed. I'm unsure of how long that may have been, but the next thing that I remember was a hazy dawn sky.

"Anna, we fell asleep." David shook me by the arm, "Let's get into the airport, shall we?"

"Are you ready to be David Sturgeon again?" I took his hand and looked into his lovely eyes.

"I think I can handle it," he spoke without a hint of British accent.

"Hmm," I teased, "I think I prefer you British," I smiled as we began to walk hand in hand across the long field.

"So, what's the plan now?" I asked. "Do you think anyone saw us? Won't we look suspicious walking from this field inside in these odd-looking suits?"

"Let's just get inside first. I'm not sure where we are," David said pensively.

"Okay. If we are not in America…we don't have any passports. We have no identification…" I began to get a sick, worried feeling in the pit of my stomach.

"Yes, but if we are on any missing person reports, we should be able to manage well enough," he reassured me.

The airport wasn't bustling with too much action right at dawn, but there were cars and buses that lined some of the surrounding roads.

"Look at all the cool old cars," I said. But David wasn't enjoying the sights as much as he was studying the details.

"What is it?" I asked.

"I'm not sure," he said dismissively. "Let's just get inside." We walked around a building to find the massive entrance with the drop-off and parking areas.

"Well, I think we are in Europe, at least," I said, recognizing the designs of sleek European architecture.

"Yes, it does look like we may be. But things don't seem quite right, Anna. This may be a little more difficult than I thought," he said shaking his head with a confused countenance.

We crossed the large parking lot and entered the tall glass doors that led to the airport terminals. Immediately we knew that we had not arrived where we thought we had.

"This looks familiar," David said. "But strange. I think we may be in London. Does this look a bit like Heathrow to you, Anna?" he asked.

I shrugged my shoulders unsure of how to answer. We moved toward the terminal entrance and started to watch the arrival and departure signs flip from one set of flight notifications to the next. The little plastic tiles clacked downward in rhythmic sound. A feeling that we definitely weren't where we needed to be made my stomach flop as we walked to an airline counter where an agent was getting ready for her morning duties, sipping on a cup of steaming coffee. We needed to speak with someone about a possible flight back to the States, but I was nervous. David had begun cordially chatting, trying not to look conspicuous in our rubber suits, as I held his hand, saying nothing.

Noticing a small desk calendar resting on the counter, I moved toward it. *September 29.* I picked up the triangular paper stand and noticed the shadowy inlay of the year. *1976.*

"David," I whispered.

He had been trying to get information on how we would go about getting back to America, asking about flight times, stating that it may be difficult for us to travel today, and nonchalantly trying to collect information. He always impressed me with how he could keep his cool in most situations.

"David," I spoke a little louder and tugged at his arm. "Look," I said.

I held the calendar up closer to his face, tracing the numbers of the year with my right index finger. He stopped speaking and turned his body fully toward me.

"Thank you for your help, Miss," he said, acknowledging the airline employee. I could see the wheels in his head turning, trying to come up with a quick plan.

"1976?" he whispered.

"What do we do now?" I asked.

"That must have been my pod, Anna," he said as we walked into the wide hallway and away from the ticket counter. He began to mentally walk through the scenario. "How did I miss it all those years? How did it return after so long? Surely they weren't reprogramming the pod after the initial two hundred days." He took a moment to think. "It must have been Professor Maxwell and Laura. That means it worked," he continued without a breath, "all the time and effort we put into the pod calculations to get me to 1977 and return were offset by my miscalculations to place me in the 1860s, but has now sent me back to 1976?" his voice drifted off in profound thought.

"David that doesn't even make sense…does it?" I asked in confusion. It didn't make sense to me, but I was no scientist. I could hardly wrap my head around what was happening or even how we had made it as far as we had. *I now have to prepare myself for another journey through time?* The thought was frightening.

"I am not sure," he continued to ponder, "but what it does mean is that they are here–Laura and Maxwell are here, Anna. I know they are because I have been here once before. We can still have hope. This isn't over yet."

I stood motionless–almost numb.

"But all I want is for it to be over, David." I pressed my head against his tall chest and held him tightly as a tear slowly traveled down my cheek.

"It soon will be, my love," he whispered lovingly, kissing my forehead. "We will get there. We've come this far; we will conquer this, I promise you."

He held me close, as we stood motionless in the spacious airport walkway. His face was pressed against the top of my head and his long arms enveloped me in warmth. People began bustling about in a busy morning of travel, but our world stood still. Frozen in time.

One thing mattered most. We were together.

287

ABOUT THE AUTHOR

Shelly Snow Pordea is a travel-loving author and teacher at heart. She taught both English and Creative Writing for more than ten years, and is a member of Author Academy Elite (AAE) where she enjoys a community of fellow authors and visionaries. Her fascination with time travel since childhood has led her to pen the stories of the *Tracing Time* trilogy and join the world of fiction writers. Shelly spent nearly fifteen years living in Eastern Europe with her family, and is passionate about charity work and paying it forward. She is a coffee and dark chocolate lover who currently resides in Missouri with her husband and three teenage children.